The Art
of
Love

Peter Stipe

THE ART OF LOVE
Copyright © 2020 by Peter Stipe

For information contact :
Blue Fortune Enterprises, LLC
Lavender Press
P.O. Box 554
Yorktown, VA 23690
http://blue-fortune.com

Cover photo by Thomas Reilly
        www.designertom.com
        tom@designertom.com

ISBN: 978-1-948979-34-4

Second Edition: February 2020

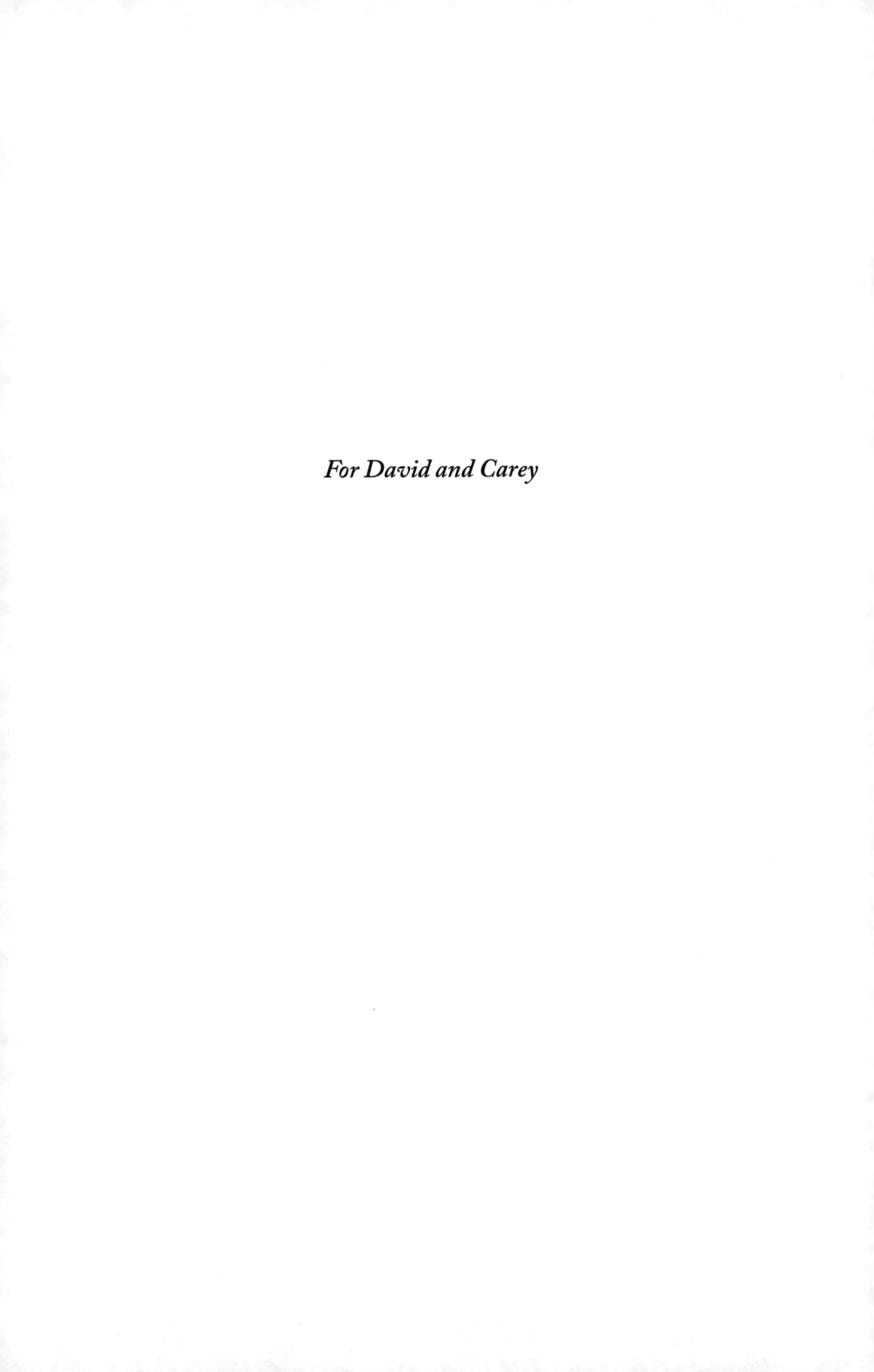

For David and Carey

Prologue

PATRICK SAT AT THE KITCHEN table watching out the apartment window as the sky lightened into dawn. Late autumn fog washed in off Great Bay; the sunrise colors filtering from violet to gray and then turning a pale, cheerless yellow. He picked up his coffee mug, handmade by a pottery-major classmate back at the art school in Rhode Island, and took a sip. The coffee was strong, the way he liked it, but cold, bitter, brewed hours ago. Out the edge of his window the façade of the church across the street began to catch the first rays of sunlight. He was so tired now of the church, of what it meant to Mary and how little it still meant to him.

He turned and looked across the kitchen at his work table and easel. The paint tubes on the tabletop were now in disorder, brushes scattered. Otherwise, the table was empty; squares of brush-stroked paint on the flat space silhouetted the places where paper had been painted. He had not been able to paint anything for a week. Tacked to the wall behind the table was the last picture he had done: a watercolor portrait of Mary painted from memory. Her dark hair cascaded, falling to her bare shoulders. Her head was turned; only the lashes of her magnificent eyes could be seen at the fringe of her profile, defined by a single, thin brushstroke.

Mary had been gone for almost two weeks now.

How had it ever gotten to be this way? It had seemed so simple, so natural at the start. He had gone off to Providence for grad school at the Rhode Island School of Design. Mary had come north from New York to Brown University. They met, dated, and fell in love. After that shared year in grad school, their careers had taken them to different places; him to New Hampshire, her to Montreal and then back to New York. But always they had remained connected, with frantic visits on the weekends and nightly phone calls. Had he been foolish? Naïve? Maybe both Mary and he had been. It had been a year since they met, he reminisced, a dreamlike time. He had never seen the end coming.

Chapter 1

One year earlier

"OH BOY! HERE WE GO, young Patrick. You're off to conquer the world."

Patrick leaned against the fender of the weathered Volvo and smiled as he looked at Uncle Win. "You sure you won't teach me anymore, Uncle Win? We've painted together my whole life."

"I could teach you more. But my approach to art is only one way." Uncle Win, always voluble, became excited. "You need to learn from other artists with different perspectives. And Bowdoin's not a true art school. Great for liberal arts, but limited for the visual arts. It's time for you to move on. Your portfolio could have gotten you into any art school in the country. You were wanted everywhere you applied. New York? Good art school, Pratt, but you're not ready for that big of a city. And Chicago, the same story. Savannah College of Art and Design? What do they know about art in Georgia? But Rizdee? RISD? Rhode Island School of Design! Providence! It's enough of a city to give you a taste of that lifestyle, but not overwhelming for a boy from Maine, from here on Casco Bay. And the tradition, the artists who've worked, studied, and taught there? The best!"

Behind them the screen door to the old white clapboard farm house banged. Patrick's father, Tom, stepped off the raw granite doorstep and started across the carefully mown lawn. Both brothers, Winthrop and Tom, taught at Bowdoin, but they were complete opposites.

Win was short, thickset, bordering on chubby, with a ragged mess of graying curls above a red face, always smiling, laughing, with his eyes squinted. His clothes were rumpled. Today's wardrobe featured paint-spattered shorts, a loose plaid shirt with the sleeves turned up, gray wool socks, and leather sandals. He hadn't bothered to shave for a week. Painting occupied his mind. He didn't worry about his appearance.

Older brother Tom was crisp, clean shaven, his white hair trimmed short and combed. He wore a blue Pinpoint Oxford shirt with the sleeves folded precisely above his wrists. His pressed blue jeans were a perfect fit for his lean body. His polished brown loafers matched his belt. Tom was a professor of English specializing in nineteenth century British authors. Tom stopped a few feet from his brother and his son. "You're all set, Patrick? All packed? Got all your art materials?"

"All set, Dad. Uncle Win helped me pack."

"Okay. You have directions to Providence?"

"Yes. I printed them off the computer, and they're on my phone."

Tom nodded and assessed his son. "I made sure the Volvo's running well. Got her an oil change. You should be okay with the car. And you can find the house where you're staying in Providence?"

"Yes. I'm all set."

"Well—good. Call when you get there so Mother and I won't worry. And stay in touch, please. We'll see you this fall sometime? Plan on Thanksgiving."

"Dad, I'll be fine. Of course I'll come home for Thanksgiving."

Tom took a step closer and gave his son a cursory hug, finishing with two quick claps on Patrick's back. "Drive carefully." He turned, walked across the lawn, and vanished through the screen door.

Patrick and Win watched him go. In a second-story window, a curtain moved. Mother. Patrick had never been further from home than Portland without one parent or another as an escort. *She's terrified of what might happen to me in a strange faraway city. She wants me to stay at Bowdoin and teach alongside Dad and Uncle Win. She's probably worried I'll never come back to her.*

Uncle Win and Patrick turned to face each other. "Well, Uncle Win, time to get on with it."

Patrick gave a short sigh and opened the door to the Volvo.

Uncle Win pulled him back from the car, gave him a bear hug and let go, pushing him off. "Go! Get on out there to Providence. Make art! Discover life! Meet a woman and fall in love! Find out what it's all about!"

Patrick laughed and got in the car. "I'll take each day as it comes. I'll keep you posted once I'm settled in, and I'll send photos of my work."

He slammed the car door and started down the gravel driveway. Win ran alongside, his short legs pumping to keep up.

"Go Patrick!" Win shouted. "Paint the world as you see it! Live your life and love! Go!"

Winded, Uncle Win stopped at the tumbled-down white granite wall where the driveway met the road. He sagged, hands on knees, red- faced, sweating and panting. A moment later he stood and waved until the Volvo crossed the bridge over the narrow, rock-bound channel and headed toward Harpswell Road. "It'll be a great trip, my boy. Portland, Boston, and Providence." Win sighed and walked back to the farmhouse. Tom might have glasses of red wine ready for the two of them even though it was still before noon.

—

The two women sat facing each other across the square oak desk. It was an austere cell of an office, cool, quiet, and filled with diffused light. Furniture was sparse; the desk, a small round table in the corner for conferences, the rock-maple desk chair on casters for Sister Catherine, and two other straight-backed hardwood chairs for visitors. Mary had pulled one of the straight chairs to the front of the desk; the other sat next to the door. Behind Sister Catherine was a low bookcase with two shelves. The top shelf held a thick Bible and a line of books on theology. The lower shelf contained French literature. The dark, polished wood floor had no rug.

The plain whiteness of the walls was broken by varnished wood baseboards and a matching chair rail. The door to the hall served as the only decoration on one wall. Above Sister Catherine hung a crucifix, the pewter body of an anguished Christ hanging on a beveled wooden cross. On the wall behind Mary was a painting of Christ, hair flowing to his white tunic-clad shoulders as he looked up toward heaven. Across from the door, a window faced out onto the college lawn, late-summer sunlight filtering through maple trees and cedars. Birds darted among the branches, but they couldn't be heard. Except for an inch at the bottom for air, the window was closed.

"What should I do, Sister Catherine?" Mary asked, shifting in her seat. "I've always done the right thing. It's the way I was raised. Everyone is telling me this is the right thing to do. My parents want me to go to grad school. But why not stay in New York? I know my way around. Why should I go to Providence?"

"It will do you a world of good to get out to a new city for a year or two. You've lived your whole life in New York. You've hardly even left the neighborhood where you were raised. This is the right thing for you to do."

Mary gave it a moment of thought before she voiced a second point. "I've been in Catholic schools my entire life. Why should I move to Brown for grad school? It's a good college, I know. But it's not Catholic."

"It's a great college." Sister Catherine smoothed back her white hair. "So what if it's not Catholic? It's the best place for you to continue your French studies, don't you think? They've accepted you and given you a full scholarship. Why would you want to go anywhere else?"

"I could stay in New York and get my Masters. And if I must go to Providence, why not Providence College? It's Franciscan."

"You could stay, Mary. And Providence College is a fine school. But you should go to Brown. It'll give you a broader perspective. You'll learn more about the world outside the church and more about yourself as well. You'll find your way around Providence and Brown quickly enough. Get out, see another side of life away from New York, and learn more than just French."

Mary sighed and slumped in her seat. She pushed her dark hair back from her face. "If that's what you think I should do, Sister Catherine. Okay, I'll go. But it scares me a little."

Sister Catherine paused for a moment to straighten her gray skirt across her lap and adjust the cuffs of her white blouse. She leaned forward, folding her hands on the desktop. Her old eyes exuded concern and warmth. "Why, Mary? What scares you?"

Mary fidgeted, tense in her chair, her hands clenched in her lap. *Should I tell her?* "I don't know. I know my way around New York. I know my limits, what to do, what not to do. Maybe I worry about things when I shouldn't."

"What worries you?"

Mary shrugged. "What if the people I meet don't share my Catholic beliefs and values?"

"Now, Mary. You haven't spent all your time at school and in church. Your family lives in the city. And they have the weekend place in Connecticut. When you're not in school, you're in New York, one of the most diverse cities on the planet. You've been around people who aren't Catholic."

"Yes, Sister, but all my friends were from St. Clare's. That was all girls and taught by nuns. And my friends in college and the boys I've dated? They've all been Catholic. Not that I've had that many boyfriends." Mary hesitated a moment. "What if a boy who's not Catholic asks me out? What should I do?"

"If he seems like a nice young man and you like him, go out with him. Is that what concerns you?"

Mary looked, pleading, into Sister Catherine's eyes. "Maybe. I know Brown is a great school, but I don't know what I'd do if most of the people I meet believe in something else."

"That's exactly why you should go there. You need to meet people of different faiths, or of no faith at all. Your beliefs are strong enough that you won't stray. You need this experience. Go to Brown and get your Masters. Enjoy Providence. Meet people. You can always come back here and teach." The old nun smiled. "And see if that boy is out there. Date him if you like him. Just remember who you are and what your values are."

"What if I fall in love? I could never marry someone who isn't Catholic."

Sister Catherine laughed and leaned back in her chair. "You're getting a bit ahead of things, aren't you? You haven't even met the boy yet, let alone gone out with him. Go to Providence. Live a little. Meet that boy — if he's there. You've been sheltered your whole life. Until now, the church and your family protected you. You need to learn about more than the things you study in your classes. Get out into the world. Experience new things and come back and tell me all about it. Call me any time."

Mary took a deep breath and pushed her hair back again. "Do you know what worries me the most, Sister Catherine? My sister Margie met a boy, dropped out of college, and moved in with him. They love each other, but it's not right, living together when they're not married. It's a sin. And my parents are both so upset with her. I would never do that to my parents. I've always done the right thing. My parents admire me because of that. I love my sister, but I can't end up like her. What if I meet a boy and am tempted to do what Margie did?"

Sister Catherine smiled and reached out to place a dry hand on top of Mary's. "Focus on your studies. If you meet a boy and you like him, you should go out with him. You know right from wrong. I trust that you won't do anything you shouldn't. Now go. Have a great year and enjoy the experience. Study hard and you'll be fine."

Reassured, Mary thanked her mentor and stood. "Thank you." She hugged Sister Catherine at the door, a warm embrace between friends. Then Mary was out, walking down the hall, silhouetted by the light at the glass door to the lawn and the parking lot beyond. Her car was packed, ready for the trip to Providence. She had said goodbye to her parents earlier that morning. She climbed into her old Honda Civic and drove away, across the Bronx and onto the highway headed north to Providence.

Chapter Two

MONDAY MORNING. PATRICK FILLED HIS backpack with a sandwich, pencils, and a small sketchpad. The studios at RISD had everything else he needed. He locked his apartment, jogged down the stairs of the old house and out onto Wickenden Street.

The early morning air was warmer than in Maine, but fresh and cool. He found a bakery and bought an onion bagel and a large coffee with milk and sugar in a paper cup before climbing the hill on Benefit Street. He studied his surroundings as he walked, seeking inspiration. It was an old city, with cobblestone alleyways and brick sidewalks. Dark, shuttered historic homes lined the streets with clapboard siding painted white or pale yellow. The more prosperous residences were brick, the windows framed with white wood. There were lawns, gardens, and brick courtyards. He glanced at his watch. Plenty of time 'til class. He leaned on a wall, cracked the top of his coffee, sipped and ate while the city came to life.

Patrick observed the steady procession of early morning pedestrians. They might populate his paintings here in this new-old city of Providence. Some were out for exercise; women walking in pastel exercise gear with iPods and earphones, men jogging on the steep hill. A few others were dressed for business and appeared to be heading from apartments to downtown offices. Most were like Patrick, college students headed up the hill to the Rhode Island School of Design or to its Ivy League neighbor, Brown.

He realized that he could sort them to their school by their appearance.

The RISD students were dressed like Patrick, many wearing black clothes that could absorb the dirt and paint of making art. The Brown students, or those Patrick thought must be Brown students, dressed in attire from fashionable stores. *I'm stereotyping. But it's important for an artist to notice details. Those details can give my paintings authenticity.*

A young woman hurried along on the opposite side of the street. She walked with her head down, watching her steps on the uneven brick-paved sidewalk. Though she wore a backpack, she clutched a short stack of books tight to her chest. Long, dark hair swung as she bustled up the hill. She turned a corner and continued up the hill toward Brown. Her intensity captured his attention. *Where is she going?*

Patrick dropped his garbage in a trash can, slung his backpack over one shoulder, and followed the girl at a distance. She rounded another corner and raced along the black iron fence that surrounded the Brown campus. Though Patrick tried to keep his distance, the girl paused and turned to look back. Patrick froze. Her eyes met his for a moment, her hair blowing in the breeze. Blue. Her eyes are blue. Her face showed no expression, not interest, not fear, nothing. Then she was gone, vanishing through a small open gate in the brick wall.

Patrick was stunned. *Who is she? What's her story? She seemed desperate, hustling up the hill and clinging to her books — why? And looking back at me before she dashed through the gate onto the campus.* Intrigued, he carried the vision of blue eyes and windblown hair down the hill to RISD for his first class.

—

Mary made sure she had everything. Books, notebooks. Good. She checked herself in the mirror one more time. Khaki pants and a white top. Aside from the crucifix she wore around her neck, her only jewelry was her grandmother's tiny diamond ring on her right hand. Mary had

14

considered switching it to her left hand while in Providence to suggest to men that she was married, but decided to take her chances. Her dark, shiny hair hung loose, and she wore no makeup. *I'm ready.*

Mary filled her backpack with a sandwich for lunch and a bottle of water and snugged it to her shoulders. She picked up her books and darted out the door of the old house. She walked past the bakery on Wickenden Street and turned up Benefit Street, toward Brown. She kept her head down, a tactic she always used when she walked in New York. She didn't want to make eye contact. She had left just enough time to walk to the campus so she wouldn't have to interact with the other students before class.

Nearing the campus, she became aware of a young man watching her from the opposite side of the street. He wore a black t-shirt with some rock band logo on it. His blue jeans were torn and looked dirty, maybe even paint stained. His hair was short but shaggy. He hadn't shaved. Maybe a street person, certainly not a Brown student. She clutched her books to her chest as she turned the corner and raced up the hill. At the next corner she peeked back. The boy was following her! *Why? Why is this stranger, dressed in dirty clothes, stalking me? What should I do? The campus will be safe.* As Mary got to the gate she steadied her nerves, stopped, and turned to look back at him. He was closer now and he stopped too, startled but almost smiling. For a moment their eyes met. Unsettled, Mary turned and ran through the gate. But in the moments before she reached her classroom, and again throughout the class, Mary thought about the boy. *He looks better up close. Yes, he needs to shave and his clothes aren't quite presentable, but his dark eyes are soft and speak of intellect and kindness.*

She bowed her head in a brief prayer. If it was to be, she would meet the boy again. If not, so be it. It was in God's hands now. After she prayed, she always felt calm. Mary directed her attention to her professor. After all, this was the reason she had come to Providence, to continue her French studies, not to meet some ragtag man on the street.

Chapter Three

THE CLASSROOM WAS DISORDERLY, WORKTABLES and easels arrayed in a loose semicircle around a raised podium. A stool and a small table were on the podium waiting for a model to pose or a still life to be set out. Today they were empty. Faded spatters of paint on the floor marked the passage of many young artists working in this space over the years.

Patrick sat on a stool in front of his worktable in the classroom. Other artists sat in front of other easels and tables, watching their new instructor, waiting to impress him with their talent. The instructor was a gaunt man, slightly built. His narrow head was shaved to disguise his baldness. He surveyed his class, looking directly into the eyes of each of his students.

"Look into your mind," he directed. "Find a vision that interests you. Paint from that. Something you've seen maybe, but paint it from memory. Don't be distracted by trying to recreate your vision exactly. Paint what you see in your memory, what you feel. Add or leave out the details. Your mind will add detail as needed. Let's get started."

Patrick looked around the room. A few of the other students set to work, blocking out their compositions on the watercolor paper, busying themselves with paints and brushes. Many, like Patrick, sat lost in thought, drawing on memories, seeking inspiration. It was obvious to Patrick what he should paint. The girl.

Watercolor demands that the artist create quickly. The paint, the water, and the paper take on a life of their own as the artist works. Patrick roughed in the shape of the girl's head, an outline of her profile and dark streaks for the hair, letting a light wash on the white paper serve for sunny highlights. He left the face blank. Then he added the eyes, making sure they were the clear, dark blue he remembered so well. A touch of her mouth showed. He obscured most of the girl's face with dark horizontal streaks as the wind blew her hair. The face finished, he began to lay in the black bars of the college gate behind her. The vertical bars contrasted with the horizontal lines of her windblown hair, forming a grid. He washed in green for the campus lawn behind the gate. Less than an hour after he began, he was finishing the picture by adding the vaguely remembered detail of the Brown coat of arms above the gate, a shield divided into quadrants by a cross.

Patrick sometimes became so immersed in painting that he lost awareness of the world around him. He emerged from this creative place as he finished the crest above the gate. He took a deep breath, sat back on his stool, and looked up. The professor and several other student artists were standing behind him.

"Very good," the professor said. "Who's the girl? A friend?"

Patrick looked back at the painting. How could he explain it? "No. She's someone I saw going onto the Brown campus this morning. I don't know her."

"Oh, you know her. Look at her eyes. You know her. You've found something there."

"I've never met her."

"You should. She's given you a fine work here. Anyway, the picture's a good start and one you should keep."

Patrick took another look at the painting. He had to admit it had turned out well. The girl was beautiful. He signed it, then almost as an afterthought titled it. In small print in pencil at the bottom he wrote, "Gone through the Gate". He let the paint and paper dry, then rolled it and slipped it into his backpack to take to his apartment. The walls there were bare, but he could easily take care of that.

Mary stayed indoors on campus throughout the day; classrooms when she had scheduled classes, then a dash across the campus to the library. She bought peanut butter crackers from a vending machine to add to her sandwich for lunch. Late in the afternoon she bolted back out the gate, off the campus, and hurried down the hill to the old house where she had her new apartment. Mary saw no signs of the man who had followed her in the morning. Her fear began to recede.

She had brought food with her when she left New York and had enough left for dinner. She made toast, heated a can of soup on the stove, and brought up some music on her iPod. She ate her soup sitting at the front window of her apartment, watching the people walking by on Wickenden Street. Finally, she began to relax. But she worried. "What do I want while I'm here? A master's degree in French. That's the easy part."

Her plan was to take extra classes and complete her Masters in one year. The intensity of that would leave little time for anything else. She knew how to get from her apartment in the old house, up Benefit Street, to the campus and back. She had found a supermarket nearby where she could buy food from her small savings. She had found the Catholic Church a few blocks up the hill. That was all she needed to know about Providence.

She remembered Sister Catherine's advice that she should experience life and meet people during her year in Providence. *Do I want that? Should I get out and explore some of the city, meet some people? Will it test my faith? And if it does, is that bad? I'm a good person, but I've led a sheltered life, protected by my family, my small circle of friends, and most of all by the Church. I'm naïve, I suppose. Maybe I should follow Sister Catherine's advice and get out a little.*

Again, Mary thought of the boy. Maybe he wasn't really a bad person or dangerous. She remembered him as seeming friendly now that time had passed. He had smiled at her. He hadn't pursued her through the gate. And here she was after her first day of classes having spent the day hiding from the boy. She had been hiding from everyone really, but mostly the boy. Stay away from strangers. That was what she had been taught she ought to do in the city. But he was probably just another Brown student. She decided that if she saw him again, and if he spoke to her, maybe she would talk with him a bit. Sister Catherine had told her it would be all right. She wouldn't go on a date with him. That was what Margie had done and now she was living with Javier. That was fine for Margie. Margie was always pushing the limits. But Mary couldn't do that. She might talk with the boy, but she wouldn't let herself go any further and be tempted the way her sister had been.

Patrick woke early on the second day, determined to go up the hill again with his coffee and watch for the girl. He was out the door of his apartment, down the stairs, onto Wickenden Street, and nearing the bakery when he saw her. She was leaving the bakery with a bag and a cup in hand. He didn't need to stop at the bakery. He could buy breakfast at RISD. He raced to catch her. Just before the corner on Benefit Street where she would turn for the Brown campus he caught up.

"Hey," he called. "I saw you yesterday." The girl paused and turned back.

Sweat broke out under Patrick's shirt. *Stay calm. Act cool. Talk to her.* "I'm Patrick. I'm a grad student at RISD. My school's up the street here."

The girl assessed him, evaluating whether or not to respond. Then she answered, the beginning of their first conversation. "I'm Mary. I'm a grad student at Brown."

Patrick waited for more but realized it was up to him to make the conversation go someplace. "What's your major?"

"French. And you? What are you studying?"

"Painting. Drawing, too, but mostly painting. I work mostly in watercolor."

"And Rizdee? What is that? I'm not familiar with it."

"R.I.S.D. Rhode Island School of Design. It's all art. A great art school."

The conversation seemed to have hit a wall. Neither Patrick nor Mary could think of the next thing to say.

Patrick did the best he could. "Well, Mary, it's good to meet you. I hope to see you around. Maybe after our classes this afternoon? Or lunch. Are you free for lunch?"

"No, not for lunch. I have a lot of work today. But I'll see you around."

"Okay. Sure. Have a good day with your French classes."

"You, too. Bye."

They turned and went to their different schools, Mary head down clutching her books to her chest, Patrick striding along, appearing confident. His heart raced and sweat trickled down his back. He was terrified of what he was feeling about this girl.

At lunch, Patrick bought a sandwich and walked up the hill to Brown. He found a shady spot under a tree just inside the big gate and sat down to eat, watching for Mary. Maybe she would wander by and he could call out to her and ask her to join him on the lawn.

Mary never came. She had gone out the other side of the campus and found a sandwich shop near Thayer Street. She was hungry, having eaten so poorly the day before. She bought a sandwich and a bottle of iced tea, took them to a booth near the back and sat alone, her head down in a book.

Late afternoon, as had already become his habit, Patrick walked down Benefit Street toward home, evaluating the neighborhood for scenes he could sketch. He found a view he liked partway down the hill; odd angles of the hilly, cobbled alleyways and the old clapboard houses. He stopped, pulled his sketchbook out of his backpack, sat on the curb, and began working. Quickly, he was deep into his drawing, shading the rough texture of the stones, stressing the straight lines of the clapboards.

"So this is what you do!"

He became aware of a figure standing nearby watching. He looked up and saw Mary.

"You're very good. I like the drawing," she said. It was uncharacteristic of Mary to approach anyone, particularly a boy she hardly knew. But when she had seen him sitting on the curb and had seen the sketch he was working on she felt drawn to him.

"Thanks. Yes, I carry my sketchpad with me all the time. It's better than a camera for capturing images I like, just the way I see them. Look at the angles here, how the street drops away. How the lines of the side of the house are different."

"Yes, I see that. And I like the contrast of the round stones in the street and the square lines and right angles on the house. Very nice."

Patrick stood. Then he leaned over his sketch pad again to add a few final accents, deft finishing touches, his pencil moving quickly. Mary stood transfixed, frozen in place, her hand at her throat, eyes wide, watching his sure-handed strokes bring the picture to life. Finished, Patrick tore the picture out of the sketch pad.

"Here, this is for you. Tack it up back wherever you live."

"Oh, I can't take this. Don't you have to turn it in to one of your professors or something? I really can't take this."

"No, this isn't an assignment. It's what I do. And I can do it again if I want to. By memory tonight, or I can stop here and do it again the next time the light is right. It only took a few minutes. It's my gift to you. Take it."

Flushed, Mary took the drawing. "Thank you. I appreciate the gift. I have nothing but bare walls in my apartment. I'll find a place for this, maybe in the living room."

They walked down the hill together. "Where do you live?" Patrick asked.

"About a block up Wickenden Street. It's an apartment in an old house."

"Me too! Which house?"

"That yellow one up there."

"Oh my god! Me too! I'm on the second floor. Top of the stairs at the front of the house."

"I'm on the first floor. Also front of the house. I'm right under you." As she said it, Mary felt momentarily distressed by what she believed to be the mildly suggestive implication of her statement. "I mean, my apartment must be one floor below yours," she corrected.

Patrick smiled, thrilled that they lived so near to each other. He didn't notice her embarrassment and failed to catch any innuendo in what she had said. Blindly, he continued their conversation. "Here we are meeting and getting to know each other up the hill at our two campuses, but we live in the same house! Who would have thought?"

"Yes, well. What a coincidence."

"Almost like it was meant to be."

They arrived at the steps to the front door. Patrick opened the door and held it for Mary. "So, Mary, do you have plans for dinner?"

"I'll probably just fix something for myself."

"I'm out of food, so I'll have to go out anyway. Why don't you join me? I found a place downtown my first night here that looks like it might be good. Not too expensive. Just a pub that I can afford on my grad student budget. Come on. Let's get a bite together."

Mary paused, reflecting on her instructions from Sister Catherine. "Get out," Catherine had told her. "Meet people. Live a little." Mary would do what she was supposed to do, what Sister Catherine had directed. She took a deep breath and let it out.

"Okay. I'll meet you here in front of the house in a half hour?"

Chapter Four

PATRICK AND MARY WALKED ALONG the river to a brew pub in an old brick basement of a converted train station. They sat facing each other in a booth, their arms resting on the varnished dark wood table. High, arched windows above them were at sidewalk level. People were striding by, framed by the window from the knees down. Behind the bar, past the televisions showing football, they saw the massive steel tanks and tubing where the beer was made. A waitress in a low-cut black t-shirt brought them two tall glasses of dark beer. She placed the glasses on square cardboard coasters colored with beer logos, took their food orders, and left.

"How did you find this place?" Mary asked.

"I came to Providence last Friday. I got in early afternoon and went out walking to see the city. Those walkways along the river brought me here. It looked like a nice spot. I checked the menu outside and decided I'd come back."

"Is it expensive? I'm on a tight budget. I don't have much money."

"Neither do I. We're both grad students, so I expect neither of us has much money. But my Uncle Win has set me up with a small allowance. 'Walking around money,' he calls it. He wants me to get out into the city and explore life. So I can pay for both of us."

Mary paused, considering his offer. *If he pays, will this be a date? Will he expect something in return? Sex has always frightened me and it's a sin. I can be strong if I need to be. That's what Sister Catherine said.* "I guess that would be okay."

Patrick continued the conversation. "Did you notice that wide passageway under the street where we cut through to get here from the river?"

"Yes, I remember walking through the tunnel." *That place was scary. In New York, it would be a dangerous place, a welcoming spot for muggers. But Patrick seemed unafraid. Maybe he's foolish and unaware of the potential dangers of such a place. I'm comforted by his fearless attitude.* She relaxed and settled back into her seat in the booth.

"That tunnel has tiles from end to end with artwork done by Providence school kids. It's their impressions of the 9/11 attack in New York."

"I didn't notice them. But I don't think that day is something to celebrate with art. It was awful."

Patrick paused, assessing her emotional response. *What's this? 9/11 must matter to her. Is it the art or the attack that's put her on edge?* "I don't think it was to celebrate the event. The art was used as therapy to help the kids cope, expressing what they experienced. What they felt. Sometimes I paint to express my emotions, to help me sort out the things I'm feeling. Where were you when the attack happened?"

"In New York. I'm from New York. Lived there my whole life. That day and that week were terrifying if you lived there. You can't understand what it was like for New Yorkers. It was horrible. Our city, our whole way of thinking about things, came crashing down with those towers."

"Did you lose anyone in the attack?"

"No. I didn't know anyone who was right there. But it was still scary. I was in elementary school. I kept thinking if people could attack a place like the World Trade Center, could they attack my school? But the nuns reassured me. We prayed about it at school, and I prayed about it every night for weeks when I was home."

"I can't imagine what it must have been like to be a kid in New York then." Patrick shook his head and looked away. Then he reached out for her hand. As he reached, she slid her hands off the table and into her lap.

For a moment she looked down at the table. But she made herself look up into his eyes. She was startled and confused by the emotions there: compassion, sympathy, maybe a bit of shared fear, his eyes almost tearing up.

"Where were you when it happened?" she asked.

"In Maine. I'm from a little town on the coast north of Portland. And I was an elementary school kid, too. I remember it, but it didn't have the impact for me it must have had for you."

That's enough about the shock of 9/11. Talking about it has never been easy for me, not even with Sister Catherine. I don't want to talk about this anymore. I've got to change the subject and talk about anything else. "What does your family do?" Mary asked. "How do people earn their living in Maine? Is your father a lobsterman or a fisherman or something?"

"No, he's a professor at Bowdoin College. English Lit. And his brother, my uncle, is an art professor there. He's the one who got me started with my art. Uncle Win. He's like a second father to me."

"Do you have brothers or sisters?"

"No. I'm an only child. And Uncle Win never married, so it's like I'm the only child in the whole family. How about you? You're from New York. What about your family?"

Mary paused for a moment. *I've already told him so much, and I've asked him questions too, so I guess it's okay. I'm comfortable talking with him. It's not like me, but it's so natural and easy.* "My father works for the subway. He's a pipe-fitter; hard work, all underground. My mom works in an office. I have a younger sister, Margaret. Margie. She lives with her boyfriend and works in an office in the city. My parents aren't happy about that, about her living with the boyfriend and not being married. I'm not thrilled by her lifestyle, either. She dropped out of her first semester in college to be with the guy. I'm the first in my family to graduate from college."

"Your family must be very proud of you. And now with you in grad school, and at an Ivy League school, too."

"Yes, they are. But it's a little overwhelming. I've never had a problem with the academic part of it. I was valedictorian of my high school class and I got good grades in college, too. That got me the scholarship here at Brown. I'm taking extra classes so I can get my Masters in a year. I went to college a few blocks from home, so I was able to go home every weekend. I could see my parents, have dinner, and do my laundry. This is the first time I've been away from home and out on my own. I don't know my way around Providence like I do New York."

"At least we have that in common. This is my first time on my own, too. Let's discover Providence together."

Mary looked down at the varnished table top. *This place frightens me. He frightens me. But Sister Catherine said I should get out and explore life a little.* She took a deep breath and looked up at Patrick. "Okay," she said. "But I came here to study French, not to wander around a strange city. If I do get out, I guess it would be easier to do it with someone. Probably safer."

"Sure. Safer for both of us. Let's do this. You study, and I'll paint during the week. Then we can explore together on the weekends."

"Okay." *It's only Tuesday. I have the rest of the week to think it over and decide if it's something I want to do.*

After dinner, they walked back to the house. Neither talked much. As they approached the house, Mary spoke. "I don't know your last name. Your first is Patrick. Are you Irish?" *If he's Irish, he might be Catholic.*

Patrick laughed. "No. I get asked that a lot, though. My last name is Chamberlain. It's an old New England name, common in my part of Maine. What's your last name?"

"Flynn."

"Here we are." Mary dodged over to the door of her apartment at the foot of the stairs. Patrick followed and put a hand on her shoulder. She turned back for a moment and he kissed her on the cheek, even as she averted her face.

"Good night." Mary fumbled with the key to unlock the door. Then she was inside.

Before she closed the door, Patrick called, "See you tomorrow." She rested against the door a moment. "Sure. Bye."

Patrick trotted up the stairs and into his apartment. He walked over and dropped on the sofa, looking out the window at the fading light of the autumn evening. *As usual, you weren't very smooth. But there's something about her. I've never been smooth with the girls. Never could flirt or chat until I know them. It's been easier with Mary than with most. But she's so hard to read, so hard to reach. There's something between us. I can feel it. I don't know if this will work. Only time will tell. I like her.*

Downstairs, Mary still stood just inside the door, leaning against the jamb. She put a hand up and touched her hot cheek, where he had kissed her. After a moment she turned and locked the door. *What if I call him back? Will he try to kiss me again? I want him to. The thought left her shaken as she made her way to the sofa. My God, it's everything I'm worried about. I've met this boy. I'm drawn to him, and I don't know if he's Catholic. Chamberlain. What kind of name is that? I'll just take it a day at a time. And I'll be cautious.*

Patrick sat at his worktable in his painting class the morning after their dinner in the brew pub. Around him other students were at work. He began to paint, washing in a brown rectangle with patchwork squares, reflections of light from above, yellow and a bit of blue. It was the glossy varnished top of the square table in their booth. On the table were two dark bottles of beer and two round glasses, half empty. The top of the beer frothed in a ring inside each glass. Two square coasters aligned under the round bottles, stark against the dark wood of the tabletop. White highlights, paper left unpainted, marked wet rings where the bottles had been on the shiny table. White napkins, also folded in squares, sat next to the glasses. Between the glasses and the bottles he added two hands, one a right hand, masculine, the other a smaller, thinner, feminine left hand. The hands rested on the table close together, reaching toward each other. They almost touched on the tabletop. Neither hand wore a ring. The composition was all squares and circles except for the two hands.

Finished, he sat back and evaluated the painting. *That's good.*

The professor stopped, hand on his chin, leaning back to assess the work. "It's almost abstract. That geometry of forms, the squares and circles, sets off the human element of the two hands reaching across the table."

"I'm not into abstraction," Patrick said. "I'm a realist. This is a departure for me."

The professor nodded. "Good. Go with it. It may be a passing thing. But see where this takes you."

Patrick picked up the painting, being gentle with it since it was still damp, the paper soft. He signed it in pencil and added a title in small print at the bottom. "Square Peg/Round Hole?"

CHAPTER FIVE

PATRICK AND MARY SPENT THE rest of the week on the neighboring campuses; close to each other but worlds apart. They cooked their meals and ate alone in their apartments, a floor apart. Patrick's footsteps were above Mary. She thought about him though she never went up the stairs and knocked on his door. Patrick was thinking about Mary as well. Sometimes faint music rose from her apartment. The days passed, and it became the weekend.

Saturday morning was devoted to errands and laundry. It was as though the dinner at the pub had never happened. Late Saturday afternoon as Patrick was bringing in his laundry he bumped into Mary at the door.

"Hey, how are you doing?" he asked.

"Fine; it's been busy. How are you?" She smiled.

"Good. Want to do something tonight? Go somewhere?"

Mary fidgeted, looking from side to side as though seeking a place to run to. She pushed her hair back from her face. "No, I'm kind of busy. Another time?"

"Sure. How about tomorrow afternoon, Sunday? Other students in my class told me about a few good places on the coast. I'd like to see more of you."

"Sure. I have church in the morning. I missed Mass this afternoon because of all my errands. But after lunch would be okay."

Patrick's plan was to go to Newport. The ride south was filled with idle talk about their classes. They missed a turn, pulled off the highway early and discovered the village of Jamestown on an island to the west of Newport across Narragansett Bay. They drove through the town and turned, finally coming to a park and a lighthouse; "Beavertail State Park", the sign said. They parked and walked the perimeter of the point. Beneath bluffs were shoals of granite, tidal pools and thundering surf. On the horizon they could make out the faint line of Block Island. It beckoned. Someday we'll have to go there. Sailboats filled the bay. Across the water was the low skyline of Newport. They climbed down a trail washed into the bluff and found a flat rock shelf above the surf and sat side-by-side.

Neither talked for several minutes, as they absorbed the warmth of the sun and the beauty of the view. Finally Patrick started.

"I should have brought my sketchpad. I'll have to lock this place into my mind and paint it, or at least draw it when I get back home. It would make a good picture, a seascape. I would want to sketch you into the picture too."

Mary brushed her wind-blown hair back and looked at him, squinting against the sunlight. "Why not take a picture on your phone?"

"That's not how I work. I paint both what I see and what I feel."

"I like your commitment to your art. You seem to see the whole world as a painting waiting to be painted."

"I like that! That's good."

"Do you draw every day? I mean, is it the most central thing in your life?"

He nodded. "Yes. Of course. You can see that already?"

She smiled. "I'm not sure, but yes. I like your work. I took that drawing you did on the street that day and put it up on my living room wall."

"Wonderful. I'm glad you liked it. So, what about you? Is French the most important thing for you, Mary? What will you do when you get your Masters? What does someone do with a degree in French?"

"No, French is important and I work hard in my studies. It's very important to me to get good grades. I always have and I don't intend to do any less here at Brown. But my Catholic faith is the most important thing for me. It defines my life. It tells me what's right and wrong, what

I should do and what I can't as a good Catholic. That and my parents' expectations of me. My dad expects me to do well and I really want to make him proud."

"Okay," Patrick replied, passing by Mary's reference to her faith and her family. "But can you get a job with your degree? You told me that you could get your Masters in one year. What do you want to do afterward?"

"I'm not sure. I'm loaded with courses this year. So there's not much time for thinking. I'll get the degree and then think about the next step. I can always teach of course, and there are businesses in France or in Canada that need bilingual people. There might be good money if I got a job with a big corporation."

"Nice. You could become a big power-broker working in two languages."

"I can't imagine I would be a power-broker as you call it, but we'll see where I'm meant to be next year. I'll wait and watch the big plan unfold. What about you?"

"I could get my degree in a year as well, though I expect it might take longer. The degree would be good to have but less important than what I learn. The key for me is to refine my art. I'd like to be able to make it by selling my work in galleries. But that's not easy. I might get a job as an art teacher to put food on the table while I wait for my paintings to start selling."

"So, we might both end up as teachers. What is it people say? People who can't do it, teach it?"

"Yes, but I can do it. And I expect you can too, Mary. Teaching is what we could do while we wait for a break that would start us on our real careers."

"Teaching might be the real career for me, Patrick. I think I might like it. My advisor in college, Sister Catherine, could find me a job teaching French."

Late in the afternoon, they found a table in a seafood bar in the village of Jamestown. They ordered dinner, the daily catch special. Patrick ordered a bottle of inexpensive wine featured on a blackboard behind the bar.

"I can't afford wine, Patrick. My budget doesn't allow it." *I hate to have to admit to him that I lack the money to chip in for another dinner. But I know my budget and I can't afford wine.*

"My treat," Patrick said. "I can handle this. It will go well with the fish."

After dinner, windblown, sunburned, and filled with food and wine, they returned to Providence. As before, Patrick leaned in to kiss Mary at her door. And as before, she turned her head allowing him only her cheek. "Good night," she said and went in her apartment.

She stood behind her locked door fretting. *He wants to kiss me. And I want to kiss him. Why can't I let him? He is frustrated when I turn away. Why can't I do it? It's a kiss, nothing more. Maybe next time.*

Patrick bounded up the stairs to his apartment. *God, what's wrong with me? What's wrong with her? Why won't she let me kiss her? It's not that big a deal, I guess. I can tell she likes me. Maybe she'll kiss me next time. I need to talk to someone.* Patrick glanced at the clock. *It's not too late. There's one person I can always talk to.* He dialed his phone. "Hey Uncle Win! How are things back in Maine?"

"Good, good. And how about you? How did the first week of classes go? Any good paintings? I got the photos you sent me of the two paintings. Did anything else turn out well for you?"

"Yes, there was one sketch. A little thing I did walking home one day. But I've done some good work this week. And it's only the beginning, the first week. I expect there's a whole lot more to come."

"Who's the girl? In the one painting?"

"She's a girl I saw walking on the street the first day. I painted it from memory."

"Did you meet her?" Interest was evident in the tone of Uncle Win's voice.

"Yeah, she goes to Brown, and she has an apartment downstairs in the same house where I'm living."

"Okay." There was silence on the line for a few moments before the Win cleared his throat. "Okay. Have you met other people? Get to know other artists. It's as much a part of your education as what you'll pick up in your classes. There is chemistry among artists. They will push you and inspire you. You can learn a lot by being with them."

"Yeah, I've met a lot of really good people. Other students and professors. It's a great environment. A lot of creative people all around me."

"Soak it all in, Patrick. Keep sending me pictures of what you've done."

Nothing more was said about the girl in the picture.

Win sat back after the call, musing about Patrick. *If he painted such a stunning picture of the girl, and if he isn't talking about her, something's going on. Sometimes Patrick leaves the most important things unsaid. He'll open up about her when he's ready, not before.*

Mary called Sister Catherine. "Well, it's happened," she began as soon as Catherine picked up the phone. "I met that boy I was worried about. It's like I knew it was going to happen."

Sister Catherine leaned back in her chair in her room at the school back in New York. "Mary, good for you. Tell me all about him. But first tell me about your first week. Let's start with your classes. How are they going?"

Mary squirmed in her chair. "The classes are fine. I can handle the academic part. It's the boy. He's the problem."

"He's a problem? How can that be? Tell me about him. Is he a student too? What's his major?"

"He goes to this art school down the hill from Brown. He's a grad student there—studying painting. He's good, incredibly talented. I saw him one day doing a drawing on the street. A sketch, and when he finished it, he gave it to me. I taped it on my living room wall."

"Tell me more about this boy. Do you like him? It sounds like you do."

"I don't know." Mary sighed, looking down, covering her face with her hand. "I guess so. He lives upstairs in the same house where I live. We bump into each other all the time."

"So, you like him. Why is he a problem? Have you gone out with him? Do young people really go out on dates these days? Have things changed in that regard?"

"We had dinner one night. And we went to this rocky point of land with a lighthouse today and had another dinner together."

"Wonderful. What's this young man's name?" A smile could be heard in the woman's words.

"Patrick. Patrick Chamberlain."

"So now then. What seems to be the big question for you is this. Is he

Catholic? Is that the problem?"

"I don't know. And you know how I feel about that."

"Yes, I do. So, do you think you'll see him again? Out to dinner twice in your first week in Providence tells me something about you and him."

"Yes, I expect we will be seeing each other again."

"So, the next time bring up your faith. Ask if he's Catholic. Maybe he is. But if he isn't, that's not a reason to stop seeing him if you like him."

"I told him I was Catholic. I told him it was important to me."

"Good. So what is the problem, dear Mary?"

"He tried to kiss me. Twice. Actually, he did kiss me. On the cheek."

Sister Catherine chuckled. "Yes. So?"

"Is that wrong? Is it a mistake to let him kiss me? Should I kiss him back? I'm not like my sister. It shouldn't get to that."

"Trust your heart. Whether he's Catholic or not is only an issue if it bothers you too much. It balances against what you think of him and what he thinks of you. The key is this; do you like him? If you do, go ahead. Let him know you like him. Kiss him, but be careful. Margie made a mistake, moving in with her boyfriend. I know you won't do what your sister did."

"I will never let it go any further than a kiss."

"Of course, you won't. So relax, dear Mary. It will be all right."

<hr>

Patrick and Mary went out for pizza one evening early the next week. They sat in the noisy, neon-lit restaurant and chatted, sharing stories about their classes and their schools. They laughed about the dramatically different cultures of Brown and of RISD. It was incidental; small talk that filled the time as they approached the moment when they would return home. At the end of the evening, they faced each other at Mary's door, awkward as teenagers on a first date. Neither said a word. Then Patrick placed his hands on Mary's shoulders. He leaned down. And Mary stretched up. They kissed.

Patrick held on to Mary for a moment to steady himself. Finally, he let go, stepped back, and smiled. "Good night." He let his hands drop down her arms, gave her hand a light squeeze, and turned toward the stairs.

Mary lingered for a moment, watching him go. Turning to unlock her door she said a harried, "Good night, Patrick."

Elated, Patrick walked up the stairs to his apartment. *Well, she kissed me! Finally, she kissed me. I've kissed other girls before, and it's never been a big deal. But oh my god. This is something special!* He pulled out paper and paint. Less than an hour later he had her portrait. Sunlight filled the painting. She was radiant. Brilliant highlights surrounded her smile. Her eyes glowed. Dark hair blew back from her face like a corona. To her left he added white, foaming, hard surf pounding the granite shoreline, ragged and wild. To her right, at the top of the bluff, the Beavertail lighthouse took shape, a square and solid tower rising against a clear sky. He signed it but gave it no title. None was needed.

He tacked it to the apartment wall next to the two earlier works; Mary at the campus gate and their hands on the pub table between the glasses and wet rings.

One floor below, Mary sat on her sofa in the dark. Her thoughts were chaotic. *I did it. I kissed him. Oh my God! I kissed him.* She felt like laughing with the thrill. *I've never dated that much. But I've had a few boyfriends, and I've kissed boys before. It was never like this. Oh my God! Sister Catherine said it would be okay. And it was more than okay. But she also warned me to be careful. I must not give in to temptation. Oh my God!*

She picked up a textbook but couldn't focus. She tossed it aside and called Sister Catherine.

"How are you, Mary? How's that young man, Patrick?"

"Good."

"Good? That's all you can say? Good?"

"I kissed him tonight." *It feels like a confession. I don't have anything to confess, do I?*

"And..."

"That's it."

"Good. What happened? How did he react?"

"I don't know. I kissed him goodnight, I came into my apartment, and he went off to his. That's all."

"Well. Good. Relax, dear Mary. He sounds like a nice young man. And you like him. Did you ask him if he's Catholic?"

"No."

"Why not?"

"I don't know. Maybe I'm afraid of what he'll say. If he is Catholic, where might all this lead? And if he isn't, what should I do? I like him and don't want to lose him."

"You need to ask him, Mary. You're going to church every weekend? Ask him to join you."

—

Patrick called Uncle Win.

"Hey, Patrick," Win answered, his voice betraying a smile over the phone. "What's up? Two calls in a couple of days?"

"Nothing, I guess. I wanted to call. Wanted to talk."

"Is everything all right?"

"Yeah. Great actually. I had another dinner with that girl. Mary. I painted her from memory tonight when I got home."

"I'd like to see more of her than in that first one you did. You show her face this time?"

"Yes. I'll photograph the new painting and send it on my phone."

"You do that."

Patrick sighed. He'd left so much unsaid.

CHAPTER SIX

TIME PASSED. THERE WERE SMALL steps, small victories in their relationship. They walked up College Hill together each morning and shared lunch once or twice each week. A kiss good night became part of their routine though it was never insignificant to either of them. Weekends they went out; to a movie or to listen to music in a Providence pub. Simple dinners out were included in their weekends as well, as much as their grad-student budgets could allow. Aside from that, they always ate alone. Mary was afraid to go into his apartment for a meal, and she couldn't allow him into hers.

After a month, Patrick offered a new idea for the coming weekend. "Hey, Mary, Columbus Day is Monday, so it's a long holiday weekend. A couple of my friends say there's a big arts festival outside Providence. They want me to go. And they want to meet you. I've told them about you. What do you say we join them on Saturday?"

Mary became quiet, thoughtful. *Should I? I've become acquainted with a few other Brown grad students, mostly French majors, but I don't know any of Patrick's RISD friends. It's time.* "Sure. Where are we going?"

"It's in a little town a few miles west of here. They tell me there will be hundreds of artists set up in booths on the town common and people buy their artwork."

"I can't afford to buy anything, but it sounds fun. Who are your friends?"

"They're a couple. He's a sculptor. Aaron. Works with steel and a blow torch and makes big, abstract metal pieces. His girlfriend is Melanie. She works with glass and makes small ornamental things, very pretty, kind of abstract as well. They live a few miles away, up on the northern edge of Providence and have a gallery there. They both make a good living with their art. He sells in galleries all over the east coast."

"They're still students even though they're successful already?"

"No, he's on the faculty. Melanie's graduated too, but she's in one of my painting classes. She believes we should always be students; always learning, always growing."

"Okay. Let's go to the art show on Saturday."

Saturday morning they drove to the old mill town of Pawtucket. Patrick parked his Volvo, checked the address, and led Mary to a door in one of the cavernous old brick mills. Signs on doors announced art galleries, dance schools, restaurants, and a bar. Posters in the window of the bar advertised concerts with rock bands. A sign stenciled on one of the vast plate-glass windows next to the door they approached read "Dragonfly Gallery". They went through the door and were in a dark, echoing lobby hallway with worn oak-planked flooring. A dark staircase went up one side of the hall to a landing and turned. A newly varnished paneled door across from the stairs had the Dragonfly Gallery logo: a fanciful art-deco insect on a reed in a rippled pool. Patrick knocked. The door burst open. A tall, broad-shouldered man, his head crowned with short curls of black hair, filled the doorway. He wore jeans with no belt, leather sandals, and a faded denim shirt open two buttons at the collar. A light-blue glass dragonfly hung from a chain, resting on the dark hair of his chest.

"Patrick!" He shook Patrick's hand and pulled him close in a quick embrace. "And you must be Mary. He's always telling us about Mary." Aaron placed a hand around the back of her head, pulled her forward, and kissed her forehead. "It's wonderful to meet you! I'm Aaron." He turned and led them into the studio. "Come on in. Let me give you a quick tour. Melanie will be ready in a minute"

Mary froze, stunned by his greeting and the kiss. *This is too much, too soon.* She gathered herself and followed the men. She looked around the gallery and was amazed by his sculptures. They were arresting and monumental; dark metal for some pieces, others buffed to a silvery sheen. Most were larger-than-life figures, heroic in attitude, abstract in form. Some incorporated parts of motors, gears, and links of chain. Mary was overwhelmed by their mass, their weight.

"Aren't these heavy?" she asked. "The floor's wood. Are you sure the floor can hold them?"

"Obviously the answer is yes," Aaron replied. "But that was a concern. That's why Melanie and I are here. We looked for a long while before we found this place. When it was a mill, they had big machinery here. The floor is reinforced. I work in this space, and I have a second studio over at RISD in the basement. Moving is a challenge, though. I have a heavy-duty Ford truck with a winch for that."

Half of the gallery, an airy section on the front of the mill, was sunlit with tall windows. This section was devoted to glass. On clear shelves were tiny figurines of blown and pulled glass. Some were crystal, some frosted. Translucent pastel colors floated in many. A few featured highlights of a metallic glaze. There were birds, insects, and fairies with wings of hair-thin strands of glass resting on the shelves, aglow in the morning light. Some were designed to hang on invisible fishing-line threads from clear acrylic stands. Others, like the dragonfly Aaron was wearing, were jewelry on tiny silver chains. They were breathtaking.

"Good morning, everyone." Melanie made her entrance. She proceeded slowly down a wrought-iron spiral staircase, turning and smiling at her guests as she came. Patrick and Mary were dazzled; drawn to her water-blue eyes and her delicate porcelain-doll features. She was dramatically beautiful, though her hair, cut in bangs, was dyed a pale blue that matched her eyes. As she got closer Mary noted that even her eyebrows were tinted a faint blue. She wore white linen pants that flowed about her legs but fit her hips like a second skin. For a top, she had selected a loose white macramé halter; no bra. Thin shoulder blades accented her narrow white back. Her only jewelry was a silver ring in her navel with a sculpted turquoise glass bead. A narrow silver chain dropped from the ring to several inches below her navel and vanished into the top of the linen pants. Delicate silver straps clasped her sandals.

Even Aaron was speechless for a moment. Recovering, he introduced Melanie to Mary. All he could say was "Melanie," his voice hoarse as he gestured in her direction.

Melanie beamed.

After introductions, they went to Aaron's BMW in a garage beneath the old mill. As they were getting in, Mary whispered to Patrick, "A BMW? You said he and Melanie are artists. How can they afford a car like this?"

Patrick leaned over and whispered, his lips brushing her hair. "They both do really well. They're a little older than us and they sell their work in galleries in Boston and New York."

"Do you think you will ever be that successful?"

"I hope so. They're already established. Art collectors know them and they get orders online. Maybe someday I'll be like them."

They drove west, parked, and walked the last half mile with crowds of other art lovers into the town of Scituate. They were part of a throng of hundreds, maybe even a thousand; suburban couples, noisy packs of high-school kids, rich and poor, young and old, all drawn to the event. Bands played. Concessions sold clam cakes and cheeseburgers to raise money for various charities and high school trips.

It was a brilliant Indian summer fall day in New England. Warm sunshine bathed the crowd. Yellow-leafed maple trees glowed in contrast to the deep cloudless blue of the sky. A white clapboard Congregational church with a black-roofed steeple watched over the town common.

Aaron and Melanie led the way, Melanie striding along, her arm wrapped around her tall man. Mary clutched Patrick's hand, nervous about losing him in the crowds. She watched peoples' reactions to Melanie. Women stared and more than a few gave disapproving looks and whispers. Men stared too, some turning after she passed, stunned by her otherworldly beauty. Melanie seemed oblivious to the reactions.

Many rows of tented booths where artists displayed their work filled the common. Mary allowed Patrick to lead her. Patrick stopped when he discovered artwork he liked, chatting with the artists, asking how they had created their paintings. They spent several hours at the show before heading back to the car.

"Did you buy anything?" Mary asked the group. "You seemed to find things you liked."

Patrick smiled but said nothing.

Aaron laughed. "Some of the work here is good. But we're that good too, all three of us. Coming to a festival inspires us, but our art is as good as what we've seen. Better than a lot of it."

"I've thought about setting up a booth here," Melanie chirped. "But I'm selling my glass as fast as I can make it. A booth costs money I don't need to spend. And it's three long days of work. I would have to be here all weekend. I'd rather spend my day out in this beautiful sunshine playing with all of you."

Aaron started the BMW. "Anyone want lunch?" he asked "I know a great place not far from here." Patrick and Melanie agreed; Mary followed the trio of artists. Aaron drove west, crossing the line into the hills of eastern Connecticut.

After lunch Aaron announced, "One more stop before we head home." There was no discussion; no debate. He turned to drive farther west and then south, cruising small country lanes past gabled white mansions, forests, and dairy farms. He finally pulled into a gravel parking lot at what appeared to be a rustic farm. "Here we are." he stated. "Sharpe Hill Winery. We'll take our time and enjoy a wine tasting. This is my treat. I sold two big pieces in New York this week. I'd hate to have that money just piling up in the bank."

Behind the old, gray wood-sided barn was a garden enclosed with a zigzag rail fence. A ridge rose beyond the fence covered with leafy rows of grapevines, hanging with dark, late-season fruit. Warm autumn sunlight sifted through the bright leaves of trees above the garden. A bar had been set up under the trees. Bow-tied waiters served the visitors who sat among the mums and other autumn flowers. Mary and the artists lingered over liberal pours of several sample wines. Neither Mary nor Patrick knew much about wine, but they were able to recognize that the wines they tasted were extraordinary.

The three artists discussed their artwork, telling tales of their recent creations. Mary listened. Melanie was in the midst of a story, her musical voice enchanting them, laughing about some silliness that had happened in a gallery in downtown Boston, when Mary felt a chill and noticed the sun was low in the sky. She checked her watch. *Four o'clock. Mass is at five on Saturday. We're at least an hour from Providence. All but one week since coming to Providence I've gone to the Saturday Mass at Saint Joseph Church up the hill on Hope Street. That one week when I missed the Saturday Mass, I went Sunday morning. I'll have to wake up early tomorrow morning to go to Mass.*

When they were ready to leave, Aaron bought a case of wine to divide among the four of them. Mary and Patrick got six bottles of her favorite, a complex white wine evocative of grapefruit, green apples, and other tart fruits. Mary had never tasted anything like it before. She liked the label too; a folk-art picture of a colonial-garbed girl.

"Ah," Aaron said as he added their bottles to the case. "You like Ballet of Angels. It's one of Sharpe Hill's best sellers."

Ballet of Angels? What a lovely name, Mary thought. *It symbolizes our day together. It has been a magical day in so many ways; the beautiful foliage in the country, the art festival, lunch, and the slow-paced leisure in the garden of the winery.* Mary sighed. *I've been swept along; following the group from one place to another, timid, and afraid to tell them I wanted to go home. I've lost control. And now I've missed Mass.*

Back at the gallery, Aaron invited Patrick and Mary to dinner. Patrick accepted before Mary could decline. As she had all day, she followed the lead of the three artists.

Up the spiral stairs above the gallery, the loft was spacious; wide open with a high beamed ceiling. It was a harsh contrast to the small apartments that Patrick and Mary each had in the old student house on Wickenden Street. Tall windows set into brick walls looked out onto a courtyard within the old mill complex. The loft was an open area furnished as a living room and dining room. At one side, two doors opened, one into a kitchen and another to a bedroom. Through the open door of the bedroom, Mary saw a wide four-post bed with a lacy canopy. Aaron and Patrick crashed onto two couches. Aaron turned on the television. "It's time for college football. The west coast games should be at halftime. What about you, Patrick? You like football?"

"I've never watched. Bowdoin had a team, but they weren't very good, and I was off painting on Saturdays anyway."

"I love football. I played in high school. Tight end. My art teachers worried that I'd hurt my hands, but think about it. I'm lifting raw metal and welding every day. If my hands are going to get hurt, welding will do it as easily as football. But I stopped playing when I got to college. Art schools don't usually field football teams. I miss the game."

Mary and Melanie went in the kitchen, leaving the men sprawled on the sofas. Melanie pulled things from the cabinets and the refrigerator. "Pasta and shrimp," she explained. "Do you like shrimp, Mary?"

"Yes."

"Great. Lend a hand. I love to cook. The way I see it, cooking's as much an art as art itself."

"How long have you and Aaron lived together?" The question was impolite, but Mary was intrigued. *I've only known a few women aside from my sister who lived with a boyfriend before marriage. There have been short-lived relationships and one-night stands among a number of my friends, but nothing sustained. I've never allowed myself even to dream of spending the night with a man.*

Melanie paused for a moment. "Let me think." She put a hand to her mouth, amazed. "Four years. Oh, my! I hadn't thought about it, but we've been together four years. That's the longest I've ever been with anyone."

"Why don't you get married? You seem like a loving couple with a good relationship."

"We are. I love him to death, and I guess he loves me too. But I'm not the marrying kind of girl. Besides, we're committed to each other, with or without vows."

"I would have thought you'd at least have been engaged. He hasn't proposed?"

Melanie laughed her quiet, musical laugh. "I've been engaged three times, to three other men, of course. I was always good at getting men to fall in love with me and want to spend the rest of their lives with me. But I could never imagine that whole 'rest of your life' thing. It's a good thing I never went through with it. None of those engagements lasted long enough for me to get married. Not until Aaron. I'm not a churchgoer, and the Justice of the Peace civil ceremony thing seems like a stupid waste of time. So where do you come down on all of this?"

"I'm Catholic. I wouldn't live with a man unless I was married. It's wrong."

"I used to be Roman Catholic. That's how I was raised. I went to my First Communion and wore the white dress and the whole thing. And I do believe in God. Or something, a supreme force I guess. But I don't think the church should tell me who I can love, or how I should love them. And not with the way some priests behave, certainly. The hypocrisy!"

Melanie diced tomatoes and dropped the pieces into a simmering stock broth mixed with a bit of olive oil.

"Not all priests are bad," Mary whispered.

Melanie looked up. Mary leaned, her back against the counter with her arms folded across her chest, her face set into a hard mask. Melanie stopped working, put her knife down, wiped her hands on a white towel, and went to Mary.

"I don't mean to offend. Please forgive me. I can see that your faith matters to you. I respect that. I value you and your viewpoint. But this is just me. This is the way I am. I'm so devoted to Aaron. I can't imagine being without him. I know he feels the same way. We're not married. But our relationship is strong. Please understand that."

Mary looked at her and gave a slight smile. She paused and took a deep breath. "Can I say something?"

"Of course."

"When I first met you this morning, I was overwhelmed. I've never gotten out that much and met people who weren't living normal, average lives. But Melanie. You with the hair and the clothes and all that. I was put off at first. But somehow, as the day passed, I've changed. I guess I know you better and I can see that deep down, you're a nice, sweet girl."

"Thank you, Mary. That's so nice of you to say."

Mary had said a lot already, but she continued, struggling to find words to explain her thoughts. "You're not exactly down to earth; you're pretty far out there in space. But I love your art, and I can see you and Aaron are happy together. It just flies against my Catholic beliefs and everything I was raised to believe. I could never do anything like that."

Melanie nodded. "I understand." She took Mary's hands and held them tightly. She smiled her incandescent smile and Mary softened. "So, can we be friends despite our differences? Please? You might not believe this but I don't really have many friends, aside from Aaron of course, and now Patrick. I scare most people and they don't know how to act around me. Too many men only want to sleep with me. And a lot of women just don't like me. I don't know why. But I need a girlfriend I can talk to. Can we be friends?"

What should I say? Mary thought.

Melanie smiled again and Mary found herself nodding "Yes, okay. Yes. Friends." *I don't see any other way. I've been following Patrick and his two friends all day; now I'm being dragged into this friendship with Melanie. I feel like I'm moving without a direction, with no guidance from the structure I find in my faith and the values of mom and dad. But Melanie is fascinating, all her eccentricities. Should I tell Sister Catherine about Melanie and this whole day? What would Sister Catherine have to say? Maybe it would be best if I don't tell Sister Catherine.*

The two women hugged, then Mary busied herself arranging silverware on the table.

Melanie went back to the dinner preparations, dropping fettuccini into a pot of boiling water. "So, then. How about you? You've been seeing Patrick since the start of the semester. How's that working for you?"

"Good! We like each other, enjoy each other's company."

"Yes. I can see that. And I understand your religious beliefs and respect that. Where do you think it's going for the two of you?"

Mary hesitated. *I want to grow this new friendship with Melanie but already the conversation is getting more personal than I want.* "I don't know. We're taking it slow. It will grow into whatever it's meant to be. I haven't even been inside his apartment and he hasn't been in mine. It's only been five weeks. We live in the same house and that's close enough. We see each other every day and that's where we are with things."

"Five weeks? In some relationships that's a lifetime. You should invite him in. I can see that you're a strong woman. It'll be okay and nothing will happen that you don't want. Make sure he knows how you feel and don't close him out."

"I don't know. I'm not closing him out. I don't want to come across as someone I'm not."

"You won't. I expect he'll be fine with it. He seems kind of traditional, kind of shy, too. But you don't want to hold back so much of yourself that you lose him, do you?"

"Of course not."

"So, invite him in. Cook him dinner."

Melanie coaxed and Mary listened while they went back to preparing that evening's meal. Mary peeled the shrimp; Melanie stirred the sauce. Feta cheese was ready to be added to the mix. The pasta drained in a strainer in the sink. Basil was chopped for a garnish.

When dinner was ready and they were at the table, Aaron opened a bottle of the Ballet of Angels from the winery. Then he turned to Mary. "Where are you from in New York? I'm down there all the time."

"The Bronx. Some of the Bronx is a sketchy part of the city but where my family lives is okay, a nice neighborhood. We also have a place up in the country about an hour north of the city in Connecticut. It's where we go on vacations and weekends."

"Really! Maybe you know the people who bought my two pieces last week. The Addisons? They wanted two pieces out of my catalog; a smaller one for the front hall of their townhouse in Manhattan and a big piece for the garden at their home in Connecticut, in Greenwich. Do you know the Addisons?"

Mary shook her head. "I don't think so. I expect my family moves in a different circle. We own a little place on Putnam Lake. My dad built it." The conversation changed to talk of other acquaintances at RISD, of gallery exhibits, things Mary knew little of. Still, she was intrigued. This was Patrick's world. She wanted to learn more.

As they were saying goodnight, Melanie pulled Mary aside. "Thank you for our talk in the kitchen," she whispered. "I appreciate that it wasn't an easy topic for you. How about we get together next week? Maybe lunch? My treat."

"Sure, I'd like that. I have a lot of time mid-day on Wednesdays."

"Perfect. I'll meet you at the front gate of your campus at noon on Wednesday."

"Thanks. I'll see you then."

Mary rode home tired but content. At last, she had another friend in Providence besides Patrick.

They climbed the steps to the front door of the house. Mary cleared her throat. "Ahh, Patrick, Tuesday night, do you have plans for dinner?"

"I don't know. Not really. Why?"

It's time to find out where this relationship is going. Mary took a deep breath. "Could you come to my apartment for dinner? I'll cook, or we can cook together, the way I did tonight with Melanie."

"Sure, that's great. I'd like that."

The evening ended with their customary kiss. When he was gone, Mary sat shaking on her sofa. It was such a beautiful day with Patrick. The kiss was so warm, so intimate, after being with him all day. *I must be strong. I can't be tempted by everything that's happening to me.*

Chapter Seven

MARY HAD NEVER DONE MUCH cooking. She checked recipes for something simple and inexpensive and settled on meatball stroganoff. All it required was ground beef, mushrooms, onions, a can of mushroom soup, and sour cream. The recipe called for wine but Mary ruled that out. She would cook everything in a deep iron skillet and serve it over egg noodles. She chose a side of salad; lettuce out of a bag bought in the supermarket.

Tuesday night came and Patrick knocked on Mary's apartment door. "Come on in," Mary said, hurrying back to the kitchen. "I chilled a bottle of the wine Aaron bought us. Could you open it?"

Patrick worked the corkscrew into the top of the bottle and poured the wine into the glasses Mary held out.

"I made meatball stroganoff. I hope you like it. I don't cook much."

"I love beef stroganoff, so I'm sure I'll love it." While Mary served, Patrick surveyed the room. The furnishing was sparse; the standard futon, tables, and chairs that came with college-owned student housing. The furniture and layout was an exact duplicate of his apartment. Lit candles adorned the tiny table next to the front window. The sole picture adorning Mary's walls was his small sketch of the cobbled street, tacked up in the middle of the living room wall. Mary's only other addition was a small television.

After dinner, Patrick refilled their glasses with the last of the wine. They settled on the sofa and found a historical drama on PBS. Outside, it was dusk. Quiet street sounds filtered through the window.

There had been the long weekend, an early morning wake-up on Sunday for Mass, and an all-day study session to make up for the weekend of play. It began to catch up with Mary. Patrick was no better. He had been up late Monday night painting a cityscape of old Providence.

Actors droned on the television, obsessing in British accents about a nineteenth century Parliamentary intrigue. Mary and Patrick dozed.

When Mary awoke, it was dark outside. The television flickered, now showing the ten o'clock news. Mary yawned and stared at the blaring television. *The ten o'clock news? It's that late?* She was startled to find she had reclined against Patrick as they slept on the sofa, leaning back against his chest. His arm encircled her shoulders, his hand resting lightly near her breast. Her hand was lying in his lap, on his thigh. Patrick's head rested against the sofa, his breathing relaxed in slumber. She snatched her hand back.

This is wrong! All of it! But it feels right, so natural and comfortable. Mary straightened and pushed Patrick's hand off her.

Patrick awoke, still dreaming, and sat up. "Mm, what time is it?" he asked.

"It's late. Get up. You've got to go." Mary stood and pulled him to his feet.

"Thanks for dinner." Patrick drew her to him and held her. "This has been a great, relaxing evening. I'll cook for you sometime later this week maybe."

"That would be nice. But it's late. You've got to go." She pushed him out the door.

"No goodnight kiss?"

"Of course. Sorry." She gave him a cursory brush of her lips. "I'll see you in the morning, okay?"

"Sure." He gave her a tired smile. "Usual time."

She closed the door. *It's too late to call Sister Catherine. And what could I possibly say to her? I can't tell her what happened tonight.*

Mary went to bed, her mind anxious and her body shaken. She couldn't fall asleep until dawn.

—

The next morning, the picture came together in the first few strokes of Patrick's brush. At the center was a white clapboard church, its plain walls broken with black-paned, shuttered windows. Vertically the picture was bisected by the church steeple at the top and a wide walkway to the church doors at the bottom. Horizontally it was divided by the tumbled- down granite walls of a cemetery. On one side of the steeple the sky was a deep blue. On the other, gray cumulus clouds gathered. Above the stone wall next to the church were maple and oak trees, the colors gold and crimson. Beneath the wall, the cemetery was a checkerboard of white headstones and long, wind-blown, straw-colored grass. Flecks of yellow and red, fallen leaves, dotted the cemetery lawn. Patrick titled the picture, writing in small print in pencil at the bottom, "Autumn Contrast — Where are we going?"

The instructor surveyed the painting. "Well done! You've turned away from the abstract forms of the last couple of pictures. This is more traditional. I like the depth of the colors."

"Thank you." Patrick nodded, continuing to assess the fresh painting.

"I sense a lot of symbolism." The instructor adjusted his glasses, leaned in to read Patrick's inscription. "Is that intentional?"

"Maybe. What are you seeing?" It seemed brazen to question his professor. He and Uncle Win had always debated their paintings, but this man wasn't his uncle. "Sorry, no offense."

"None taken. It appears to have religious overtones. Besides the obvious of the church and cemetery, the picture itself is designed with a cross pattern, centered on the church. And there's the tension between the blue sky on one side of the steeple and the gathering clouds on the other."

"Okay. Maybe." *It wasn't my intention, but it makes sense.*

The instructor continued. "Is this a new direction for you?"

Patrick shook his head. "I'm comfortable with landscapes."

"Don't always do what's comfortable. This is good, but it's safe. Don't be afraid to try new things. See what happens. You'll know when it's working."

The advice made sense. An image of Mary flashed in his mind. Patrick smiled. It could work for his painting and his relationship with Mary. "Try new things. See what happens."

"Mary. Over here."

Mary turned to find Melanie waiting at the gate. At first, she didn't recognize her, but Melanie's distinctive soprano voice called out. Today Melanie was dressed in black; from baggy black pants tucked into black high-laced boots to a black turtleneck. Her hair was now dyed black as well. She wore oversized black sunglasses. Her face was pale, almost white, devoid of any makeup.

"What happened to your hair?"

"I dyed it."

"I can see that. Why?"

"People change their clothes every day," Melanie said. "I figure why not go all the way, so I change my hair color every month or so."

"Sure, okay. But with a look like this there's got to be a tattoo somewhere I haven't noticed. Am I right?"

Melanie laughed. "Of course there's a tattoo. Here, let me show you." She unbuttoned her pants and started to unzip the fly. A flash of black lace sent Mary into a panic, appalled that Melanie might drop her pants right there on the street in front of strangers. Is she going to drop her pants? She can't! "Stop!"

Melanie laughed again, seeing the shock on Mary's face. "Mary, I'm kidding. I don't have any tattoos. Tattoos are permanent. They last forever. Nothing about me is permanent. I have piercings, yes. But those grow closed if you leave them alone." She zipped and buttoned her pants.

Mary laughed, her unease evident. "You got me. I thought you were going to—"

"No. Of course not. Even I have boundaries."

Melanie gave Mary a quick hug then wrapped an arm across her shoulder, steering her down the hill to a sandwich shop

"I liked the blue hair," Mary said, surprising herself. *Now I'll have to come to terms with Melanie's new black look.*

"This is the new me. It's my fall look in preparation for winter." Melanie ushered Mary into the restaurant and found a booth near the windows. A heavily tattooed waiter, dressed in black, took their orders.

"I cooked dinner for Patrick," Mary said.

"How'd it go? What'd you cook?"

"Meatball stroganoff. I found a recipe. It was good!" *I need to sound enthusiastic so she'll believe it was a good evening. It was a good evening, almost too good. But I was surprised how well the meal turned out. I'll talk about that. It'll be safer than delving into what happened after dinner.*

"Wonderful. I knew you would turn out to be a good cook. Did Patrick like it? Did the two of you have a good time?"

"Yes. It was good."

"Okay…" Melanie let a lift of her tone turn the single word into a question, suggesting that she was waiting for more.

Mary offered nothing.

"So, after dinner? What did you do after dinner? Don't tell me you both went off to study."

"No, we watched television. It was boring. We dozed off."

"Okay. And then what? Where did things go from there?"

"Nowhere." *Leave it alone.* "We just nodded off for a few minutes. That's all. We woke up about ten and he went to his apartment. Nothing happened."

"Okay, okay. But come on, Mary. Would it be the worst thing in the world if something did happen? It's obvious you like each other."

"Yes, it would. I'm not like you, Melanie. I'm not going to do that. I can't. It flies in the face of everything I believe in; my Catholic faith, my parent's expectations, everything that matters to me."

"Okay. Okay." Melanie rested a hand on Mary's forearm. "Just relax with him. Be yourself."

Mary hung her head. "I am being myself. We are happy. Very happy. We're letting things move at their own pace. We're fine."

"Of course you are. Let's change the subject," Melanie soothed. "Tell me about your classes."

—

Patrick and Aaron sat in Aaron's RISD basement studio with subs bought off a food truck parked near the river. Wide doors allowed a flood of sunlight, warming the concrete floor. The room was clean but held the odor of burnt metal. Patrick had helped Aaron hoist a small piece of sculpture into the back of Aaron's truck. Now they were eating their sandwiches while resting on wood crates filled with scrap metal. Bottles of tea and paper napkins were spread on a nearby pallet.

"Thanks for the weekend out in the country," Patrick said. "And for dinner. It was nice to get out of the city for a while."

"You're welcome. Yeah, Melanie's a good cook."

"Mary and I should have you guys over some time. It turns out Mary can cook too."

Aaron paused. He finished chewing and lifted a paper napkin to the corner of his mouth. "Sure. Melanie and I would love to come to dinner. Mary can cook? She's cooked for you?"

"Yes. Last night. It was the first time. She invited me to dinner."

"Hey, that's great, man. Good for you. And good for her, too. I didn't expect that. The two of you seem a little more conservative. Not the kind of people to be spending time together in each other's apartments. Nothing wrong with that." Aaron waved a dismissive hand. "Just not what I expected of you two."

Patrick nodded. "Yeah. We're kind of conservative. Maybe we've both been raised in sheltered homes. I guess that's part of why we're hitting it off so well." He hesitated a moment. "Can I ask you something?"

"Sure."

"You're pretty experienced, right?"

Aaron nodded.

"If I wanted to move things along with Mary—do you have any suggestions? I've done it a few times, to see what it's all about, but this is different."

"Different how?"

Patrick ducked his head. "I've just never loved anyone enough to do it again. I want it to be special when it happens. With a girl I really love. And I won't do it till I'm sure."

Aaron shook his head, sat back, and looked at his friend. "Love? What's love? You think you're in love? With Mary?"

"Maybe." Patrick busied himself with his sandwich.

"You don't know where to start with Mary?" Aaron's tone was gentle, like an older brother ready to offer guidance. "Good for you. Things will move along when you're both ready. I think it's kind of refreshing that you're getting to know each other so well first."

Patrick stared out the open door of the studio. "We've almost started a couple of times, I guess. But one or the other of us always backs off. I guess I need help. We want to—I want to. I think she does too, but we've both got some baggage. For me it's my family. Sheltered home. Mother was always concerned that I would get in trouble with girls. Put the fear of God in me about it. And after that one girl in college, things didn't go so well with her. But now I'm ready. I want it, but Mary and me, we dance around the edge and I can't seem to move things along."

Now Aaron was embarrassed too. He smiled to himself for an uncomfortable moment and shook his head. "I guess you do what comes naturally. Explore her body the same way you've been exploring her mind. You'll figure it out. Don't worry about it."

"What if I scare her off? I don't want to do too much and drive her away."

"She comes across as just as much afraid of things as you are, but she wants you, too. It's in her eyes and in the way she stays so close to you. Trust your instincts. Make a move on her, but carefully. She'll probably be happy that you made the first move."

"Maybe. Okay. I don't know."

"Be careful, man. Just do what comes naturally, what's comfortable for both of you. And go buy some condoms, just in case."

Patrick nodded several times. "I'm going to see her tonight. I'll ask her about having you and Melanie over for dinner."

Aaron crumpled the empty sandwich paper, his big hands crushing it into a tight ball and pitched it across the room into a steel barrel. "We'll be there whenever you'll have us. Now give me a hand lifting this metal."

Chapter Eight

MARY WENT TO PATRICK'S APARTMENT for dinner on Friday night. He planned spaghetti, a simple meal he knew he could cook. Ingredients were on the counter in the small kitchen when Mary arrived.

Mary stopped the moment she came through the door from the hall into the living room. The floor plan and the furnishings of Patrick's apartment were the same as hers. But the walls of Patrick's apartment were covered with artwork. There were cityscapes, landscapes, and still lifes. There were watercolors, pencil sketches; some big, some small. Mary thought of the one little sketch he had given her that she'd hung in her living room.

"It's like an art gallery in here," she exclaimed. "It's your own personal one-man show."

Patrick smiled, pleased that she liked his work. She began to walk along the wall reviewing the paintings. She paused, looking at the first portrait he had done of her at the gate the morning they met. "I love this one. Is this me?"

"Yes. I did that the day I first saw you. Do you like it?"

"Yes." *He painted this portrait of me before we even met! He didn't even know me then. And look. This is our hands on the table at that pub where we had our first date. What does he mean by the title, "Square Peg/Round Hole"? This is me at the lighthouse we went to that Sunday afternoon. It's overwhelming to see how much of his art involves me.*

"This is me again! At the lighthouse we visited a few weeks back. You paint or draw something every day?" Mary was overwhelmed.

"Yes, at least one thing I do each day is good enough to keep, sometimes two. Here, this is my portfolio." Patrick opened the flat, black-leather case to expose a stack of other artwork. "Here are a bunch of other things I haven't put up. I've done all this since I got here in early September."

He handed her the case. She thumbed through drawings and painting while Patrick watched. She came to the picture of the church he had painted after their weekend in the country.

"Here's another one, from another day we were together," she noted. "They're amazing. I really didn't understand till now how good you are. They're incredible. I love every one of them."

Patrick was quiet. *It's embarrassing whenever people make a fuss over my work. But I'm thrilled that she likes it.* "Yes. I paint the way some people keep a diary. You mentioned it yourself the other day when you said I see everything as a picture waiting to be painted."

"Yes, but it's me you've painted several times. I didn't even pose for you."

Patrick answered cautiously again. "You don't have to. I have you in my mind's eye. I hope you don't mind. It's not like I've been stalking you. But we're together every day. And I paint what I see every day, what I'm thinking about, what interests me. You know I like you. You're beautiful and I want to show that."

How can he think of me as beautiful? How should I respond? She blushed. "No, it's okay. It's fine. Thank you. Would you like me to pose for you sometime?"

"If you would, yes. But I can paint you from memory. I know you by heart; I know your face."

Mary smiled and continued to flip through the stack of artwork, pausing at each one.

Oh, my god. I can't let her see the rest! What will she think? Patrick caught her by the arm and closed the portfolio. "Come on. Let's cook dinner," he insisted.

Mary pulled away and opened the folder again. "Just a minute. I want to see the last few pictures."

Patrick let her go and stood back waiting. At the bottom of the stack were two pencil drawings; nude figures of a woman, one standing, the other sitting on a stool. The woman appeared to be middle-aged and overweight with a round belly and sagging breasts.

"What's this?" Mary turned to confront Patrick.

"I have a drawing class once a week; Thursday afternoon. Sometimes we draw still life; bowls of fruit, flowers, that sort of thing. Sometimes they have models pose for us."

"What's her name?"

"I don't know for sure. Everyone calls her Sadie. She's been posing for RISD classes for years, they tell me."

"Why did you keep these drawings? They're pornography."

"They're art. The human body is a beautiful thing. Even imperfect bodies, like this woman. Don't you see that? I think they turned out pretty well, so I kept them. There's one you saw earlier in the portfolio? The one of the pile of vegetables is from the same class. Back near the top of the stack of pictures. Go back there and take a look at that one."

Close the portfolio. Why can't she let it go, look at different pictures, anything.

Mary closed the folder. "I don't have to go back to look at a drawing of vegetables," she said. "I'm not at all comfortable with you looking at a naked woman, even if it is for an art class. Staring at her, capturing every little detail of her body. And then you keep these drawings? A still life is one thing but not this."

"I shouldn't have to apologize for this!" Patrick argued, red in the face with anger. "We had a male model once, too. I didn't keep those drawings because they didn't turn out as well as Sadie did. And when I draw her, it's absolutely the same as drawing a still life. It's capturing the shapes, the light, the shading. No more, no less. Another shape."

"And when you asked if I'd pose for you?"

"First, you offered. And yes, I'd like to paint you, draw you. But not nude."

"Good." Mary closed the portfolio. "Let's cook dinner."

"Thank you!"

They moved to the kitchen. Tension remained. Patrick tried a new tack as he began filling a pot with water for the pasta. "How are your classes going?"

"Fine."

"What are you working on? What are you reading?"

"Victor Hugo."

"Oh, really. Tell me about it."

Mary stopped and turned to face him, hands on her hips. "Look. I like you a lot. But I need time to come to grips with what you do with your art. Those drawings of the woman? That's hard for me to deal with. Okay?"

"Sure. Give it time. Think it through. It's art, that's all. You're the woman I spend my time with. There's no reason for you to be jealous. She's a model. We've never even talked. She comes in, poses for an hour. Nothing more."

"I'm not jealous!"

"Fine. Then drop it. Forget you ever saw it."

Mary remained silent but she was more composed, the tension leaving her shoulders. She poured the spaghetti sauce into a pan and began to heat it.

"Victor Hugo's okay," she began, regaining her composure, trying to restart the conversation. "I enjoy his stories. I'm not sure it does much for me or my education except to make me comfortable thinking in both English and French. I don't think it does anything more to help prepare me for a career of some sort where I would use my fluency in French."

Patrick nodded, allowing her more time to elaborate. He brought the meat out of the refrigerator and dropped it into a frying pan. *Maybe we can cook together and enjoy our dinner. Maybe she can move on from her aversion to the nudes and the argument will be forgotten.*

Mary continued, "My advisor says that some companies will be on campus in the spring looking for people like me. They'll be international companies of one type or another. They recruit for bilingual fluency more than expertise in the business world."

Patrick nodded again. "Yes, you mentioned that. Where do you think you'll end up working?"

"France. Canada. Anyplace where French is commonplace. Where do you think you'll end up?"

"I don't know. We both might become teachers. But where I go to work is wide open. I can paint anywhere. As long as it's near enough someplace where there are galleries to sell my art."

Mary stirred the sauce, concentrating on her cooking, not looking at Patrick as she answered. "Wherever I end up living and working, could you move there to work?"

"Maybe. I'd like that. We have the rest of the year to sort all of that out. But I like the idea of us staying together after we graduate. It's still early in the year. We have time."

"Yes, it is. But I want to be with you or at least near you." It was a significant admission for her. She hadn't intended to say it. Once again she had let her thoughts come out before she could stop herself. Now it was out there for both of them to consider.

They finished preparing the meal and sat at the small table next to the front window to eat, just as they had downstairs in Mary's apartment. Patrick had put a lit candle on the table between them but the lights were still on, the room bright, diminishing the atmosphere of the candlelight. As they cleaned up from dinner Patrick offered, "I had lunch with Aaron today. I asked if he and Melanie would be interested in coming over for dinner sometime. We owe them after this past weekend. He said yes."

"I had lunch with Melanie today, too. I like her, eccentric as she is. That would be fun. Maybe we could have them at my place. We could cook together for them."

"Good. Any evening is okay for me next week. How about you?"

"Any evening will work for me too."

They ended the evening with a lingering close hug. For Patrick, the fuss over the nude drawings was forgotten. Mary's anxiety about nudity remained though she couldn't bring herself to talk with anyone about it, certainly not with Sister Catherine or Patrick.

Saturday morning was devoted to errands and laundry. They had plans to meet for a movie in the evening after Mary returned from Mass. On an impulse at the laundromat, Patrick took out his sketch pad and began to sketch her face life-size from memory while he waited for a load of wash to dry. He swept her hair back from her face as though caught in a breeze. Her eyes were wide. Her mouth was slightly opened and smiling as though she were about to laugh. The dryer hummed to a stop as he completed the sketch.

Back in his apartment, Patrick propped up the sketch on the kitchen table. *It's perfection.* The likeness captured her beauty as well as her restrained happiness. He tore the sheet from the sketch pad and laid it on the kitchen table. With his watercolors he added faint hints of color to the pencil sketch. Pale green framed her head, bringing it out from the paper. He washed in darkness over her hair, giving it depth. He touched light peach to her face and cheeks and a stronger rose on her mouth. He added vibrant dark blue to the irises of her eyes. The effect was stunning. As a final touch he painted in a narrow chain around her throat. A crucifix hung from the chain, resting between her collarbones.

When it was finished and dry, Patrick signed and matted the portrait and set it into an old black-steel frame he had brought with him from Maine. He hung it on the wall above the sofa, directly across from the door into his apartment. It would be the first thing anyone would see when they came through the door.

When they returned from a movie later that evening Patrick paused inside the door to their old house. "Could you come to my apartment for a moment?"

"Okay. For coffee?"

"Sure, we could have a cup. But I want you to see the new painting I did today."

Patrick unlocked his door and turned on the lights. Mary stopped. Her hand went to her mouth.

"Do you like it?"

"Oh! Patrick, it's beautiful. I know it's me, but I'm not that beautiful."

"You are to me."

"I love it!" She hugged him and held on, turning to look at the picture again. "I'm flattered. I don't know what to say. You did this from memory?"

"Yes."

"And I was going to pose for you. I thought maybe you could paint a portrait for my parents for Christmas. But you've already done it."

"Do you want it? I could hang it for you downstairs in your apartment if you'd like. Then you could give it to your parents."

"Would you? You don't want to keep it for yourself?"

"No, that's all right. It's yours."

Patrick took the portrait and followed her down the stairs to her apartment, bringing a hammer and a picture hook with him. *It doesn't matter; I can do another one. Mary will always be with me, locked in my mind.* He hung the painting in the same spot he had hung it in his apartment.

—

They met at the end of the day Monday and walked to their house. "Let's cook dinner together tonight," Patrick began. "It'll give us practice for when we have Aaron and Melanie over."

"Did you ask him?"

"Yes. They're coming Thursday. I was worried he might have the Jewish holidays to contend with. I don't keep up with these things but I think there's a Jewish holiday sometime in the fall and then Hanukkah sometime before Christmas. But he said it's not a problem and Thursday works for both of them."

"Aaron's Jewish?"

"Sure. You didn't know? Aaron Goldschmidt? Of course he's Jewish."

"I didn't realize. I didn't know his last name, and I didn't think about the name Aaron. It's not always a Jewish name. I guess I should have realized."

"Is that a problem? I don't think he's Orthodox. I don't even know if he goes to temple."

"No, it doesn't matter. Melanie told me she used to be Catholic." *I know so little about these new friends of ours.*

"Maybe she is. I never ask a person about their religion."

"What's her last name?"

"I don't know. She goes by just Melanie. That's all anyone calls her. No last name."

They sorted through Mary's refrigerator looking for something to cook.

"I have some chicken." Mary held up a package. "As long as we're on the subject of religion, tell me, are you Catholic?"

"No. Protestant. Methodist, I guess. There's a Methodist church I go to sometimes when I'm home."

"It doesn't seem as though it matters to you."

"I'm not like you when it comes to religion," Patrick confessed. "I go to church, but if I miss it once in a while it doesn't bother me. I guess I'm okay with any church."

"Have you gone since you got here in Providence?"

"No. I've been kind of busy." *That sounds like a weak excuse. But I shouldn't have to apologize for my beliefs. I guess if it matters to Mary I ought to explain.*

Mary frowned, then continued. "I've been busy too, but I make sure to find time to go every week. And I pray every day. You could find time if it mattered to you."

"I guess."

"Come to Mass with me this weekend." *Why am I so assertive with him, practically ordering him to come to Mass with me? I've never done this before. But I've never dated a boy who wasn't Catholic before either. It matters so much that Patrick comes to church with me.* Mary watched him. *He seems lost, unsure how to reply.*

"Please?" she added.

"Okay."

⌒

After dinner, when Patrick went up to his apartment, Mary called Sister Catherine.

"Mary! How nice of you to call. I haven't heard from you for a while. How are you?"

"Good, very well, thanks."

"How are your studies going?"

"Also, good. There's just been a lot going on. I'm sorry I haven't called." *Or told you about Melanie or sleeping on the couch with Patrick.*

"That's all right," Sister Catherine said. "Are you still seeing that boy Patrick?"

"Yes. We had dinner tonight. We baked chicken in my apartment."

"That's nice. What else have you been up to?"

"Mostly just going to my classes, studying, and doing things with Patrick. He's nice. I asked him tonight if he was Catholic. He's not."

"Oh, Mary. Don't give up on him because he's not Catholic."

"I'm not giving up on him. Yes, I do like him. I asked him to come to Mass with me this weekend."

"What did he say?"

"He said yes."

"That's good. Don't push too hard to convert him though. He'll become a Catholic if it's right for him. Please don't pressure him."

"I won't. He's not religious at all. He's not even sure what kind of Protestant he is, maybe Methodist, he said."

"Okay. But a person's faith is a personal decision. Respect his beliefs. And don't stop loving him because he's not Catholic."

"I won't. But who says I'm in love with him?"

"You do, Mary. Every time you talk about him, I hear it in your voice."

"Okay. Maybe. But is that wrong?" *Am I in love with him? He's all I think about. What should I do? I'm not ready to discuss this with Sister Catherine.*

"Of course not. You know him. You know what you want."

"Okay."

"Good night, Mary. Take good care of Patrick."

Mary set her phone on the sofa and sat, restless, fidgeting. She pushed her hair back with both hands and closed her eyes. *Oh, Sister Catherine. There's so much I want to tell you. About Aaron and Melanie. Patrick and my feelings for him. Why can't I tell you? I'm so drawn to him. Why can't I bring myself to talk about all this? What am I doing? What should I be doing? I have no one to talk to about any of this except Sister Catherine and Melanie and maybe my sister Margie. But I'm afraid to ask any of them. What would they tell me to do?*

Chapter Nine

AARON AND MELANIE ARRIVED FOR dinner. Their entry into Mary's apartment was boisterous. Aaron hugged Patrick, then embraced and kissed Mary as he came in, holding her against his wide, hard chest. Mary pulled back. *He's always so physical with me. It's disturbing.* Melanie greeted Patrick with a light brush of her lips on his cheek and a soft embrace. Mary she held for a long moment, looking into her eyes and smiling without saying a word.

They brought bottles of wine. "We didn't know whether you were cooking for a red or a white wine so we brought two bottles of each," Aaron said.

"Is it red meat tonight? I hope so. I love the red wine we brought," Melanie said. "And red meat." Her black attire seemed to have turned her into a serious carnivore.

"I'm afraid it's chicken," Mary answered. "It'll have a bread crumb and parmesan crust. It's another recipe I found online. I hope it comes out okay."

"So, white wine then," Aaron said. "And I'll leave the reds here for you to enjoy later." He set the two red wines aside and began working a corkscrew on one of the whites.

Melanie noticed the new portrait of Mary on the wall. "Oh, wow!

Patrick, you did this? Oh my God! I love it."

Aaron assessed it. "I've seen a lot of your work," he said. "But this is exceptional. When did she pose for you?"

"She didn't. Not yet. I did it from memory."

"Wonderful! Beautiful," Aaron praised. "Mary, you're a lucky woman to have a guy like Patrick. This is good work."

Patrick grinned. *This is great, the attention the portrait's receiving from people who understand quality art.*

Mary blushed. *Everybody's looking at my portrait. It displays me so beautifully.*

Patrick changed the subject. "Let me take your coats. Let's get into that wine while we cook."

Mary brought out the chicken she had prepared and set it inside the oven. Aaron poured from the first chilled bottle of wine; Melanie handed around the four glasses. Patrick turned two of the dining area chairs to face the futon.

The evening was cordial, light talk about art, laughter always following Melanie's contributions. Dinner was good. Shortly after nine Melanie yawned, brushed her black hair back from her face, and pulled Aaron's arm. "We should go," she said, standing. "I'm tired. And I'm sure Mary and Patrick want some alone time. They don't need us hanging around till all hours."

The evening ended; Aaron and Melanie were gone. Patrick and Mary cleared the dishes and began washing them. Patrick was drying the last pieces and Mary was putting them into the cabinets when she said, "I like both of your friends. I guess I should call them our friends now. I wish I knew more about art so I could understand everything the three of you talk about. But I enjoyed this evening."

"You don't need to be an artist to understand what we do. I'll explain it."

"Please do. And you're coming to church with me Saturday? You need to see that side of my life. I need to learn about your art and you need to learn about my faith."

"Yes, I said I would. And we can go somewhere afterwards and do something?"

"Of course."

They kissed and Patrick left to go upstairs to bed. Mary sat on the futon and began to read. Precious study time had been lost with the dinner. She had to catch up.

Saturday afternoon was cold and gray, hinting at snow. They walked up Hope Street to Saint Joseph's, a small stone church a few blocks up the hill from their apartment house. Patrick held open the thick, red-painted wooden door and followed Mary in. She paused for a moment inside the door, dipping her fingers in a shallow bowl on a pedestal, and then made the sign of the cross. They walked up the aisle and he stood behind her as she genuflected and slid into a pew. Patrick sat next to her. While she waited for the Mass to begin, Mary pulled her rosary out of her purse, closed her eyes, and began to pray, her lips moving.

Patrick sat quietly, respectfully, observing the décor of the building, the people, and the priest preparing for Mass. He noted the way the evening light flooded through the stained-glass windows surrounding them, coloring the sanctuary. Racks of small glass jars were along the walls in the back. Candlelight flickered in many of them. Above it all was the grisly image of the body of Christ suffering on the cross.

People of all sorts filled the pews; college students and working- class people of all ages, races, and ethnicities. He compared their rough clothing with the crisp white, the dark velvet and gold trim of the priest's robes.

Mary opened her eyes, turned to Patrick, and handed him a small booklet. "Here's something you can read to help you follow the Mass," she whispered.

Patrick began to read. As the Mass began, he discovered the prayers printed in the booklet, but the Mass skipped around, leaving out sections, repeating some prayers. Mary followed without the booklet, quietly intoning the prayers and responses. Patrick was lost. He stood when Mary stood, sat when she sat, knelt when she knelt. *How does she remember all this?*

The priest's words echoed in the quiet. *What did he say?* The people around him rumbled in response. It was something about sin and the lamb of god. He picked up the last words. "Have mercy on us." Then, "Give us peace."

This is surreal. It's like watching a strange play in a foreign language. The priest walked around the altar trailed by two boys wearing robes like those worn by the choir back at Patrick's church in Maine. The priest swung a metal globe on a chain, spreading smoke around the altar. Then he picked up a tiny white disk, broke it, and held it above his head toward heaven. *Communion. They have communion at my church in Maine with little cups of grape juice and tiny cubes of bread they pass up and down the pews. But this is different.* The bread appeared to be the disk the priest held, and the wine was in a large, decorated silver cup which the priest lifted the way he had raised the bread.

People stood and walked up the aisle toward the altar.

"Stay here. I'll be right back," Mary whispered. She pushed past him into the aisle and followed the line of people to the front. The priest mumbled as the people stood before him. One by one, he placed something in their mouth. Bread. He tipped the big silver cup and they seemed to sip. Then the people returned to their seats, hands folded, heads bowed. A few walked to the back of the church and out the door. Mary sat next to him again. She closed her eyes and resumed her prayers.

Moments later the Mass was over. Mary tucked her rosary into her bag, stood, and smiled. "There. We're done. Let's go find dinner."

⌒

"So, what'd you think of it?" Mary took a bite of her burger.

"Interesting. I've never gone to a Catholic service before."

"Is it much different from your Methodist services?"

"Yes, but I don't know if that's the difference between the rural seacoast of Maine and urban Providence, or more a theological difference."

"What was different?"

"The prayers. A lot were unfamiliar. And you leave out the last few lines of the Lord's Prayer."

"That's the Lord's Prayer we say. What do we leave out?"

"The last few lines. 'For thine is the kingdom, the power and the glory forever.' You stop after saying, 'Lead us not into temptation and deliver us from evil.'"

"Oh. Well. That's the Lord's Prayer. That's how we say it."

She hesitated a moment, considering the last lines she had repeated so many times. *I've never given them much thought.* "Lead us not into temptation, and deliver us from evil." *I need to remember those lines. Now, more than ever.*

Patrick smiled. "The service was more elaborate than I'm used to, almost theatrical, and the sermon was a lot shorter than ours."

"We call it the homily. It's a short message."

"Ours is longer. It can take twenty minutes, sometimes more. It's a big part of a Protestant service."

"Our Mass focuses more on the prayers and communion."

"I should take you to a Protestant service so you can see what we do," Patrick offered.

"Sure. Maybe. But will you come to Mass with me again?"

"Sure. I can do that."

"Next week maybe?"

"Sure."

Chapter Ten

THEY SETTLED INTO A NEW routine. The days were consumed by classes. Every evening they cooked dinner, sometimes in Mary's apartment, other times upstairs at Patrick's. After dinner, they separated, Mary studying and Patrick painting. They went to Mass together every Saturday. Even so, they both felt like they never had enough time with each other.

Then it was Thanksgiving. On Tuesday evening before Thanksgiving break they ate an early dinner and walked to their already packed cars in the dirt parking area behind the house.

Silence accompanied their farewell hug and a kiss. After a moment Patrick spoke, his voice choked. "This will be the longest we've gone without seeing each other since we got here in September. I'll miss you. Will you miss me?"

Mary buried her face in his coat. "Of course. We'll call each other. And we're both coming back on Sunday. It's not that long, just five days."

He nodded. "Drive carefully. Call me when you get to your house."

"You too. Drive safely."

Mary and her sister, Margie, walked down the narrow road from her family's vacation house on Putnam Lake. Thanksgiving had dawned, bright and sunny but cold. Frost dusted the brown leaves next to the road. Margie swung her arms the way she did when she walked the Manhattan streets. Mary hurried next to her, her arms folded at her chest.

"Tell me all about Providence," Margie said. "I know we've talked on the phone, but it isn't the same as being together. And this is the first time we can have a sister talk without mom and dad hanging around. How's it going?"

"Great! I love Brown."

"Ivy League. Very impressive. You know I'm proud of you. Mom and dad are too. Tell me everything."

"My classes are going well. The school is nice."

"Come on, Mary, details. What have you been up to?"

"Give me a moment. I'm out of breath. You're walking so fast." Margie slowed down.

Mary began again, strolling now, having caught her breath. "It's a good school and the professors are great. I'll be interviewing for jobs in the spring."

"Cool. What else have you been doing? What's Providence like?"

"It's an old city. I live down the hill from the college. There are a bunch of student apartments there. Lots of historic houses and cobblestone streets. Very pretty."

"Nice. And you hang out with other grad students?"

In spite of the different paths their lives had taken the sisters were close. Next to Sister Catherine, and now possibly Melanie, Margie was the one person Mary could confide in.

"I have a boyfriend."

Margie stopped and turned to her sister. "What? Oh, Mary! That's wonderful. Another grad student?"

"Yes, but he's at an art school a couple of blocks away from the Brown campus. He lives in an apartment in the same house as I do."

"Okay. What's he like? What's his name? Details. This is important."

Mary paused. How should I answer? Sister Catherine recognized from my tone that I'm in love. Will Margie? Does it matter if Margie knows?

"His name is Patrick. He's amazing. He's an incredibly talented artist. He does watercolors mostly. And we just plain connect with each other. We understand each other like I never have before with a boy. Things are really good."

"Oh, Mary!" Margie hugged her. "I'm so happy for you. Are you going to tell mom and dad?"

"I don't know. You know how they are. They want you and Javier to get married. It's all they talk about. And they want the same for me. If I told them I had a boyfriend, it would start with me too. You know me, always trying to do the right thing. Always trying to live up to their expectations."

"Yeah, I understand. Your secret is safe with me. Tell me more."

"There's not much more to say. We hang out together, the two of us, and sometimes we do things with a couple of his friends who are also artists. Sometimes we cook each other dinner. We go out together on the weekends."

"What else?" The tone of Margie's question carried with it a desire for more key information.

"What else?" Mary answered, blushing. "We're not intimate, if that's what you're suggesting. We're not sleeping together. You know I can't do that. It's a sin, and anyway, it's not what mom and dad would want me to do."

"Why not? Do you love him?"

Mary hesitated. "Yes, I think I do."

"And have you told him?"

"No."

"You should. And does he love you?"

"I think he does."

"Then sleeping with him would be the most natural thing in the world."

Mary spoke with a touch of anger in her voice. "Maybe for you. You've always been a rebel. You defied mom and dad and turned your back on the church. Dropping out of college and moving in with Javier. But it's not that simple for me. It would be a sin and I can't do that. It's wrong. I know where the line is and I can't cross it."

"Go to confession afterwards. Use precautions. Get the pill or something. Talk to a doctor and then go to confession."

"It's a sin, confession or not. It's wrong. I won't do that." Mary was adamant.

Margie stopped. "Okay. Let him know you love him. Tell him at the very least. Please let him love you. And love him back."

The sisters resumed walking. There was no more discussion of Patrick. Mary became thoughtful. Patrick's choice of religion didn't even come into the conversation. *All that seems to matter for Margie is that I love him and he loves me. Maybe that's all that should matter for me. But it does matter. Right is right. And wrong is wrong.*

That and so much more. *It's obvious that he wants more from our relationship. I want that physical part, too. But I can't. What Margie does with Javier is Margie's business, but this is different. This is me and Patrick. I know what mom and dad expect of me. The Church has taught me that it's wrong. But how, if we love each other, could it be so wrong? Maybe if there was just a bit more to our nights together?*

As long as there's no sex? That alone would not be a sin, would it?

Mary continued thinking, trying to work out the puzzle, trying to reconcile what she was feeling with what she believed, what she knew to be right.

—

Patrick led the way down a path to a cove through dry branches of bare blueberry bushes and barren beach roses. Uncle Win followed. The warmth of the Chamberlain house was across the meadow a quarter mile away on a bluff. Mother was in the kitchen puttering with the turkey, the vegetables, and the pies. Tom was attempting to straighten the living room and set the dinner table, aligning the forks, putting everything in its place.

The path opened to a rocky beach, slag, water-worn pebbles that slid rattling beneath Patrick's and Win's feet. Barnacles and bits of kelp spotted the rocks. The high tide line was defined by a long, dark mound of dry seaweed, spongy beneath the men's feet.

They came to a spot sheltered from the bite of the wind; large rocks and drift logs forming a barrier. It was a place they had come many times in the past to talk without the distractions and clutter that dominated the Chamberlain house. They sat side by side, facing the channel on a driftwood log.

Win took off his gloves, zipped his jacket part way down. The day was chilly but he basked in the noon sunshine. "Okay, let me hear about the past months. I know your painting is going well. But I want to know what your life has been like. Are you enjoying yourself?"

Patrick smiled, thinking of Mary. "It's been a great experience. I've been knocking out at least one good drawing or painting almost every day. Maybe it's the environment at RISD. Maybe it's the city itself. But I'm inspired like never before."

"Maybe it's the girl." Win winked. "What's her name? Mary?"

"Yeah, it could be her." Patrick tried to sound casual, unemotional like his father. "She's a good friend. And I have a few artists who have become good friends, too. I've told you about Aaron and Melanie."

"Yes, I knew about Aaron already. I'm familiar with his work. I've seen his sculpture at galleries in Boston. And Melanie. Glass has always been a strength at RISD ever since Chihuly was there. RISD is a great environment. But tell me about this girl Mary. I've seen plenty of pictures of her. There are the paintings you've done of her. And you showed me that photo of her you have in your wallet. She seems pretty."

"Yes, she is pretty."

"What's she like? You told me she's studying French at Brown. That's fine, but what makes her tick?"

"She's smart like you might guess from her being a grad student at Brown. We enjoy each other's company. And she's a good cook."

Uncle Win laughed. "You include her cooking skills as a virtue? I know you. This kind of thing isn't common for you with a girl. Do you love her?"

Patrick smiled. "I've had girlfriends before this."

"Sure you have. But none that you've painted over and over again. Your time in Providence has changed you and it's not just the city or RISD. It has to be the girl."

Patrick nodded and looked down at the rocky beach at their feet. "Yes, Mary's something. I guess maybe I'm in love."

"You make it sound like it's something you have to apologize for. I think it's wonderful! Fantastic!" He clapped Patrick on the back.

"Yes. I'm not apologizing. I wake up every morning amazed that this is happening, that I have her. I don't know what's going on half the time with her and me. I don't always know what to do with her. I've never really been here before. But it's great."

"Now don't get like your father, all laconic, like having emotions is a bad thing. And don't let your mother scare you off of this. This girl's inspiring you in more ways than just your painting. Don't lose that."

"Okay, but I'm not ready to tell father about Mary. Or mother; I can imagine how she'll react when she learns that there's another woman in my life besides her."

Uncle Win laughed. "Yes, when you're ready for that conversation you might want me to be there to back you up. I'd want to be there anyway to see her face when you tell her."

Patrick laughed too. "Do you think they'll be aware enough to notice that so many of the paintings in my portfolio are of the same person?"

"Probably not. Maybe your father, but not your mother. And he won't talk about it if he does notice. What do you and Mary do together? She cooks dinner for you?"

"Yes, we cook together and we go out on the weekends. We spend time together most evenings after we get home from our classes. She studies a lot, has a lot of reading to do. But recently she's been cramming her study time into the days so she can be with me at night."

"She's with you at night?" Win asked, his eyebrows arching.

"Yes, in the evenings." Patrick thought about what Uncle Win might be implying. "Not like 'in the night'," he added, making quote marks in the air. "We're not at that point."

"Okay Patrick. I know you. I know how you are. I know how you've been raised. But don't be afraid. Let this happen if it's meant to be."

Patrick nodded. "I'm not afraid. I'm just moving with a bit of caution. We're both moving slowly."

"You know how to be careful? Buy some condoms before you get too far along."

"Uncle Win! Come on, I'm not there. Not yet."

"No, not yet. But if you and this girl Mary are in love with each other, that moment will come and you need to be ready."

"Got it." Patrick shook his head, already dismissing this last piece of advice.

"Okay." Uncle Win clapped Patrick on the shoulder. "Thanksgiving dinner should be almost ready. We'd better start back. I'm glad we were able to grab a few minutes alone to talk about this. It's a conversation that we needed. It's one we need to continue."

They stood and began the slow walk back along the rocky beach.

The low surf of Casco Bay washed in, shushing through the pebbles.

Mary drove Margie back to the city on Saturday then headed across town to Fordham to meet Sister Catherine and have lunch at a small restaurant.

"It's good to see you again." Sister Catherine settled into a chair. "It seems like ages since you left for Providence. Bring me up to date. Are you still enjoying your time there?"

"Yes. My classes are going well. I've added extra classes so I can graduate this spring. I might even have a job by then. Companies are coming to interview people."

"Good. What else are you doing? What about Patrick?"

I don't want to talk about Patrick. "I'm learning to cook. From recipes on the internet. It's fun and most of them turn out pretty well."

"Wonderful. What about new friends? What about the boy?"

"Yes, I've told you about Patrick. And I've become friends with a couple of other artists Patrick hangs around with."

"That's nice. How are things with Patrick?"

Mary paused, considering how much information to give Sister Catherine. *She knows me too well. I can't hide anything from her.* "He's great. We're doing well."

"Now Mary. Tell the truth. Is he 'the one'?" Sister Catherine made quote signs in the air with her fingers as she said it. "We've talked about how you seem to be in love with him. Where do you think this will go with the two of you?"

Mary broke down for a moment, her confusion and anxiety bringing her to the edge of tears.

"I don't know. I think I might love him. But I can't. He's not Catholic. And I don't know what to do about him. I can't leave him. And there's so many things I can't do with him. There's the sin of course; it's wrong. Sex outside of marriage. My sister and her boyfriend, and my parents and everything. I don't know what to do."

"Take your time. It's not like you two have talked marriage—have you? If it does come to that, yes, you could marry him. It happens all the time with couples who aren't both Catholic."

"No, but what do I do till we get to that point? Everyone keeps telling me what I ought to be thinking, what I ought to be doing with him. But I'm not that girl. It's a sin."

"I can imagine what they are saying. Do what you know to be right, Mary. Not because of what your friends are saying. Look into your conscience. Do what is right for you and right in the eyes of the Church. If you need to go to confession, then go. Confession won't make everything right. But it will help you be at peace with it. You need to find that harmonious balance within your Catholic beliefs."

"Maybe I should just give it all up and become a nun. That would be a lot simpler. And you said you could get me a job teaching French. Maybe that's what I should do."

"Oh, Mary. You're not ready to go down that path. Not even close. You shouldn't become a novitiate in order to run away from the things in your life. Go back to Patrick. Go back to Providence and do what's right."

After lunch, Sister Catherine offered one last piece of advice. "Be very careful, Mary. Look for that balance between what you know to be right and what sins you are drawn to. But if you love this young man, tell him. Don't lose him because you're afraid."

Mary drove back to Providence and stocked up on groceries. Patrick wouldn't be returning till Sunday afternoon. She was alone. *I need him. I just want to hold him.* She began to wait, counting the hours till he would be back.

—

Patrick sat with his parents and Uncle Win in the cluttered living room.

Books and magazines were piled on tables, under tables, next to tables. It was claustrophobic but Mother was too consumed with her reading and other academic interests to be bothered with cleaning or straightening. To her the house was fine. She sat on the edge of the sofa, her straight graying hair pulled back in a ponytail. Her hands were clenched in her lap.

The only room in the house that wasn't chaotic was Tom's study. Patrick's parents had come to a tacit agreement. Tom would accept the way the rest of the house was if Mother stayed out of his study. That room was his haven. Tom required things to be orderly so that he could think. He kept his office tidy. Papers were filed away. Books were lined up on the bookshelves that covered one wall of the room, the spines of the books aligned like a regiment of soldiers. The only things on the desk were the computer, the keyboard, a mouse, and a pottery cup filled with a handful of ballpoint pens. Even the trash basket was empty.

"You're heading back after lunch on Sunday?" Uncle Win broke the silence.

"Yes, I don't want to get caught in Boston traffic."

"Couldn't you stay till after dinner in the evening? Why the rush?" Mother pleaded.

"Sorry, Mother, but I need to get back and settle in. Classes start Monday morning."

"Do what you have to do, son." Tom was fine regardless of whenever Patrick chose to leave.

"You'll be okay, Patrick," Win said. "You need to get back and catch up on things with your friends. Let me know about all of that."

Chapter Eleven

AS PATRICK PULLED INTO THE parking area behind the house late on Sunday afternoon, he was excited to see that Mary's Honda was there. He parked, grabbed his duffle bag and portfolio, locked the car, and ran to the house. Mary waited at the front door. He had called her when he left Maine and she had been watching for him for the last hour.

He dropped the bags and held her. Mary buried her face in his shirt, diving into his scent. Patrick kissed the top of her head. After a long moment, they pulled back.

"Come on in," said Mary. "I have dinner in a Crock-Pot I brought back from home."

"Thanks. Dinner would be nice. Can I put my things upstairs first?"

"Later. That can wait. Just come in with me. Put your bags here by the door." *Now that he's back I don't want to let him go for even a moment.* She pulled him in and hugged him again.

Patrick dropped his bag and portfolio and Mary closed the door. They sat side by side on the sofa.

"I told my sister about you," Mary said.

"And your parents? What did you say to them?"

"They're not ready for me to tell them yet. Maybe later. At Christmas."

"Me too. Uncle Win and I talked about you. But not my parents, either. Mother won't take it well that I have a significant girlfriend."

"Why not?"

"No matter what, you won't be right. No one would be. She's always afraid she'll lose me; to a faraway place like Providence, to a girl, to anything. I'm still her little boy."

Mary gave it a moment of thought. Then she teased, "You're not a mama's boy, are you? Still tied by the apron strings?"

"Do I seem like that?"

"No."

"For her, maybe she wishes I was, but no, I'm on my own; my own man. My father and mother have influence I guess, but I don't always follow their advice. They don't talk much to each other and they talk even less to me. Uncle Win is the one I listen to. He's my advisor."

"That's what you've told me. So what did Uncle Win have to say to you while you were back in Maine? What advice did he have?"

"He said I should tell you that I love you."

"Did he? And do you? Do you love me?" She snuggled closer.

"Yes, of course. You knew, didn't you? Does it even need to be said?"

"Yes, I knew. But yes, it needs to be said. My sister and Sister Catherine told me the same thing."

"What?"

"That I should tell you that I love you." She looked down, unable in the moment to look him in the eyes.

They sat quietly next to each other. Nothing could add to the enormity of what had just been said. They had been back together only minutes and now it was done. Patrick put his arm around Mary and she leaned in to him.

"I missed you these past few days," she said.

"Me too. It was a long time. Not being with you and so much happening, so many things I wanted to show you in Maine. So many little things I wanted to tell you. I can't remember them all now. They seem trivial. But every moment; I wanted to be able to share them with you."

They sat with nothing more to say for several minutes. Mary finally ended the silence. "Let's get dinner," she said.

She served the beef stew she'd made in the Crock-Pot; another recipe she'd found online. They ate quietly. Then they sat together again on the sofa watching television. The evening passed into nighttime.

"I've got to go," Patrick said. "We both have to get ready for our classes tomorrow."

"Don't go. Stay." Mary surprised herself, letting the words slip out.

She turned to Patrick and held him, hiding her face in his shirt.

"You think we should?"

"Yes. I want you to stay. I need you here with me tonight. Spend the night with me. There are boundaries, though. We can sleep together but without sex."

"Okay." It came out as a tense whisper.

"Come on," she said, standing and taking his hand. She led him to the bedroom.

She found that she was shaking. *I've never done this before. Even though Margie and Melanie both urged me to take this step, it still frightens me. I want Patrick; I know I love him. And the days we've spent away from each other make me need him even more. But it's a sin. Sister Catherine counseled balance; to hold on to him but to do what's right and to steer clear of sin. I'm so confused by these emotions. I need to be strong.*

"What should I wear?" Patrick asked, his voice tight in his throat.

"Whatever you'd be comfortable in. I sleep in a t-shirt and panties."

She went in the bathroom and closed the door. Patrick heard water running. He went to his duffle bag. In it were freshly laundered clothes. He brought the bag with him into the bedroom. He found his toilet kit and took out his toothbrush and toothpaste. His heart was racing; he was almost out of breath with anticipation. No sex, she said.

Mary came out of the bathroom carrying a bundle of clothes. A long t-shirt came to the tops of her bare thighs. "Your turn," she said, avoiding eye contact.

Patrick went in, brushed his teeth, and paused, looking in the mirror, evaluating where he was in his life, what this moment, this night might become. He unbuttoned and took off his shirt then his jeans. Wearing just a t-shirt and shorts he returned to the bedroom. Mary was under the covers, tugging them to her chin, lying on her back.

The bed was the standard furnished-student-apartment issue; a narrow double bed. Without a word Patrick got in. Mary turned out the light. He put an arm across her and kissed her quickly on the cheek.

"Good night," he said.

"Good night."

They lay together for a while in a half embrace, eyes open in the dark, neither talking, neither able to sleep. Patrick's hand came up to her shoulder, but then it slipped down to her breast. He had rarely touched a woman like that before. And never a woman he loved. Her body shifted and she sucked in her breath. She said nothing. He left his hand there, exploring, discovering.

Mary pulled away as best she could in the narrow bed. "No. I said no. I want you to stay. But no. We can't."

"No, but you want me to stay?"

"Yes, stay please." She turned and kissed him, hard on the lips, her hands on each side of his face. "But no. We can't do that."

"Okay."

They lay together in the dark, both wanting everything, neither able to go any further. They finally fell asleep so close together.

—

The seven o'clock alarm startled them both awake.

"We've got to get up and get going. I'll shower first," she said. "Then you." She ran from the bed to the bathroom. Her t-shirt was bunched above her waist, showing her bikini panties.

Patrick pulled a fresh shirt from his bag. He put on his jeans, went into the kitchen, and started a pot of coffee.

Mary hurried back out of the bathroom wrapped in a towel, her hair hanging wet. "I put a towel on the sink for you."

"I've got coffee going."

"Good."

He took his toilet kit and went into the bathroom. It was the mirror image of his bathroom upstairs except for an assortment of bottles and tubes in the tub. Body wash, shampoo, conditioner, all in scents of a variety of fruits and vegetables. Patrick was learning about women, more and more by the minute. He showered, shaved, dressed, and came out to find Mary sitting at the table by the front window with a bagel and a cup of coffee.

"There's another bagel in the toaster. Come join me. It's a beautiful sunny morning."

They sat quietly, sharing breakfast, watching as the city woke up outside their window. Neither spoke about what had happened the night before. Or about what had not happened.

When breakfast was finished, Patrick stood and leaned down to give Mary a kiss.

"Give me a moment," he said. "I've got to go upstairs to get my stuff for my classes."

He took his portfolio to his apartment but left his bag in her bedroom.

He grabbed his backpack with his sketch book. When he got back to Mary's apartment she had her coat on.

"Come on," she said. "We can't be late."

—

Late in the afternoon, Patrick stood by the campus gate, their usual meeting place for the walk home. Mary wasn't there. He waited a few minutes and then called her phone.

"I'm at the house. I got done early today. Come on down." Patrick jogged to the house, eager to see her.

She met him at the door to her apartment and handed him his duffle bag. "Let's have dinner at your place tonight. Do you have any food?"

"No, but we can call out for pizza."

They went up to his apartment, ordered the pizza, and settled in to watch television for the evening. They talked little.

Mary stood. "I've got to go. See you tomorrow morning?"

"You won't stay?"

"No. Listen, last night was special. We'd been away from each other so long. I needed you to stay with me. But that can't be a regular thing. Occasionally, maybe, but not every night. And like we agreed, no sex whenever we do spend the night."

"Okay." Patrick hung his head like a scolded puppy. He had no option. *Let it go. Things have to happen at her pace. I want more, but it would be dangerous to argue.*

—

Mary sat in the shadowed confessional off the side aisle in a dark Saint Joseph's. She knew how close she was to the priest behind the screen, yet she was isolated. Isolation is good. "Father, forgive me. I have sinned."

A voice responded from behind the screen. "How, my child? What have you done?"

"I slept with my boyfriend." *Dear God, this is so hard for me to admit.*

"I see. You understand that sex outside of the covenant of marriage is wrong?"

"Yes, but we didn't have sex. We were dressed the whole time. We slept together. Spent the night together. Nothing else happened."

There was silence for a moment. "I don't think that constitutes a sin. But it could lead you in that direction. Be careful."

Mary left the confessional and knelt alone in the middle of the sanctuary saying the requisite prayers assigned by the priest. When she finished, she remained seated, praying and thinking in the presence of God in the church. *This is so confusing. Sin is a black and white, right and wrong set of absolutes. But now areas of gray are invading my world. If Patrick and I love each other, how could it be a sin? Still, the priest didn't tell me anything I didn't already know.* "You understand that sex outside of marriage is wrong?" he had said. *He offered no advice. And all my friends, even my sister, speak as though sleeping with Patrick is inevitable. Sister Catherine warned vaguely about the sin of sleeping together. The delicate euphemism, "sleeping together," doesn't begin to cover what I'm thinking. It's "making love" rather than "having sex".*

She had hoped that confession and time spent in prayer would ease her mind. Instead, she left the church more troubled than when she went in. She kept returning to Sister Catherine's advice. *Balance. I must work to find a balance between love and sin.*

Patrick bounded down the stairs to meet her when she got home late the next evening. "I went shopping. I bought shrimp. I can't cook like Melanie, but come on up and let's try to make a shrimp dinner together." Mary dropped her things in her apartment and followed him upstairs.

While he got things sorted out in the kitchen, she checked for a shrimp scampi recipe online. They ate and settled in. Later in the evening, Mary rose from the sofa and stretched.

"Is it time for you to go already?" Patrick asked.

"I'm tired. I need to get to bed. Could I stay here?" She looked around the room, pulling her hair away from her face. Her hands were shaking. *Mother Mary, help me to be strong tonight.*

Patrick paused, assessing her. "Of course." *What does she want? What should I do?*

"Okay. I've got the bathroom first." She walked into the bathroom. He straightened the covers on the bed. He found an extra pillow on the shelf in the closet and dropped it into a pillow case.

Mary came out of the bathroom still wearing the t-shirt she had worn all day. Bare legs. She placed her clothes on a chair and pulled back the covers. "Your turn."

Patrick returned from the bathroom, turned out the light, and climbed in beside her. She lay stiffly, on her back with her arms at her side. As on the first night, he kissed her quickly on the cheek and wrapped one arm across her.

"Good night."

"Good night."

Patrick resisted the urge to let his hands explore. Mary's breathing became deep and regular. Then she rolled from beneath his arm onto her side, edging away from him. Patrick pulled his arm back and let her rest. Her presence filled the room. Her scent filled the bed. *What are we doing? I want her and she's right here. But she can't. I have to respect that.* He fell asleep, waking often during the night, aware of her lying next to him.

Chapter Twelve

THEIR MERGED LIVES CONTINUED TO evolve. As before Thanksgiving, they still walked to and from their campuses together. They cooked and ate most of their meals together. They spent most evenings together and went out on dates on the weekends. But there was a new wrinkle; they slept together several nights a week. Sometimes they were in Mary's apartment, sometimes in Patrick's.

In early December, Melanie and Aaron met Patrick and Mary for drinks on a Friday evening. "It's almost Christmas," Aaron said. "Time to begin thinking about the holidays."

Melanie picked up the conversation. "We'd like to have you two come by our place for a Christmas feast next week. It'll be a way for the four of us to celebrate the holidays before we take off for vacation." Her cheery voice was a contrast to the gothic black of her late autumn costume.

"What should we bring?" Patrick asked.

"We'll take care of dinner and wine," Melanie said.

Aaron added, "What about gifts?"

"What can one artist give another?" Melanie continued.

"A work of art?" Patrick suggested.

"Okay." Aaron nodded. "Yes. But one thing from the two of us to both of you, and one thing back from both of you to us."

They settled on a date for the dinner the following week.

Patrick and Mary arrived for the dinner carrying a large, flat, wrapped package. Aaron met them in the lobby of the old mill building. He was dressed in jeans and a white sweater; comfortable winter wear for Providence. His dark whiskers were a rough contrast above the cabled wool of the sweater. Patrick and Mary were dressed in similar casual attire: jeans and sweaters. Rather than entering through the gallery, Aaron escorted them up a dark staircase at the side of the lobby and through double doors into the loft apartment. Patrick leaned the package against the wall inside the door.

Melanie's touch was throughout the apartment. White twinkle lights were the only light source in the loft, but the tiny lights were everywhere. They lined doorways and windows and hung with pine garlands in festoons. The big space was brightly lit as if by hundreds of fairies. Silver bows linked the garlands spanning the space between the old oak beams that lined the ceiling. The room smelled of pine. Christmas carols played quietly. A Christmas tree stood against one of the brick walls, also decorated with white lights and dozens of Melanie's glass figures; angels, birds, butterflies.

Melanie came in from the kitchen. She had changed her look again. Her low-cut, long, silvery gown shimmered as she moved. She wore a necklace, bracelets, and rings made of crystals, possibly diamonds, though the sheer number of gems defied the budget of even artists as successful as she and Aaron. Her hair was platinum blonde, her lips a bright red like a 1940s movie star. Her smile dazzled. Melanie threw her arms up and out, posing. "For Christmas I shall be the Snow Queen," she proclaimed. Patrick clapped, admiring her performance. Mary laughed, giving her an embrace and a tiny kiss.

"Do you like what we've done with the place?" Aaron asked. "It's Melanie's concept. We worked together all week on the decorating."

"Nice. Well done," Patrick said.

"But you're Jewish, aren't you?" Mary asked. "And Melanie, you told me you don't go to church, either. It's Christmas."

"So?" Aaron looked puzzled. "I'm Jewish. Right now, it's Hanukkah. And the holidays are the holidays, whatever you believe. It's a wonderful time of the year."

"I simply love the whole season." Melanie gestured to encompass the room. "The songs, the decorations. I just wish we had a fireplace and a fire. Let's have fun. Here, I've got mulled red wine. Spices!"

Mary picked up a glass of the wine and took a cautious sip. Melanie had cooked a goose. Cranberries dominated the recipe, adding both their red color and a tart flavor to the gamey flesh of the bird. They finished the meal with plum pudding.

After dinner, the men stayed on the sofa talking while the women went to the kitchen to clean up.

Mary rinsed the dishes. Melanie began stacking the plates and putting them in the dishwasher. "So, Mary, any new developments with Patrick?" It was a brazen, direct question, but Mary and Melanie had been eating lunch together for several weeks. A comfortable relationship between the two women had developed where they could talk about anything. They spoke often about their men but only in general terms.

The details of Mary's relationship with Patrick were delicately avoided. Mary gave the question a moment of thought. "We're doing well."

"You still cook together several nights each week?"

"Yes."

"So, you and he are comfortable being in each other's apartments? I know that was a big step for you back when you first did it."

"Yes." Mary leaned closer to Melanie and whispered, "We sleep together from time to time as well."

Melanie squealed and hugged her, wet hands marking the shoulders of Mary's sweater. "Oh, Mary! That's wonderful! I'm so happy for you. I know how big this is for you. And for him. How was it?"

"What's going on in there? Are you two okay?" Aaron called from the living room.

Melanie answered. "Yes, we're fine. But Mary's got some—"

Mary interrupted, shouting, "Everything's fine. We're good."

She pulled Melanie close again and whispered, "I don't want to talk about it with them. This is between you and me. It's like this. We sleep together, but there's no sex. Maybe it's a compromise. We like the closeness, falling asleep and waking up together. It's how I avoid the whole 'sin' issue."

Melanie leaned back, scrutinizing her friend. "Really? How can you do that? Don't you want to do it with him? How can you fall asleep in bed with him and not do it?"

"It's not easy. It's hard sometimes. But we manage."

"Yeah, I bet it is hard sometimes," Melanie said. "You two need to be careful. Have protection handy. And you've been to confession?"

"As long as we don't do anything else we don't need protection. And yes, I'm going to confession every week now."

"What'd the priest say?"

"He gives me the standard prayers to say, just as he would for anything I had done. And he tells me to be careful. But he says that if we don't do anything more it's okay. I always try to do the right thing. And right now this is the right thing. It's not just my faith that's involved here, though that is important. I guess I have high standards for doing what's right and not doing what's wrong. I don't want to disappoint my parents."

"Do you want me to set you up an appointment with my OB GYN? Maybe you should start on the pill?"

"No, thanks. Like I said, we aren't doing anything."

"Be careful, Mary."

"Don't tell Aaron, okay? I don't want everyone else to know about this. Just you."

"Of course."

They rejoined the men on the sofa.

"Time for gifts." Aaron produced a wrapped box, dragging it from behind the sofa to the floor in front of Patrick and Mary.

"Open it!" Melanie clapped her hands, sitting on the edge of the sofa.

Mary and Patrick pulled the box nearer and peeled off the paper. Inside was a small interpretation of a tree made of thin silver and black steel cables. It sat on a crystal base; its branches spreading wide, spanning two feet. Throughout the branches of the tree were tiny crystal birds, some clear, others in pale colors. It combined the skills of both artists.

"Wow! It's amazing. Oh, it's beautiful. Patrick where should we put it?" Mary sat back, flushed with excitement, and hugged Patrick, who was still admiring the sculpture.

Patrick was speechless. "Thank you." Then turning to Mary, he added,

"Let's put it in your place. I have plenty of art in my apartment."

"It could be a Christmas tree," Aaron explained. "But it really is a tree for any season."

"We'll keep it out all year. It's too nice to pack away after Christmas." Mary retrieved the package from beside the door and handed it to Melanie. "This is for the two of you."

Melanie tore the paper. "I'll bet it's a painting. I can feel the frame." Aaron shifted forward on the sofa. Melanie lifted out the painting.

It was a watercolor. In a classroom studio, four artists were cleaning up at the end of a day. Two easels faced away from the viewer with their paintings unseen. Two faced front, showing half-finished still lifes, roughed in on canvases. The floor, the tables, every surface was dirty. Palettes were cleaned, rags thrown away by the artists. At the side of the picture the leg of a departing painter was seen through a half-open door. The room was lit with late afternoon light. Shadows crossed the floor, making the figures of the three remaining artists stand out. The overall feel of the picture was of messiness. But it centered on the artists.

Aaron was the first to speak. "It's wonderful, Patrick. It's unconventional, not like most of your landscapes. I mean, I like your work, but this one is special. It's very good. We'll find the perfect place to hang it here in our apartment." He stood and took a closer look, admiring the way Patrick had worked the colors.

Then Melanie noticed something else. In careful calligraphy, a quote had been inked beneath the painting in small letters on the matte. Melanie read, "An artist never really finishes his work, he merely abandons it. – Paul Valéry." She looked up, puzzled. "I like the quote. It fits the picture; and maybe all of us. Where did it come from?"

Mary beamed. "Paul Valéry was a French philosopher and a poet from the early twentieth century. I've studied his life, read his writings. And I dabbled with calligraphy back in high school. I'm not an artist like all of you, but it's the best I can do. It's my contribution."

"Well, that's perfect," Melanie praised. "Aaron and I collaborated on our gift to you. And you did as well. It's wonderful." Melanie leaned down to Patrick and gave him a hug and a kiss. Then she turned to Mary. As she hugged her, she whispered, "You two can do amazing things together."

Then she kissed her.

Chapter Thirteen

CHRISTMAS BREAK CAME. MARY TURNED in papers and took her exams. Patrick submitted his portfolio from the semester for review. Again, they faced days apart. They made plans to meet each other's parents during the holidays.

They exchanged gifts. Patrick gave Mary a small framed watercolor he had done showing a view of their old yellow apartment house from across the street. Mary gave him a book filled with prints of Monet and other French Impressionist painters. They slept together. Late the next morning, they left, heading their separate directions.

They got through the days before Christmas with frequent phone calls. On Christmas Eve, Patrick called Mary. "I miss you. It's only been a couple of days, but it feels like forever."

"I miss you too, but we'll see each other in a few days."

"Yes. I can't wait."

"Are you going to church tonight?" she asked.

"Of course. It's Christmas Eve."

"Tell me about your church. What do you do on Christmas Eve?"

"It's like most other services except there are more hymns, more carols. Then they turn the lights down low and we light candles, passing the flame along the aisles while we sing 'Silent Night'. It's pretty moving."

"Our Mass is like that, too. I used to go to midnight Mass in the city but my family is going earlier, at seven this year, at a church out here in the country."

"Not so different, then. And you open presents Christmas morning?"

"Each of us opens one present Christmas Eve. Then we do the other presents and the stockings on Christmas morning. I'm going to insist that my parents open the portrait you did of me on Christmas Eve."

"I hope they'll like it."

"How could they not? It's wonderful! What does your family do for presents?"

"We do everything Christmas morning. The stockings are predictable. I'll get chocolates and an orange. A pair of socks and maybe a book about art. The regular presents are a bit more than that, but we don't go all out with gifts. Mother and dad always give clothes from L.L. Bean. Uncle Win will surprise me with something amazing. He always does. He might give me paints or a block of watercolor paper."

They talked again early on Christmas morning. Patrick asked, "Did they like the painting?"

"They were overwhelmed. I'd told them a little about you so they knew you were an artist, but they had no idea how good you are. They hung the picture before we went to bed. Right over the sofa."

Patrick sat facing his parents on sofas in their cramped living room. Uncle Win was by his side. Opened gifts were stacked carefully under the tree as was Tom's custom. Wrapping paper had been folded and stored away with the used bows. Everything was ready to be re-used next year. The sparse tree was decorated with handmade ornaments, decorated Styrofoam balls and paper crafts. Lights added to the tree decorations but it was daylight so they weren't lit.

Patrick had called them together after the Christmas turkey leftovers had been put away. "Dad, Mother, I'm going south tomorrow morning. But I'll be back in a few days. I have a girlfriend, and I'd like to bring her here before New Year's so she can see where I come from and meet both of you."

They sat in silence. Uncle Win looked at his feet as though this didn't concern him, while stealing quick glances at Patrick's parents, observing their reactions.

Mother was white, her eyes squinted and darting.

Tom was placid; he was always placid. "Tell us about the girl. How did you meet her? What's her name?"

"Mary. Mary Flynn. She's a grad student at Brown."

"What's she studying?"

"French. She might end up in international business. She might become a teacher."

"A teacher," Mother stated. "That's nice. She would teach French, then? In a college, I should hope."

"I don't know. She might graduate in the spring and then we'll see how things turn out for her."

Tom nodded. He had nothing more to say, no questions to ask. He'd let Mother take care of that.

She did. "Where is she from, this Mary Flynn? What does her father do?"

"New York. Her father works there."

"I see. And you'll be bringing her here?"

"Yes." After a few moments, his mother nodded. "When will you arrive?"

"We'll get here on the twenty-ninth. We plan to stay two nights. We want to be back in Providence for New Year's Eve."

"Of course you do. I guess I'll have to set an extra place at the table. And make up the bed in the spare room." Mother stood, her hands clenched at her sides, and walked out the door.

Tom stood. "It will be nice to meet this young lady. She must be important to you if you're bringing her all the way up to Brunswick. Now I'd better go see about Mother." He followed his wife upstairs.

Uncle Win grinned and reached over to pat Patrick's hand. "That went well."

Patrick left the day after Christmas. Only Win knew he was headed to Mary's home in Connecticut rather than back to Providence. It was late afternoon when he pulled into Mary's driveway.

Mary ran to his car as soon as he pulled up. "Hi, how was the trip?" Mary opened his car door.

"Long—better now that I'm here."

They hugged self-consciously in the driveway and kissed quickly, aware of her family watching from the front doorway.

Patrick grabbed his bag and sketch book and followed Mary.

The house was a low ranch, painted white. The yard was small, landscaping minimal, the grass browned by winter frost. A rail fence lined the lawn next to the street. "Mom, Dad, Margie, this is my friend Patrick. And Patrick, these are my mom and dad and my sister Margie."

Mary's mother smiled and shook his hand. "It's nice to meet you, Patrick."

Mary's Dad was more effusive. He clapped Patrick on the back and reached to shake with a hand that was thickly calloused, stained from work, with cracked fingernails. He draped an arm over Patrick's shoulder. "Patrick! Come on in out of the cold. So, you painted that picture of Mary? Good job with that. Can I get you a drink?"

"Sure. It's been a long drive. I'll have whatever you're having."

Margie stepped forward with a smile. Mary had shared with her that she and Patrick were sleeping together, being sure to include the chaste nature of the arrangement. Margie hugged Patrick and brushed his cheek with her lips. "Love my big sister," she whispered.

Mary's dad returned from the kitchen with two small glasses. "Here, we still have leftover Gluck. It's an old family tradition. We only drink it during the holidays. It's not Irish. I don't know where we got the recipe or how we started with this."

"Dad," Mary scolded. "Give him a moment to get settled. Patrick, be careful with that stuff. You'd better sit."

Patrick sat on a narrow sofa, next to an artificial Christmas tree, its lights blinking on and off.

Mary's dad leaned down and clinked his glass against Patrick's. "Cheers! Merry Christmas and Happy New Year's." He downed his drink with a quick tip of his head. Patrick took a big sip. The amber liquid was good, a sweet mixture tasting of honey, raisins, and nuts. It was warm. He looked at the almost clear drink. He downed the rest of it in one gulp.

"Good stuff, huh? You want more?" Dad grinned.

Mom, Margie, and Mary insisted, "Come on, Dad. Be good. Patrick, don't do it."

This is a challenge. Okay. Patrick nodded. "Sure, Mr. Flynn, but only one more."

"Coming right up. And then I'll show you around the house." He brought back two more full glasses, giving one to Patrick before settling into a recliner to nurse the second glass.

"It tastes like a mince pie in a glass," Patrick said.

"Drink up, boy." They each took a sip.

Dad wiped his mouth on the back of his hand and motioned to the portrait hanging behind Patrick above the sofa. "You did that?" It was a statement as much as a question.

"Yes." Patrick flushed with pride. *Or maybe it's the drink.* He took another sip.

"It's great having a picture of Mary. Could you do one of Margie, too?"

"I expect. She'd have to pose for me."

"Mary posed for you?"

"No, but I know her face, so I sketched it from memory and then painted it."

"Well, it came out pretty good."

"I think so. I'm glad you like it."

"You painted it from memory?" Mary's mother stood in the kitchen doorway. Mary and Margie crowded right behind her. "That's amazing," she said. "It looks just like her. But there's something else. It has a special life to it. In the face or the eyes, maybe. I don't know what it is. You really captured her spirit."

"Thanks."

Mary came to sit next to Patrick. "You could paint my sister?"

"Sure. I could sketch her while I'm here and do the rest when I get back home."

"Okay, great," dad announced. "Enough of the art talk. Get up. Let me show you around."

When Patrick stood, he felt the floor tip. It was like being on a fishing boat rolled by an ocean swell. He sat back on the sofa.

Dad laughed. Mary rested a warm hand on Patrick's forearm.

"That Gluck is good stuff, isn't it?" Dad continued laughing, his breath wheezing. He pulled out a pack of cigarettes, tipped one out, and lit it. "You sit down and drink it, and you never know. It sneaks up on you. I'll show you around later. We'll both be okay in about an hour or so."

Patrick sat elbow-to-elbow with Mary at the kitchen table. A saucepan on the stove simmered with more Gluck. Even the aroma was intoxicating.

"I'm glad you got here okay. I've missed you."

"Yes. Me too."

"You really think you can do a portrait of Margie?"

"Of course. I'll have to do it live, with her posing. She's not in my head, in my soul, the way you are."

"Maybe she can pose tomorrow."

"Whenever she's free."

"I thought we'd take Margie back to the city the next day. Then I can show you around and you can meet Sister Catherine."

"Ah, yes. Sister Catherine. You're always talking about her; I'd love to meet her."

Dinner was a noisy event, full of conversation and laughter; a stark difference from the austere environment at Patrick's home in Maine. It was his first view of Mary's world.

Late in the evening, Mary showed Patrick the fold-out couch in the basement. They were alone in the darkened room as the woodstove ticked, radiating heat. Mary, in her robe, moved close to Patrick and kissed him.

"I'll be right upstairs. My dad built the house. We lived down here in the cellar for a year before he framed the regular house on the foundation. It's warm. You'll be fine."

Patrick studied her face in the dim light. "And you'll be only one floor above? It's almost the same as our house in Providence."

"Except this time, it's me upstairs, not you."

"Maybe I'll sneak up once everyone goes to sleep."

"Or maybe I'll sneak down."

"Okay. I'm fine either way."

Mary held him close, pressing her body to his, arms wrapped around him. "We'd better not. My dad likes you so far. Let's not risk messing that up. Just a couple of days and we'll be back in Providence. Good night." She climbed the stairs with a wave.

Patrick stretched out on the sofa-bed. It was quiet. Alone in the warm darkness, he slept.

Patrick sat at the kitchen table with his sketch pad. Margie sat across from him in a low-necked sweater that showed her throat and collarbones to advantage. Mary and her mom stood behind Patrick. Dad had gone off to run errands; a planned visit to Dunkin Donuts and a trip to a hardware store. Morning sunshine filled the room. Hand-washed breakfast dishes were stacked beside the sink.

He roughed in the shape of Margie's head, then the flow of her light hair as it framed her face. He laid in the position of her eyes and the shape of her nose and mouth. He extended the line of her throat and the cleft between the collar bones.

Mary's mom brought a hand to her mouth. "Oh, look at it. It's not even finished and already you've got her."

"Mom. Quiet. Just watch him work." *He's so good.* Mary felt a stir at her diaphragm whenever she watched Patrick draw or paint. It was a peculiar feeling, watching the delicate movements of his pencil give shape, form, and then life to a blank piece of paper. She wanted the room quiet so she could concentrate and enjoy the feeling. Margie laughed for a moment and then resumed the stillness of her pose. Patrick said nothing, deep into his sketch.

Shadows filled the spaces on Margie's face; beneath the thick waves of light-colored hair, beneath her chin, under her eyebrows. The mouth Patrick drew was open and laughing, that was what he knew of Margie's character. It was unlike the look of excited anticipation he had given

Mary's face in her portrait.

He sat back for a moment and looked at his drawing. It was good. He turned it for Margie to see.

"Oh my God! This is how you see me? I'm beautiful. I want Javier to see this."

"Yes, that's how I see you. Yes, you're beautiful." Patrick smiled and looked at Mary as he added, "Almost as beautiful as your sister."

Mary blushed and swatted him on the arm. "It's wonderful, Patrick."

Mom pulled out a chair and sat. "How do you add the color?"

"With Mary's portrait, I just added some light colors; watercolors washed over the pencil sketch. But I did too much shading on this one for that to work. Maybe I can do a second one of Margie with less shading so it can handle the paint. And Margie, I'll get this one framed for you and Javier."

"Oh, my God! You'd do that for me? That would be amazing!"

"Maybe it could be a wedding present from Patrick to you and Javier." Mom looked grimly at her second child.

Patrick was startled. "You're getting married?"

"Eventually."

"Congratulations! When?"

Mom interrupted. "June, maybe?"

"Oh, mom," both girls answered in unison. Then Margie went on, "Sometime probably. Not as soon as June though."

"Just think of the portrait as a Christmas gift then." *I don't want to be a part of some family feud.*

"At least Mary knows the difference between right and wrong." The girls' mom turned and left the room, but her words lingered.

"Do you have a bit more time this afternoon?" Patrick asked. "I'd need about a half hour. Or I could do the second one right now."

"Let me take a short break. It's hard to sit still for such a long time."

After lunch, Patrick did the second sketch and then he and Mary went for a walk along the lake. It was their first time alone since he'd arrived. They spoke little. Being together was enough.

"Do you see what I mean about my parents?" Mary asked as they started back up the hill to the house.

"What do you mean? They seem nice."

"You see how they're after Margie to marry Javier? They want me to do the right thing too, with you, I expect."

"But we're not engaged or living together or anything."

"Exactly. Now do you understand why I feel the way I do about things?"

"Sure," he answered. *I'm still puzzled. I don't have a clue why she feels this way. I love Mary. Why is this such a big thing for her? What is she asking of me? Does she want to get married? Should I propose to her?*

—

The next day, after dropping Margie at her apartment, Mary drove Patrick to Fordham, pointing out Saint Clare's as they passed by. "That's where I went to high school. All the teachers are nuns." Mary led the way to Sister Catherine's office.

Sister Catherine was waiting for them. "Mary! Merry Christmas! And you must be Patrick. Mary's told me all about you." She hugged Mary and shook Patrick's hand, clasping it between her thin, old fingers.

They sat in the straight-backed chairs at the round table across the office from Sister Catherine's desk. Patrick surveyed the room, taking in the crucifix, the painting of Christ, the bare walls.

Mary was proud to show off her boyfriend to Sister Catherine. But, as she always did, she let the nun direct the conversation. They chatted at first about incidental things; how the drive from Maine to Connecticut had been and about their drive into the city. They discussed cold weather and the threat of flurries for that evening. They talked about Christmas gifts.

Patrick was aware that Sister Catherine was watching him, evaluating him, attuned to his every mannerism, noting particularly how he and Mary interacted. Then Sister Catherine turned to him and asked, "So, Patrick. You and Mary met back in the autumn?"

"Yes. Right after we started our classes in September."

"And you're at an art school near Brown?"

"Yes, the Rhode Island School of Design. Our campus is right next door to Brown. Mary and I have apartments in a house a few blocks away. It's a place reserved for grad students from both schools."

"That's convenient."

Patrick smiled. *What does she mean about it being convenient? That it's an easy walk to our colleges, or that it's convenient for us to be living in apartments that share the same building? I'd better play it safe.* "Yes, it only takes us a couple of minutes to walk to our schools."

"Of course. And Mary tells me you're very talented."

Patrick looked to Mary for help.

"He is," Mary replied for him. "He did an incredible portrait of me that I gave my parents for Christmas. They hung it in the living room of the house up in Connecticut. And he's starting a second portrait of my sister."

Sister Catherine smiled and nodded. "So, you're a portrait artist? Is that what you'll do when you graduate? How do you plan to earn a living with painting?"

"No, I'm not really a portrait painter. I can do it. But I paint mostly landscapes. I work in watercolors. There are lots of great places to paint in New England. I've been inspired being in Providence." He looked quickly at Mary and smiled. Sister Catherine noticed.

"And do you plan to make a living painting landscapes?"

"Yes, I do. I know I can do it."

Sister Catherine turned to Mary. "Is he good enough? You and he seem to be serious about each other, so this might impact you someday."

"Yes, he's good enough. He's very good. You should see some of his work. And yes, you already know that we're serious about each other."

"Mary, dear. Don't be angry with me. You too, Patrick. I just want to know that you are thinking things through regarding your future."

Her old face, usually pleasant, showed her concern for the two college students. She reached a veined hand out and took hold of Mary's hand. "I care about you, Mary. About both of you," she added, looking at Patrick and reaching with her other hand for him. "You're a beautiful couple. I want the best for you." She held both of their hands.

They sat for a tense moment. Sister Catherine ended it. "Well, I won't keep you two. I'm sure you've got a busy day ahead. When do you go back to Providence, Mary?"

"We're leaving tonight. We'll go to my parents' house at the lake, have dinner. Then Patrick will follow me to Providence."

They stood. Sister Catherine hugged Mary. "Keep in touch, Mary. Call me. Anytime."

Then she turned to Patrick. Again she shook his hand, clasping it warmly. "Patrick, you're every bit as impressive as Mary had described you. You're a good man; good for Mary. I know she loves you. Now you love her back. Take good care of her. She's a very special young woman."

Finally, Patrick relaxed. *I did it! I passed her test!* He smiled. "I do love her. I've told her and I don't mind telling you. And of course I'll be good to her. She's a very special woman to me, too."

"Good. God bless you both." Sister Catherine pulled Patrick to her and held him for a moment, a hand on the back of each of his shoulders.

She walked them to the door that led out to the parking lot. "Drive carefully."

The drive back to Putnam Lake was quick. Holiday traffic was light. They drove without talking, watching as dusk dimmed the countryside.

Chapter Fourteen

PATRICK AND MARY GOT BACK to Providence late and made a quick run to the supermarket. The food would be there, ready for New Year's when they got back from Maine.

"Do we need to get an early start tomorrow to go to Maine? How long is the drive?"

"Four hours. It depends on traffic around Boston."

"I've never been to Boston. We should go in the spring."

"Okay, we will. It's a nice city. I don't know my way around there, but from the few times I've been, I like it."

They went through what was now a regular bedtime routine. Mary went in her bathroom first and came out in her t-shirt and panties. Then it was Patrick's turn. He came back to the bed wearing his t-shirt and shorts. Mary was under the covers, lying on her back, rigid, her arms at her side. Patrick turned out the light and climbed in next to her.

It had been nearly a week since they had shared a bed. Patrick rolled to her and wrapped his arm over her tense body. She turned and kissed him, raising her hands to the side of his face, the way she always kissed him in bed at night. "Good night. I love you."

"Good night. I love you too."

She rested then, still turned toward him.

This is new. The kiss and then staying turned to face me. It's always been me initiating our small activities in bed. Tonight, she led the way, or at least she's allowing me to take her further.

He kissed her again. She kissed him in return and rolled away onto her back. But she took his left hand, caught between their bodies, and held it tightly with her right. His other hand moved across to her shoulder and rested. Her face was illuminated by the faint light from the window, her eyes were closed, and her breathing was steady, slow and deep. *What if I move my hand?* His hand shifted lower to her breast. She did nothing. As he had the first time, Patrick caressed her. Her breathing remained unchanged. He continued. Mary's body tensed. Her mouth was open, her eyes still closed, her brow wrinkled. He stroked her breast again. She gasped, shook convulsively, pushed his hand away and rolled onto her side.

Patrick lay awake. *What just happened?* He touched her back. She pulled away. He tried to make sense of it. He wanted more but how could that happen? *How are we ever going to get past this?* The thought lingered, and he woke at dawn, restless.

Mary rolled to him and smiled. "Good morning! Did you sleep well?"

"No. I couldn't seem to get settled."

"Oh, poor baby. I was out the moment my head hit the pillow. I don't remember a thing." She hopped from the bed and trotted into the bathroom.

Patrick crawled from the bed, found his clothes, and got dressed. *Is she serious?*

Mary returned, wrapped in a towel, shaking out her wet hair. Patrick headed to the front door. "Listen. I need to go upstairs and pack. I'll be back in a few minutes. Okay?"

"You can shower and get ready here if you want to."

"I know, but my clothes are upstairs. I'll be back for breakfast." He left.

—

"I don't remember a thing," she said. *Was I the one dreaming last night? How could she not have known?* He puzzled over her response while he showered and dressed.

After breakfast, they drove up interstate 95, past Boston, and on to Portland. The day was sunny, a pale blue winter sky streaked with white, the air outside the car biting and cold. In Boston a dusting of dirty snow remained on the ground, but by Portland, the snow was deep, with banks edging the sides of the road. They turned toward the shore and Brunswick.

Patrick pointed out the Bowdoin campus before turning down Harpswell Road toward home.

"Tell me about your family," Mary asked. "I know the facts. Your father, the professor, and all that. But what am I getting into? What should I expect?"

"My father's reserved, very much an academic. He doesn't talk a lot except about Dickens, which is his specialty. He can also get a bit worked up about some of those later nineteenth-century romantic authors. If that interests you, he'll be happy to talk with you for hours. Once I've introduced you, you can call him Tom. His students don't; they call him Professor Chamberlain, or Doctor Chamberlain. But you're not one of his students.

"Mother is even quieter than my father, but she'll be evaluating you. She's probably not going to like you because you might lure me away from her. You can't do anything about it, so don't worry."

"What should I call her?"

"Mrs. Chamberlain will do."

Mary nodded. "What about your Uncle Win? Will he be here? I hope I get to meet him."

"He'll be here. He lives in Portland. The city is a better environment for an artist than up here on the coast. But he'll be here. He's looking forward to meeting you."

"What's he like?"

"He's an artist. You know Aaron and Melanie, and you've seen a few of the other artists around RISD. He's like that, but older. He's outgoing and can be a clown at times. He'll do or say anything at any time. I could tell you all sorts of stories about him, but I'll let you meet him first. You'll like him."

"Why are artists like that? I mean, why are they eccentric as a group?"

"I don't know. We're not tied down by convention. Artists can't be limited by the rules. If we always do what we should, we'll always make conventional artwork. Creativity has to do with exploring the other side of the boundaries, seeing things differently, painting things in a way that's never been done before."

"Can't a person be creative and still act and dress conventionally?"

Patrick nodded in agreement as he drove, still looking ahead at the road. "Creativity comes from a different place. It's easy for someone to act oddly if they want to try to be an artist. That's pretending to be an artist. But it's not easy to be an artist. The good art, the creative stuff, comes from someplace unique, an unconventional place. I believe we can't always do what we're expected to do. We can't always color within the lines."

"And Uncle Win—what about him?"

"Uncle Win is unconventional. Meet him first. Then tell me what you think of him."

—

They crossed a causeway and bridge. Seaweed-coated rocks, polished with ice, lined the narrow channel. Sheets and blocks of ice were piled by the tide on rocky beaches. Above the granite shore, snow had drifted on bluffs and open fields. Only the water was moving. It was as frozen and still as one of Patrick's landscapes, a study in shades of gray, black, and white.

Patrick turned onto a snow-packed, plowed road and followed it to the white farmhouse. "Grab your things and follow me." He was out of the Volvo and heading toward the house with bags banging against his legs in his haste. *Oh god! Here we go. Let's see how Mother deals with Mary. It's only two days. I can get through this.*

Mary followed him up a shoveled footpath to the granite doorstep.

He knocked. After nearly a minute, his father opened the door.

"Well, if it isn't our Prodigal Son, come home! Come on in out of the cold. And you would be his girlfriend, Mary." He held the heavy wooden storm door wide. "May I take your wraps?"

They surrendered their coats. Patrick dropped his bags in the hall; Mary did the same. The bleached floor boards of the front hall were age-worn and covered with threadbare oriental rugs. Patrick led Mary into the living room. Table tops were cleared, but bookshelves were lined unevenly with books with papers and magazines tucked on top of the rows of books. The Christmas tree, its brittle branches now drooping, stood by the window. A black wood stove sat on a brick hearth, pulsing with dry heat. *Dad must have tried to straighten up. Where is Mother?*

The room still looked cluttered. Furniture was crowded together. One sofa had an old quilt draped diagonally across it, a tattered end hanging off one arm to the floor. When Tom returned from hanging the coats, Patrick introduced him to Mary. "Mary, this is my father. And Dad, this is my friend, Mary."

"Doctor Chamberlain. Professor Chamberlain." Tom extended his hand and shook. "It's very nice to meet you, Mary. I'll go round up my brother and my wife. Why don't you two kids take a seat? Anywhere on that sofa is fine." Tom circled back into the hall and climbed the stairs.

Patrick and Mary hadn't time to sit before Uncle Win came bounding in through the kitchen door, red in the face, beaming at Patrick. "My boy. Welcome! And who do we have here?" He stopped, leaning back, his arms opened, palms out, grinning at Mary. He looked at her like she was a lost jewel suddenly discovered.

"This is Mary. And Mary, here he is, my Uncle Win."

Mary looked over Uncle Win, appraising. *Why, Uncle Win's an older version of many of the art students I've met at RISD.* His hair was all over the place and too long; graying curls to his collar. Even though he was indoors, he was dressed in layers. A flannel plaid shirt covered a long sleeved woolen shirt with a third shirt beneath all of that. Baggy blue jeans dropped to the tops of lace-up rubber boots. Tom was natty; a cashmere sweater over pressed corduroys. Uncle Win was like a Panda bear with no sense of fashion.

"I've heard all about you, Uncle Win. It's a pleasure to put a face with everything Patrick's told me about you."

"Well, aren't you a sweetheart," Win said, turning on the charm. He clasped his hands together. "Patrick, she's lovely. Why, you're just like a fairytale princess."

Mary blushed and smiled.

"Now Mary, you need to forget everything Patrick might have told you about me. He does go on sometimes. Maybe half of what he's probably told you is true."

"I'll make up my own mind," she said with a quick laugh.

The three of them sat on one of the sofas. Tom returned leading his wife. Patrick, Mary, and Uncle Win stood back up quickly. Mother was dressed more formally than either her husband or Uncle Win. She wore a long, plaid skirt, a ruffled blouse buttoned to her throat, and a navy-blue velvet blazer. At her throat she had a cameo pin. Her gray hair was pulled back in a tight bun.

"Mother, this is my friend, Mary Flynn. She's the grad student at Brown I told you about."

"It's so nice to meet you, Mrs. Chamberlain." Mary reached out her right hand.

"It's very nice to meet you as well." Mother pursed her lips and turned without shaking Mary's hand, tugging her jacket close. She sat on the sofa across from Win, her son, and Mary. Tom sat next to her.

There was an uncomfortable moment as they all settled into their places on the two couches. Nobody spoke. Patrick looked from his father to his mother. Win grinned as he took in the tense room. Mary sat, waiting for the next move.

Uncle Win opened things up. "Mary, is this your first time in Maine?"

"Yes."

"Well, you just got here. It's still too early to pass a final judgment. But what do you think so far?"

"You have more snow than we do in New York. Or even in Providence or Boston. But it's very pretty. I loved coming across that bridge just before we got here."

"Ah yes, that is a pretty spot. But you think we've got snow? You can't imagine what it's like up in the mountains, away from the coast, over toward the New Hampshire border. We had a clipper storm blow through last night. We got a little less than a foot; just a nuisance really. But the mountains got pounded. Great for the ski resorts."

The room settled back into silence. Mother sat, looking at her hands folded in her lap, unable to look at this new girl in her house.

Tom made an attempt at conversation. "Mary, are you a skier?"

"No, Professor Chamberlain. I grew up in New York City. I've never been skiing. This is all new for me."

"Oh, we don't all ski here," Tom said. "I won't waste my money on lift tickets. I like to go cross country skiing, though. Nordic skiing, you know. It's like going for a jog in the woods in the winter. Good exercise. I do it to clear my brain when I'm writing."

"Maybe I'll try it sometime." Mary's comment was met by an enthusiastic nod from Uncle Win.

Tom and Mother sat in silence. After a moment, Mother spoke. "What would you like to do during your short stay here?"

"I don't know. It is a short stay. Just today and tomorrow. We go home to Providence on New Year's Eve day. Maybe I could get out. Patrick could show me the sights."

"We shall go for a walk tomorrow morning," Mother stated. "Just you and me. We can talk. I can get acquainted with you that way."

"Okay." *What else can I say? I can't argue with Patrick's mother, and it would be rude to decline her invitation.*

Patrick looked uneasily from his mother to Mary. Tom sat staring straight ahead without registering any emotion on his face.

Uncle Win brought things to a close. "Mary, why don't you join me in the kitchen? I'm preparing a pot roast for dinner and I could use some help." He stood and Mary followed him through the door to the kitchen. Patrick stayed in the living room with his parents. He looked from one to the other. "Okay, so?" he asked. "There's Mary. My girlfriend. What do you think?"

Mother and Tom looked at each other for a moment. Neither spoke for a long moment.

"She seems like a nice enough girl," Tom said. "Pretty. And from what you've told us she's very smart; a good student. Studying French at Brown you said?"

"Yes, she is," Patrick confirmed. He looked to his mother.

She kept her face a passive mask displaying little emotion. "I'll reserve final judgment until I've had some time to observe her. I'll wait till I've talked with her tomorrow morning. She seems pleasant enough but I want to know what she wants with you. Why is she seeing you? I don't know enough to trust her yet."

"Mother, she's seeing me because we like each other. A lot. Why can't you accept that a woman might want to be with me?"

"Oh, I know all about that. You're a highly eligible young man. There are lots of girls who will want to be with you because you are becoming such a successful artist. I need to be sure her intentions are good."

Tom gave a terse laugh. "Isn't it usually the girl's parents who are checking to be certain about the boy's intentions? Here we have you evaluating the young lady."

"All right! Be that way." Angrily, she stood, preparing to leave. "I need to know. She seems quite taken with our Patrick. And you, Patrick, seem quite taken with her. I can see it just looking at the two of you. I'm not going to risk losing my son to someone who isn't worthy of him," she announced to Tom. She stalked into the hall and up the stairs.

Patrick turned to his father, hands out like a supplicant. "Dad? What can I do?"

"Leave your mother to me. I'll talk with her. Why don't you see about your girl out there with Winthrop in the kitchen?"

Mary and Uncle Win rolled out a sheet of dough on the kitchen counter. Patrick walked up behind Mary, wrapped his arms around her, kissed her neck and buried his face in the back of her shoulder.

Uncle Win teased, "None of that, you two. Not here. Not in your mother's kitchen. Behave yourselves!"

"We're making biscuits," Mary explained. "From scratch. It's Uncle Win's special recipe."

"Nothing fancy. I add caraway seeds to the dough. Then we make the biscuits and bake them on a cookie sheet. They'll go great with the roast."

Uncle Win looked at Patrick, stopped, and put down his rolling pin. "Are you okay? You look like you got kicked in the stomach. What happened out there?"

Patrick answered, looking at Mary, taking her hands. "Dad's okay with you, but Mother's reserving judgment. She'll be checking you out the rest of the time we're here."

Mary looked into Patrick's eyes, her anxiety showing, her eyes pleading. "What can I do? I so much want your mother to like me. Why does she hate me?" She brushed her hair away from her face then retook his hands.

Win shook his head. "Oh well, would you have expected anything different from your mother? This will take time but she'll come around."

They continued with the dinner preparations. Outside the sun began to set, turning the sky to the south and west into a mix of reds, oranges, and yellows. The snow on the meadow behind the house glowed in the light. For a moment, Patrick and Uncle Win paused by the window absorbing the sight. Mary noticed.

"You're looking at that beautiful sunset with what Patrick calls his artist's eye and storing the image in your minds so you can paint it later, aren't you?"

Uncle Win wrapped an arm around Mary's shoulder. "You're a very perceptive young woman. Yes, that's what we're doing. We see it; we feel it. And we both know the other does as well."

Patrick added, "I guess that's why Uncle Win and I get along so well. We see the world the same way."

"Why is Uncle Win doing the cooking? Why not your mother or father?"

Both men laughed, looking at each other. "Let me bring you in on a little family secret. Maybe it's an inside family joke," Win said. "Mother is a terrible cook. And my brother, Tom, doesn't cook at all. So when they have company Tom always asks if I can come join them for dinner. I'm a pretty good cook. And Susan, that's Patrick's mother, she lets me do it. We all know what the plan is, but nobody talks about it."

"So, your mother doesn't come down and help?"

"No, right now she'll be holed up in her bedroom waiting for your visit to end so she can get on with her life."

"She wants to go for a walk with me tomorrow."

Patrick nodded. "Bundle up. And you brought good walking shoes, didn't you?"

"Yes, I've got my sneakers. As long as we stay on the roads and don't go into the snow I'll be fine."

"She'll stay on the roads." Win checked his roast. "She hates the snow. She usually walks over the bridge and back. She'll probably do that with you." Patrick nodded in agreement.

"What will she ask me? What should I expect?"

Uncle Win counseled, "Who knows? Be prepared for anything. Just be yourself. You'll be fine."

Patrick held her for a moment. "She'll end up liking you. Don't worry."

Dinner was over. Everyone crowded into the living room again. It was early in the evening from the viewpoint of the two grad students. But for adults in rural Maine it was late. Uncle Win bundled into a tattered, down-filled parka. "Got to get going. Icy roads between here and Portland."

Patrick and Mary stood. Win gave Patrick a pat on the shoulders. "I'll come back over in the morning. I'll keep you company while Mary is out for her walk."

"Thanks."

"And Mary, what a pleasure it's been getting to know you this evening. Patrick's found himself a wonderful young lady." He embraced her in a bear hug that was amplified by the bulk of his down parka.

When he released her, Mary smiled. Win leaned over and gave her a small peck on the cheek. "You have fun, young lady." It was an order.

"I will, Uncle Win. Thank you. I'll see you in the morning." Mary couldn't stop smiling as Uncle Win exited the room.

Next it was Tom's turn. "It is getting late. I'm heading up. Mother, are you joining me?"

She remained on the couch until Tom reached to her and pulled her to her feet. "Come along, Mother. Patrick and his girlfriend will be fine. And Patrick, you'll be in your old bedroom. Mary, you're in the guest room down the hall. You know where the bathroom is." Then they were gone.

When Patrick heard the bedroom door at the top of the stairs latch, he let out a long breath. "Whew! We made it. One day down; one to go."

"It's not that bad. Your dad is nice. Quiet, but nice."

"What about Mother?"

"She'll come around. Let me spend time with her tomorrow on that walk."

"Okay. About tonight." Patrick spoke in a whisper. "You know where your room is. I'm right down the hall. And I can tell you, even if we wait an hour to go up, mother will still be awake, listening. So, we should say our good nights down here. When we go up, we can put on a little show for her benefit."

"A show? What do you mean?"

"We won't even kiss up there. And we certainly won't be talking about how we're sleeping so close by each other. Or how we can be together when we get back to Providence. Just a quiet 'good night' in the hall and then off to bed."

"Got it. Should we go up now or stay down a while?"

"Let's stay down a while."

They sat on the couch and kissed. "What time will everyone get up in the morning?"

"Early. Maybe six. There's a belief that time spent lying around in bed in the morning is time wasted. If you wake up and hear water running somewhere, get up and get ready to move."

"Got it."

They kissed again and stood, only to stop at the top of the stairs. With a mischievous smile Mary leaned up and kissed Patrick on the cheek. "Good night, Patrick. I had fun today. It was great meeting your family."

Patrick smiled and leaned down, kissing Mary on the lips. "Good night, Mary. See you in the morning."

As they went to their separate rooms, Patrick noticed the door to his parents' room was ajar a thin crack.

In her room, Mary crawled into the bed, an old maple four poster. The sheets were icy cold and felt damp. She remembered that the house was within sight of the ocean; even in winter the sea air penetrated the walls. She tugged the thick down quilt to her chin and lay alone on her back. Reaching across to a delicate china lamp on the table beside the bed, she snapped it off. She lay listening to the wind outside and the quiet stirrings of Patrick and his parents in their rooms.

The silver light of winter dawn woke her. A small alarm clock beside the bed showed quarter to six. She heard footsteps and quiet voices. She pulled the window shade aside and looked out on the snow-covered meadow that ran down to the bay. A pale light, not yet sunrise, lit the icy water. She dressed quickly in the chilly bedroom and tiptoed downstairs in her socks.

Tom was in the kitchen cooking sausage in an iron skillet. "Good morning," Mary said. "Can I make coffee?"

"Sure. It's in the jar right there. And you see the coffee maker on the counter."

She busied herself filling the pot with water and ladling coffee into the filter. At first, neither she nor Tom spoke as they went about their work.

Tom began. "Did you sleep all right?"

Mary smiled. "Yes."

"Not too chilly for you?"

"A little chilly, but I had the down comforter."

"Yes, that helps. I keep the house cool. Sixty degrees. I don't like wasting money on heating oil. Do you like sausage?"

"Yes."

"I didn't know if you were a vegetarian or a vegan or something. So many kids these days…"

"No, I like sausage. And I ate the roast last night."

"Oh, that's right."

Mary set four places at the table in the dining room.

"I should have told you. You can set the table in the kitchen. The dining room table is for dinner. And three places will be enough. Mother will take coffee in her room. And a piece of toast."

"Oh, okay. I'll take her coffee up to her when it's ready."

"No, you'd better let me do that. We ought to let her get into the day a bit before she's with you. Let's give her some time."

Patrick trotted down the stairs. "Good morning!" He gave Mary a quick kiss on the cheek then pitched in on the breakfast set up. The day was off to a good start.

⌒

By mid-morning Tom had gone to the college to do some work. Patrick and Mary sat in the living room waiting for Mother to come downstairs and take Mary on her walk.

Uncle Win burst in, dropped his parka on the sofa, and peeled off a red stocking cap. His tangle of gray curls was matted and out of place from the cap. "Not too cold today. It's starting to melt a little out there."

"Good. I was concerned for Mary if Mother takes her for a long walk in the cold."

"I'll be fine," Mary said.

Mother came down the stairs. She wore two sweaters, flannel-lined blue jeans, and lightweight L.L. Bean boots. She took her parka out of the closet and zipped it up. Finally, she pulled on wool gloves and a stocking cap. She looked at Mary. "Are you ready?"

Mary was dressed in a turtle neck and sweater over blue jeans with her sneakers. She pulled on her navy pea coat and tugged a navy blue ribbed wool hat down to her eyebrows, pushing her hair behind her ears. She wrapped a wool scarf around, tucking it into her coat. She had woolen mittens. "Ready. Let's go."

Patrick and Uncle Win watched from the front window as the two women walked down the shoveled path, past Win's truck and off along the plowed driveway. They turned onto the road toward the bridge. "I hope she'll be warm enough," Patrick said as he and Win left the window.

"Mary? She'll be fine. They'll only be gone about an hour. It's sunny and warm out there."

"I hope neither of them kills the other."

"That would be news, wouldn't it?" Uncle Win chuckled. "I can see the headlines in the Portland Press Herald now. 'New York woman indicted in the murder of pillar of the Brunswick and Bowdoin community.'"

"Not funny, Uncle Win. It could happen. And what if Mother kills Mary?"

"Mary's just a little thing, but she seems tough enough. I'm sure she can take down Mother if it comes to that."

Patrick laughed.

They sat at the table in the kitchen with fresh cups of coffee. Looking out the window over the meadow they watched geese gathered on the snow. From time to time the big birds swarmed to the water.

"How are you and Mary doing?"

"Good."

"Come on, Patrick. You can share with me. I'm not your father."

"It's good. We've spent the night together a few times. I can't seem to get enough time with her. And I think it's the same for her. We just can't go our separate ways at the end of the day."

"Are you being careful?"

"Yes, we're careful. We're close, but we haven't taken that final step. She's not ready, I don't think."

"Are you?"

"Yes."

"But she's not? How does that work?"

"We fool around a little and then we go to sleep. And she doesn't talk about it much, but she's going to confession every week. I don't ask. I've gone to church with her the past few weekends now."

"She's Catholic? Are you okay with that? Going to a Catholic church?"

"Yes. It's not a big deal. A church is a church as far as I'm concerned. Catholic, Methodist, it could be any church. And if I miss a week, it's okay with me. But she goes to Mass every week and confession as well."

"And so, you go with her?"

"Yes. It's important to her, so I make it important to me. I'm actually able to follow the service now that I've been several times."

"You two definitely come from very different worlds."

"We do. I went with her and saw New York City for the first time a couple of days ago. I met this old nun who was her college professor. They're close. I can't think of a time when I'd ever talked with a nun before."

"Being here must be as much of a shock for her as it was for you going there."

"I expect."

"Well, let's see how Mother and she get along when they get back. You're here through dinner tonight?"

"Yes. We'll go back to Providence after breakfast tomorrow."

"Stop by my place on your way south. I'll treat you both to lunch."

"That'll be nice, thanks. It'll do her good to see how you live. It'll give her another perspective on our family after meeting Mother and Father and staying here. She's trying to figure out what artists are all about."

"Then coming to my place will give her another look at our lifestyle. She knows Aaron and his girlfriend Melanie. It'll do her good to have a peek inside my world."

A few minutes later the front door opened and Mary and Mother came in, stamping snow off their feet, peeling off gloves and shedding coats. Patrick was up and out to the hall to greet them. "How was it?"

Mary, her face reddened from the wind, smiled. "Wonderful! What a pretty area here. There isn't a center of town, but we walked for a while over that bridge and then turned around and came back."

Patrick looked to Mother.

"Oh, she's a fine young lady," Mother fussed, shooing Patrick into the living room with a dismissive wave of her hands. Then she conceded, "We enjoyed ourselves. Had a nice talk. Didn't we, Mary?"

"Yes. A nice talk."

Mother followed Patrick into the living room and sat on the sofa.

Patrick relaxed. *This is a good sign. I expected her to retreat upstairs.*

Mary and Win joined them. There was talk about the weather, about the flurries expected as another cold front approached. Little of real importance was discussed, but the tension was gone.

After lunch, Patrick bundled Mary into his Volvo and gave her a tour of the region. The Bowdoin campus was first, then north through Bath past the huge shipbuilding cranes and on up the coast to Boothbay Harbor. The town was quiet, snowbound for the winter, all the tourists gone. They found a small café that was still open and shared glasses of wine, understanding that there would be no alcohol served at dinner back at the house.

"You and Mother had a good time on your walk this morning?"

"Yes, she walks fast, the way I do back in the city. We talked a bit."

"What did you talk about?"

Mary turned coy. "Girl talk. Nothing important."

"Come on, how did you win her over?"

"I don't know if I did."

"Well, she seems to have thawed a bit." *I'm baffled. How has it happened that Mother now has this sudden acceptance of Mary?*

They returned home in time for dinner. Uncle Win heated leftover pot roast and potatoes. Then he left for his home in Portland. Patrick's parents went to bed shortly after nine as they always did. Patrick and Mary lingered longer downstairs and then went up to their rooms as well.

—

After breakfast on New Year's Eve morning, Patrick and Mary brought their bags down to the front hall. Tom patted Patrick on the shoulder. "Drive carefully, son."

Then he shook Mary's hand. "It's been a pleasure meeting you, Mary. Come back anytime. Maybe in the summer when it's not so cold."

"I'd like that. The cold's not that bad."

Then it was Mother's turn. She hugged Patrick and held on, kissing him before finally letting go. She turned to Mary. "It was nice to have you here for a visit. You take good care of my Patrick." She gave Mary's hand a brisk shake, turned, and hurried back up the stairs.

—

They rolled off the interstate, followed the streets down to the waterfront in Portland, found a place to park and walked down a cobblestone alley to a door on the side of an old brick building. Patrick knocked, opened the door, and called out, "Hello! Uncle Win? Are you here?"

Uncle Win's cheery voice answered, "Come on up. We're upstairs."

"We?" whispered Mary.

"Uncle Win's partner."

"Oh." Mary absorbed this disturbing news about Uncle Win.

Homosexuality is sinful. But Uncle Win is such a good person, such a supportive friend to Patrick and me. Now I discover he has a partner. Not a girlfriend or a wife. It's unsettling.

They went up to a vast loft not unlike Aaron and Melanie's. Tall windows looked out across the harbor to a bay scattered with dark, pine-covered islands. Light glinted off the water. The room was filled with late morning sunlight. Uncle Win was barefoot, in jeans and a navy t-shirt sporting an image of Superman flying with his fist extended. He came bounding to greet them with hugs. A lean man sat on the couch, clean shaven with a gray crew cut. He too was barefoot and wore a t-shirt and jeans. "This is Robert. He's a potter. And Robert. You know Patrick. Now this lovely being is his girlfriend, Mary."

Robert came forward, embracing Patrick, and shaking Mary's hand. "Good to see you again, Patrick. And, Mary, Winthrop has told me about you. It's a pleasure to meet you."

He smiled sincerely and went back to the couch.

"Let me show you around," Uncle Win said. He stood in the middle of the loft, pointing. "This is the living room, of course. Over there's the dining room and the kitchen." He gestured to the other side of the loft. "My studio is over there. And the bedroom's through that door. The bathroom's off the bedroom if you need it. There. That's the tour. And now we're back here in the living room. Hope you didn't get lost."

Mary walked to one of the brick walls of the loft where a wide oil painting hung. It was abstract, hot colors applied in thick palette-knife layers to the stretched canvas. From across the room the painting was a view of the harbor at sunrise, the light reflecting off the water, islands and the waterfront docks silhouetted against the sunlight. It lost its clarity up close, becoming no more than thick paint. It seemed to glow. She noted the signature in the bottom corner. Winthrop Chamberlain.

She turned to Uncle Win. "This is yours?"

"Yes. Do you like it?"

She stepped back, assessing it again from a distance. "Yes! It's magnificent. I love it."

She began to study several more works on the walls of the loft. "Wow! I knew you were an artist. But it's eye opening to see your work."

Win chuckled. "Eye opening. I like that." He looked to the couch. "Robert, we're going out for lunch. Would you care to join us?"

"No, I've got things ready to come out of the kiln downstairs. I'll stay here and have some soup."

"Can we pick something up for you? I'm taking them downtown."

"No, I'll be fine. Patrick, it's always good to see you. And Mary, it's been a pleasure."

Uncle Win grabbed a pair of shoes and socks next to the couch and pulled them on. He found an old sweater on a closet shelf and dragged it over his head. "Ready to go."

They rumbled down the wood stairs and out into the alley. Win led the way, stepping over grainy dark banks of old ice at the curb, dodging snow-melt puddles, steering Mary by her elbow, pointing out the sights. Patrick followed. They came to a small restaurant on the waterfront. The interior was all varnished wood, giving it the feel of a cabin on a fine old yacht.

Uncle Win handed around the short, laminated menus. "They have great soups here; clam chowder, lobster bisque. Good sandwiches and such. What'll you two have?"

Patrick guided Mary. "You said you wanted lobster while we're in Maine. The price is a little high this time of year. But get the lobster bisque. I'm having the fish sandwich."

"Everything's fresh caught," Uncle Win added. "And get a glass of wine with that soup."

Patrick and Win ordered fish sandwiches with a dark beer from a local microbrewery. Mary got the soup and the wine. They lingered over lunch, watching the traffic on Commercial Street. After lunch they walked together back to Patrick's car.

Uncle Win held Patrick for a moment, then stepped back and looked him full in the face. He became serious. "This girl's a good one. Take good care of her. Don't let her get away." He hugged him again.

Then he turned to Mary. "I ought to give you the same speech. Love him. Don't let him get away. But I think you know that. You're a wonderful pair." He hugged Mary and gave her a kiss. "Come back and visit me soon."

Chapter Fifteen

BY LATE AFTERNOON, PATRICK AND Mary were home and settled on Mary's couch with a glass of wine. Steaks and potatoes were ready to be prepared. On the table in front of them was Aaron's tree with Melanie's crystal birds sparkling in the candlelight. Mary put on music by Camille Saint-Saens, a French composer.

"Finally," Patrick sighed. "It feels like forever since we've done this."

"I know, but it wasn't that bad with your parents. I think they were as much afraid of me as I was of them. And Uncle Win, he's a big teddy bear. I love him."

"How did you win over my mother?"

"You keep asking me that. I told you. We talked. I told her a bit about my family, my sister and my parents. Of course I didn't tell her that Margie is living with her boyfriend. But mostly we talked. She wanted me to tell her about French literature. So I did, talking about my favorite authors and what they had written. She liked Balzac when I mentioned him. Do you really think I won her over?"

"Time will tell. But she seemed friendlier than I expected by the time we left."

"Your father's quiet."

"That he is."

"And Uncle Win. Why didn't you tell me he's gay?"

"It never occurred to me to tell you. I didn't think it mattered. Does it?"

"No, not really, My Catholic faith doesn't condone that lifestyle, but he's a good man."

"It's his character. It's his art that that defines him. Who he lives with is irrelevant."

"Yes, I guess it doesn't matter. He's a wonderful friend, and I love watching the two of you together. I like your family."

"It's a good start for us with our families."

"Yes, it's a start."

They baked potatoes and grilled steaks for dinner and started on a second bottle of wine as they watched the raucous festivities in Times Square on television. Then it was the New Year. Patrick and Mary kissed long and slow. "Let's go to bed," Patrick whispered.

"It's been a long week. I'm exhausted." Mary switched off the television and headed for the bedroom, followed by Patrick.

Once in bed Patrick kissed her again. "Happy New Year, I love you."

Her hands went to his face, the way they always did, holding him as she kissed him. "Yes, Happy New Year. I love you too."

Their breath mingled in the small space between their faces. She kissed him again and rolled onto her back, taking his left hand in her right, tight between their bodies the way she had the last time they had slept together.

As before, Patrick rested his hand on her breast. She relaxed. His hand moved down, found the hem of her t-shirt, and slid under it.

She tensed, but let him continue. Her hand moved to his thigh and then moved higher.

Clumsy movements on both their parts brought release. No sin was committed in Mary's eyes; there had not been actual intercourse. Patrick was frustrated but found enough pleasure to sustain him for the moment. *The intimacy is good. I hope it's enough for Mary. I want more!* When it was over, still clothed as they were when they first went to bed, they slept.

—

They woke late to sunshine. Mary got to the bathroom first, then it was Patrick's turn. When he came back, fresh, showered, and dressed, Mary was finishing in the kitchen.

"Scrambled eggs and bacon! With toast," she announced as he walked into the kitchen. "It's what my father calls a proper breakfast. Could you pour the coffee?" Mary beamed at him as she dished the eggs onto a platter.

They sat at the window looking out at Wickenden Street. There was no traffic, it still being early on New Year's Day. Bits of litter blew between the parked cars and snow banks. Sparrows darted in the bare branches of a tree, hopping at the curb, chirping and fluttering as they sought food.

"Our first meal together this year," Mary said.

"We have enough food to stay here and eat for several days."

"Not a bad idea."

"And last night!" Patrick smiled and watched Mary. "Last night was special."

"New Year's Eve always is."

"How did you sleep?"

Mary looked away, out the window. "Like a New Year's baby. I fell asleep as soon as we got in bed."

What? This is the second time she's denied what happened between us. I know what we did. Sooner or later, she's going to have to acknowledge what we're doing.

—

They lived as though their two apartments were one, separated by a flight of stairs and two doors. There were two bedrooms, two bathrooms, two kitchens, dining areas, and living rooms. They moved easily up and down the stairs, sometimes eating and sleeping in one apartment, sometimes the other.

The new semester began. Their days were focused on Mary's reading and study time and Patrick's painting. They felt compelled to do everything they needed to do before their evenings together. The evening was their time. They always slept together now, often waking up still dressed, but sometimes their clothes were discarded beside the bed. They discovered many ways to love each other while never crossing the line that for Mary was the divide between perfection and sin.

◆

"Father, forgive me for I have sinned," she said.

"What is your sin?" The voice was quiet, controlled, coming from the shadowed man behind the screen.

"I have been sleeping with my boyfriend."

The priest answered patiently but with a trace of exasperation. "Young lady, you have been coming to confession every week now for nearly two months. You always tell me that you are sleeping with your boyfriend. And each week you tell me that you have not had sexual intercourse. Is that still the case?"

"Yes, Father. We spend the night together in the same bed. We love each other but we have not had intercourse."

"Is that possible? You are sure you have never done anything that might be wrong?"

"No, Father. We have never had sex. We have not sinned."

"You love this boy?"

"Yes, Father."

"You are sure?"

"Yes, Father."

"And does he love you?"

"Yes, he does. He's told me he loves me."

"You believe him. Do you intend to marry him?"

"I would like to. We haven't talked about it. But I think he wants to stay with me for the rest of his life too."

"If your relationship with this boy is what you say it is, you should get married."

"He's not Catholic. But he comes to Mass with me every week."

"Good. That is good." The priest paused. "Would you like to meet with me together for counseling? Would he consider becoming a Catholic?"

"I don't think he's ready. When he is, yes, we should meet with you. Or with my priest or a nun I'm close with back home in New York."

"Very good. You need not worry so much though, young lady. You have not sinned if what you say is true. But until you and this boy are married, you need to be very careful not to succumb to temptation. It would be easy for you and this boy to do something you shouldn't, something that would be a sin. Then you would need to confess."

"Yes, Father."

He gave Mary her prayers to say and sent her out into the church. She sat hunched in a pew near the back of the shadowed church, quiet and alone. Red votive candles flickered. Footsteps of parishioners echoed as they came and went. She said her prayers and stayed, sitting alone with her thoughts. *I haven't sinned. The priest said, "You have not sinned if what you say is true." We've never had actual intercourse. It all feels so right, so good, but it isn't a sin as long as we never go further. It couldn't be wrong, could it? What if Patrick and I got married? Both Sister Catherine and the priest advised it. But I can't propose. It's not what a girl does. Maybe I'll mention it to Patrick and see what he says.*

She continued to finger her rosary as she prayed, repeating the same prayers and adding new ones specific to her worries. She heard no response. *Where are God and the Virgin when I need them? What is the answer?* She dropped the rosary beads into her purse, stood up, and left the church.

I'm so drawn to Patrick, so wanting to give in and let it all happen. But I'm so terrified. A lifetime of needing to do what's right, to not commit a sin... Right now I need Sister Catherine. But I need Patrick more.

Chapter Sixteen

MARY CALLED MARGIE TO TELL her the two portraits were done. Margie planned to take the train north to Providence after work on Friday. It was a long weekend, Martin Luther King Day on Monday, so they'd have nearly three days together before Margie had to catch the train back to New York.

Mary and Patrick waited together in the echoing lobby of the Providence train station. The train from New York roared in beneath their feet. Moments later, passengers began walking through the lobby. Among them strode Margie in knee-high leather boots, a patterned Vera Bradley bag swinging from one shoulder. When she saw her sister and Patrick, Margie twirled in the middle of the station lobby, arms out, her bag swinging. Her bright eyes flashed. "I'm here!"

She embraced both of them and off they went, out into the cold, laughing as they climbed into Mary's little car for the short ride back to Wickenden Street.

In Mary's apartment, they chatted about the train ride over glasses of wine. But it was late.

"Okay." Mary set her glass on the table. "Sleeping arrangements. Patrick and I share both his apartment and mine. So, here's how it will work. You sleep in my apartment. Patrick and I will be upstairs in his apartment. Is that okay?"

Patrick looked at the two sisters. *This is the first I've heard of Mary's plan. I was prepared to go along with whatever she decided to do. But I expected her to share her apartment with Margie and that I would sleep alone upstairs till Margie left. Mary could've preserved the image that our relationship is still pure. This is unexpected, but good. Maybe Mary is showing off to her sister that she really is sleeping with me.*

Mary showed Margie the bedroom and the bathroom. They hugged, sisters who share things in a way that Patrick couldn't understand. Margie gave Patrick a small peck on the cheek. "Good night Patrick. I'll see the two of you tomorrow morning." She smiled and patted him on the shoulder.

"We'll come down as soon as we're awake," he promised.

"Lock the door," Mary instructed her sister.

———

Above her, Mary and Patrick settled into their familiar positions. His hand came to her shoulder as it always did. But tonight she tensed and pushed it away.

"No, Patrick. Not tonight. She's right downstairs. She might hear us."

"She knows we're sleeping together."

"Yes, but she might hear us."

"We can be quiet. We don't make much noise."

"We're not doing anything bad," Mary said. "But no. Not tonight."

He put his hand on her thigh and began shifting it up. She pushed it away. "No! Behave yourself. Not tonight."

He gave a sigh and eased away from her. She relaxed. It was a restless night for both, waking often, seeking each other again and again in the dark room, then stopping and backing away on the narrow bed. Patrick's frustration mounted.

Early the next morning they went down to Mary's apartment. Margie was already up, sitting with a cup of coffee by the front window in the sunshine. Mary toasted three bagels and joined Patrick and Margie at the table. After their breakfast, Mary led her sister upstairs. Patrick followed. "You've got to see this place." Mary opened the door. Margie walked in and stopped.

As Mary had done when she first saw it, Margie walked along the wall of the living room, surveying each of Patrick's paintings. "These are wonderful. All I'd seen were the two portraits you did, the one of me and the one of Mary. And then last night one or two more that Mary has downstairs in her place. But this is awesome. You should put them in a gallery and see if you can sell them."

"I sold a few things in Maine while I was in college. And I have a couple in a student exhibit in a gallery on the RISD campus. We'll see if they sell."

Mary came to stand by Patrick. "Our friends Aaron and Melanie make a living selling their artwork. And they're going to see if they can get Patrick's work placed in galleries in Boston."

"Bring some down to New York," Margie suggested. "People will spend a lot of money for things this good in New York."

"We'll see," Patrick said. "It's not easy getting a gallery to accept your work. In the end, it's like any other business. If they can make money on it, they'll take it."

Mary pulled Margie to the bedroom. "He's got your two portraits finished and framed in here."

The pictures were propped against the wall across from the rumpled bed. Margie smiled. "Beautiful."

Patrick shifted from one foot to the other. *Mary's usually so reticent to admit to our almost chaste living arrangement. Why did she lead Margie into the bedroom? Is she showing off to her sister again that she's sharing her bed with a man? She could have brought the two portraits out to the living room. And look at Margie. She has to be seeing the unmade bed, and she's not disturbed by it. It's embarrassing for me to have her here in my bedroom.*

—

Later in the morning the three of them walked up the hill for a quick tour of the Brown and RISD campuses. Patrick's whole life had centered on college campuses. Raised with a professor for a father, it was a comfortable place for him. Mary, too, was most at home in academia. But this was new for Margie. The snow-covered lawns inside the gate and the old brick of the Brown campus, the students, even on a Saturday, walking across the campus and reading in the library; all of it was impressive to her.

RISD was a different experience than the insular academic environment of Brown. The campus hummed with the vibrant energy of art being made. There were messy studio rooms, eccentrically dressed student artists, and the music, mostly rock, that played in the background. "I like this place," Margie said. "I wish I was an artist so I could live here and hang out with artists."

"You've got me," Patrick answered.

Late in the afternoon they walked to Saint Joseph's for Mass. Patrick noted that both sisters dipped their fingers in the font and crossed themselves once they were in the church. He and Mary had developed a set of unspoken rules when they attended Mass. Patrick entered the pew first, since he wouldn't be going forward for communion. Mary genuflected before she entered the pew and sat next to him on the aisle. This time Patrick slid further into the pew, allowing Mary and Margie space between him and the aisle. Both of them genuflected.

Patrick observed and followed the Mass in the booklet. Mary and Margie prayed next to him. When it was time for communion, Mary stood and was up the aisle first. Margie leaned to Patrick and whispered, "Do you take Communion?"

"No. I'm not Catholic."

"I don't go to Mass every week like my sister. But when I'm with her, I do. It matters to her."

Margie followed her sister up the aisle.

As they were leaving after Mass, Margie whispered to Patrick again. "You're really good going to Mass with her. It's important to her that you be here." She gave him a brief hug of thanks.

After Mass, they drove downtown and parked near the river to visit the brew pub where Patrick and Mary had gone months before.

"This is where Patrick and I came on our first date. It's a special place for us. And we're meeting our friends here. Those two artists I told you about."

Aaron and Melanie sat in a booth near the back. Aaron was wrapped in a thick, cable-stitched fisherman's sweater, the sleeves pushed up, showing his big hands and black hair on his forearms. He had several weeks' growth of dark beard.

Melanie, still platinum blonde, had her hair in a bouncing ponytail. She wore a pastel blue cashmere sweater with a scooped neckline. Pearls ringed her throat. She looked like anybody's ideal 1950s prom queen.

Hugs and light kisses were exchanged in greeting. Mary did the introductions.

Their time in the pub was filled with loud laughter, large portions of food, and beer. They talked about art at first. But Aaron and Melanie were full of questions for Margie. What did she do for a living? Where did she live in Manhattan? What about her boyfriend?

Margie answered, explaining that she had a job in accounts payable in an office in New York, she lived in an affordable apartment fifteen blocks from her office with her boyfriend, Javier, who worked construction jobs, mostly in the city but sometimes on projects in other parts of the country.

When dinner was over, they went separate ways. While driving back to the apartment house, Margie reviewed their friends. "They seem nice. I'll have to keep an eye out for their artwork if I ever go in a gallery in New York."

"They both have things there," said Patrick. "Aaron sells a lot in New York."

"He's impressive," Margie admitted. "Tall, dark, and handsome; a good-looking man."

"He and Melanie make a tight couple. They're so devoted to each other." Mary shook her head. "I wish he'd shave more often. He's been letting himself go the last week or so."

Patrick explained, "He grows a beard every winter because of the cold."

Margie grinned. "I like it. It's rough. It looks good on him. It gives him a dangerous sort of look. Melanie is cute. What a sweetheart. She seems nice, maybe a little young and innocent for a guy like Aaron."

Patrick smiled. *If she only knew what Melanie's really like!*

Mary laughed. "Young and innocent? Are you kidding? Everything about her is an act. Her appearance is a performance. Yes, she is a sweet girl. But she's got an unbelievable wild side to her, a crazy past. She gave you the innocent look tonight."

⎯⎯⎯

They spent Sunday in Newport, driving the deserted winter streets, past ancient buildings, and then along Bellevue Avenue with the columned mansions. It was too cold and windy to be on the edge of the bay so they returned to Newport and found a seafood bar for dinner.

After lunch on Monday, they brought Margie back to the train station. Patrick had wrapped the two portraits for the trip back. "Will you be okay with these on the train? Be careful with the glass."

"Yes. Javier is meeting me at the station in the city. He can help with the pictures. I'll take the one for mom and dad up to them in a couple of weeks."

Patrick and Mary went to bed earlier than usual. After two nights together with no attempts at lovemaking, they were both eager. They awoke at dawn. Both sets of their clothes were on the floor near the bed. But still, that fateful line had not been crossed.

Chapter Seventeen

AARON AND PATRICK SAT ACROSS from each other on stacked wooden pallets in Aaron's concrete-floored studio while they ate their lunch.

Aaron turned the conversation away from art, eager to talk about the dinner with Margie. "Interesting girl, Mary's sister. I can see they're sisters; they have the same eyes." Aaron smiled. "But Margie is more self-assured. I understand her better than Mary. She has a little edginess to her that I don't see with Mary. Mary is still a mystery to me at times."

"How is that?" Patrick took a drink of bottled tea.

"I can't figure out Mary, the way she was struggling with herself before the two of you started sleeping together."

"I never told you we were sleeping together. Did Melanie tell you? I think Mary told her."

"No. You never came right out and told me. And no, Melanie and I haven't talked about it. But I saw the way things changed between you two before Christmas. I asked Melanie, but she dodged the question which confirmed it for me. I knew you were trying to figure a way to go down that path. So good for you."

"Yes, Mary and I are there."

"But her sister. Margie. She lives with her boyfriend. Mary we see all the time, but it took her a long time to take that step, and she still can't talk about it. Margie's interesting."

"Yes. Margie was intrigued by you, too. She thought you were good looking."

Aaron laughed. He put down his sandwich and continued laughing. "Ho! Did she now? Well, that's something. She's a pretty girl. When's she coming back to Providence?"

Patrick paused. *Where's this going? What's Aaron thinking?* "She's got a boyfriend. And anyway, you and Melanie? You can't do that. I thought you and Melanie were tight."

"We are. She's my soul mate. My life partner. That doesn't mean I don't notice an attractive woman."

"Okay, but it sounded like you wanted to get together with Margie."

"Yes, she's a new friend. I would like to get to know her better. Here, if she comes back into town. Or on one of my trips to New York. That doesn't mean I don't love Melanie. Just that I enjoyed meeting Margie the other night at the pub. Margie would be a friend. Don't get me wrong."

"Sure. Okay." Patrick nodded. Would he cheat on Melanie? *This is a side of Aaron I haven't seen before. It's disturbing. Aaron's my idol. I see myself getting a life with my art and with Mary like he has with his sculpture and Melanie. It might not be so simple with Aaron.*

Aaron changed the subject. "On another note, I was talking with a gallery I work with in Boston. They sold a piece of mine, so I need to replace it. I'm going to deliver it next month and I mentioned your work. They're familiar with your uncle's paintings, and they agreed to look at your work. Do you have anything ready to sell?"

Patrick took a moment, reviewing his recent work, picture by picture, in his head. "I have two pieces in the gallery here at RISD. I might need a couple of weeks to pick a few other good things and get them framed and matted, ready to show. How many are we talking about?"

"I have contacts with two galleries in Boston that might take your work on consignment. Get three or four pictures ready. You have a few weeks till I'm going. I'll bring you along and introduce you to people."

"I'll be ready."

Melanie and Mary met for their weekly Wednesday lunch. "My sister thinks you're too young and innocent to be with a dangerous, dark, handsome man like Aaron," Mary said with a smile.

"Young? I'm nearly thirty. Innocent?" Melanie leaned toward Mary to whisper, as though they were two sixteen-year-old girls gossiping in the high school cafeteria. "You told her she was right, didn't you? Told her how much of an innocent, young thing I am?"

"Of course! She believed it."

Melanie giggled. "I was wild for so long. But not anymore. Now I'm with Aaron. What was it you called him? Dangerous, dark, and handsome? Yes, he's all of that. He could have anyone. But he loves me. I'm not one for fantasies. Except maybe with the little fairies and butterflies I make out of glass. But Aaron and me?" Melanie paused. "Being together is amazing. I never knew it could be like this with a man."

"I hope we get that, Patrick and me."

"I couldn't wish for a more wonderful thing for the two of you." Melanie reached over and gave Mary's hand a squeeze. Her smile was incandescent.

Chapter Eighteen

IT WAS FEBRUARY, THE DARK New England winter wearing on everyone. Patrick burst through the door of Mary's apartment. "I sold a painting! In the gallery on campus. It's the last day of the show and someone came in and bought it just before we took down the exhibit." Mary sat on her couch with a French novel open on her lap. He was in front of her in three strides, pulling her up from the couch her book flying to the floor.

She hugged him. *I'm overwhelmed! Someone actually paid money for one of his paintings. I knew he was good and that he'd sold a few back in Maine. But maybe he really can earn money with his art. And he's so excited.* "Congratulations! Which one sold? The city scene or the country landscape?"

"The cityscape. The cobbled alleyway with the old brick and the doorway. A law office downtown wants to hang it in their lobby."

She kissed him. "Perfect! They can have the city scene. I love that country landscape, so it's good you get to keep that one. I'm so proud of you!"

"It's a lot of money. But I loved that picture. The paintings become like my children and parting with them can be difficult. I'm not good at letting go of any of them. Just as long as they get displayed in a good setting or a good home with people who love them."

"This is wonderful. You're on your way. You want to earn a living with your painting? Here you go."

"It's a lot of money right now. But it's just one picture. It needs to be consistent for me to make a living. Aaron's introducing me to people with galleries in Boston in a few weeks. We'll see how that goes." He pulled Mary down on the couch next to him. "We don't have plans on Friday night, do we?"

"No more than any other Friday. Why?"

"Here's the thing. I just came into all this unexpected money. And next week is your birthday. I was thinking. There's this fancy French restaurant Aaron told me about, across the river in the financial district. I've already made a reservation for Friday."

"I didn't know if you would remember."

"Of course I did. I've been planning it for several weeks. And Valentine's Day is next week, too. So I was thinking."

"Oh, dear. You're a painter. You're creative. Leave the logic and the thinking to me. What should I wear? How fancy is it?"

"We could probably go dressed like the grad students we are. They would let us in as long as we could pay. But this is special. I'm going to get all dressed up. I'll wear my tie and everything."

"I'll be ready. Just tell me when."

⁓

The restaurant was small. Low walls of worn bricks and heavy block granite surrounded them. Thick tables, the oak tops inset with antique tiles, lined the walls. Patrick wore his blue blazer, and a pinstriped shirt with an out-of-style striped necktie. Mary was in a navy dress with a daring, low neckline. Melanie had loaned her pearls.

The waiter brought menus. "Don't even look at the prices," Patrick instructed Mary. "This is our special night. Valentine's Day and your birthday."

"It's also our five-month anniversary. Did you realize that?"

"Of course." Hastily, beneath the table on his fingers, Patrick counted the months since their first date at the pub. She was right, of course.

"Let's do Valentine cards on the real day," Mary said.

"Agreed. Tonight is just the dinner."

"Okay." Mary smiled. "I'll cook something special for Valentine's Day."

"And I'll cook on your birthday."

Patrick puzzled over the menu, struggling to understand the French. It was as alien to him as when the priest lapsed into Latin during the Masses he went to with Mary. "Mary, I'll need your help ordering dinner tonight."

"Certainement."

The waiter filled their water glasses. "Would you like a drink before dinner?" Mary reviewed the wine list. It was long, with wines from all over the world, featuring those from France. "What do you recommend for an oak barreled chardonnay?" she asked, hoping she sounded knowledgeable about wine but exposing her innocence on the subject.

The waiter named one, pointing it out on the wine list. It was expensive. Mary nodded. "I think we'll have this one." She pointed to a different wine. "Number seventy-eight."

"An excellent selection." The waiter headed to the bar.

"I know you told me not to think about the prices, but the wine he suggested was 128 dollars a bottle. If I'd ordered that I'd have been thinking about the cost all through dinner. I couldn't enjoy that."

Patrick nodded. *I picked the restaurant and made the reservation. But Mary's taking control of the meal. She's doing that more and more frequently.*

"Compared to that price, the one we got is cheap," she added.

Patrick weighed in. "But it's more than we're used to. Remember, we don't need to hold back on the food."

Mary smiled. "What would you like for dinner?"

"Do they have chicken?"

She ordered a chicken dish in a pastry crust for him. She got duck. They shared pâté as an appetizer and crocks of onion soup. When the waiter brought dessert menus they ordered one chocolate mousse and two spoons. The bill came to twice their shared grocery bill for a week. Neither of them cared.

After dinner, back at Mary's apartment, they settled onto the couch. He kissed her. Their near lovemaking usually began after they went to bed. Tonight was different. They couldn't wait. It began on the sofa.

They woke Saturday morning in Mary's bed. They were fulfilled as always, but Mary still worried. *Nothing sinful happened. We stopped short of complete intercourse. So I still don't need to go to confession. I didn't commit a sin according to the priest. It's a literal interpretation of his words, but it saves me. I need to be the good girl and do the right things. But if it isn't a sin, and if I'm not really living with Patrick the way Margie is with Javier, how could it be wrong?*

Saturday passed simply after the extravagant Friday night at the French restaurant. They went to Mass and returned to their apartments for a dinner of macaroni and cheese out of a box. They dressed it up with sliced hotdogs and drank tea.

"You take care of the food for Valentine's Day." Patrick winked. "I'll take care of the mood."

On Valentine's Day, Mary prepared boeuf bourguignon. She found the recipe on her computer, noting that it was not expensive, but the results might be special. Patrick put red candles on her table, played music by Chopin, and presented her with a new painting: a large watercolor showing the ocean channel in winter near his house. He hung it where they would both see it from the table while they ate. They exchanged store-bought valentines.

A week later, Mary went upstairs to Patrick's for her birthday dinner. "I've got something special for you," he said.

"Another painting?"

"Yes—two. But something special for dinner."

"What?"

"Open the refrigerator. Bring me the brown paper bag." He went to the stove where a big pot of water steamed.

Mary brought him the bag. He took the bag, folded the top open, and instructed her, "Now, lift the top off the pot."

Again, she did what he told her, releasing a cloud of steam. Patrick reached into the bag and pulled out a large, brown-green lobster, claws waving. He dropped it head-first into the pot. A second one followed.

"Put the lid back on and hold it down!"

Again, Mary did as she was told. For a few seconds they heard scrambling inside the pot, claws scratching against metal.

Patrick set out two salads and placed a large bowl on the table. "What's the bowl for?" Mary asked.

"The lobster shells."

"How do I eat a lobster? I've never had a whole lobster. Just lobster rolls."

"Don't tell me you got lobster at a fast food place?"

"Yes, I can't afford anything else. But I like it."

"This is better. I'll show you how to get it out of the shell. Be prepared to get messy."

"You're steaming them. What else do we have to do?"

"That's it. Just eat them. It's not tricky like your French beef meal we had for Valentine's Day. But it's good." He pulled a new bottle of the Ballet of Angels wine out of the refrigerator.

"Where did you find the lobsters? And our wine?"

"I asked people. They sent me to a seafood market a couple of miles away that had a big salt-water tank full of the lobsters. And I found a wine store that had the wine."

After dinner, Mary settled onto Patrick's couch. He presented her with a hand-painted birthday card. Unlike the standard valentines they had exchanged, Patrick had created his own special birthday card for her. It was a portrait of Mary, standing, hands on hips, next to brick steps on the Brown campus. As always, Patrick showed her full of energy and passion. Inside he wrote, "You are the most beautiful thing in my life. Happy Birthday."

For a moment, Mary flushed. "You're amazing. I could never imagine getting a handmade birthday card before I met you."

"There's more. I have a gift for you, too."

He went into the bedroom and returned with the landscape that hadn't sold in the RISD gallery show. "You said you liked it. We'll have your apartment decorated before the year ends."

"I love it. Thank you. You need to keep selling those paintings." She rested her head on his chest. "I like the way we've been living and eating the past few days."

"If I keep selling, we'll keep living like this. But I can't count on a steady income from my paintings. Not yet."

"That's okay. Lent starts in a few days. I'm not sure if it would be right to be eating fancy dinners during Lent."

"Your religion defines a lot for you, doesn't it?" *Does it dictate how she is in bed with me?*

"Yes. It defines everything. What defines right or wrong for you?"

"I respect all people. That's what right is for me. Anything else would be wrong, I guess."

"Religion doesn't play into it?"

"Of course it does. Maybe not the way it does for you."

"My faith defines right and wrong. It's absolute."

Patrick sat back. *How do I explain this?* "Remember when I said artists aren't limited by rules or convention?"

"Yes."

"So, that's it. I won't hurt other people, but I do whatever I like. I paint whatever I want to, however I want to. It's a real feeling of freedom."

"But this freedom, that's just with your art. Not your faith? Not your life?"

"No, it's with both my art and my life. It's not tied to my religion the way yours is."

"My faith is important to me. But it goes further. My mom and dad have always expected a lot from me. They want me to do the right things. That's why I always got perfect grades in school. But my Catholic faith tells me what right and wrong are."

"Yes, and I respect that. That's why I go to Mass with you every week."

"Do you observe Lent? And Easter?"

"Of course. I'll go to church with you on Easter."

"Ash Wednesday? Good Friday?"

"I don't usually go to church on those days, but I will if you want me to."

"I would. These are Masses that matter a great deal to me. They're a central part of what it means to be a Catholic."

"Then I'll come with you." Patrick paused. *Be careful.* "Mary, would you come to a Protestant church with me?"

Mary thought for a moment. "I could do that. You've been coming to

Mass with me for months. I suppose I could go to a service at your church, but we'd still need to go to Mass on Saturday. Then we could go to your church on Sunday morning. Let's go before Lent begins."

"Good. There's this big church just a couple of blocks past RISD. It's not really 'my church', it's a famous old Baptist Church, but it's a beautiful old building; I think it's on the national register of historic places. I'll see the inside and you'll see a Protestant service."

"Baptist? I thought you were Methodist."

"It doesn't matter. Baptist, Methodist, it's a church. Come with me."

They walked past the RISD campus then turned left, heading down a steep hill toward the river. The First Baptist Church, vast white clapboards and tall windows, loomed beside them. They turned onto a wide flagstone walk and up stone stairs to a heavy wooden door. Inside they were directed up more stairs that curled along either side of a vestibule.

The wide sanctuary was lined with rows of pews boxed in by low, white painted walls. They found their way to a pew near the back, opened a waist-high door, and entered. Patrick noticed that Mary genuflected even though it wasn't a Catholic church. As they sat waiting for the service to begin Mary slipped her rosary out of her purse and began to pray in silence, the beads sifting through her fingers, her eyes closed and her lips moving.

Patrick studied the old building. Tall columns, painted dove gray, lined the side aisles, supporting a high arching ceiling. Enormous Palladian windows dominated the cream-colored walls. The sanctuary was filled with light, mostly from the tall windows but also from an enormous crystal chandelier hung in the middle of the space. The building found a balance between austerity and beauty.

A man moved from a front pew to sit at a piano. He played a classical piece, baroque, possibly Bach. The minister entered and climbed to stand in the pulpit. During the service, Patrick glanced several times at Mary from the corner of his eye. When the congregation prayed, she sat quietly. When there was a hymn to be sung, she stood silent by his side while he sang. During the sermon, she listened, but showed no emotion. The service ended. Patrick and Mary left, dodging the minister at the top of the stairs.

Walking home, Patrick asked, "That was a Protestant service. Your impressions?"

"There was no crucifix, not even a cross. It was a nice church, but a very plain building. Nothing in the church for me. Some of the prayers were familiar; others were new to me. I enjoyed the music. But the service wasn't what I'm used to."

"Did you like the sermon?"

"I admit the sermon was interesting. Thought provoking. But what did it have to do with worshiping God?"

Umm, how do I answer that? Maybe I should've paid less attention to the architecture and more to the sermon? They walked a while in silence.

"Are you okay just going to my Masses at Saint Joseph's? I'm not comfortable in that church."

"Okay. I want you to be comfortable in church."

"Come to Mass with me on Ash Wednesday." He nodded.

Patrick joined Mary at St. Joseph's for a long Mass on Ash Wednesday. When they left, Mary's forehead was smudged with ashes. Patrick's face was clean. Mary spent the day praying before joining Patrick for a quiet dinner. In bed, she rolled away from him without even a kiss.

I guess we're both giving up things for Lent. I really want her right now. I hope this doesn't last till Easter.

Chapter Nineteen

THE NEXT MORNING, WHILE MARY was in the shower, Patrick walked into the living room. The apartment was hushed, chilled, and it was snowing heavily, filling the street outside the window. He checked the internet; both of their colleges were closed for the day.

He began cooking a full breakfast. Mary came out of the shower, smelled bacon, and joined him in the kitchen, still wrapped in her towel.

"Bacon? You're cooking bacon? What's going on?"

"Look out the front window. School's canceled!"

She grinned. "Excellent! What should we do with the free day?"

"Stay home and play? We can't go to school, and it's too much of a mess to go anywhere else right now."

"Fantastic. A free day together. I'll pick up the cooking while you get your shower."

He showered. She pulled on her light-blue fleece robe and finished cooking their breakfast. They dawdled over the meal, and then Mary settled on the sofa with a book of French poetry. Patrick sat next to her. For a moment, her robe fell open, the shawl collar hanging, exposing a bare shoulder and breast. Mary saw Patrick's eyes and reached up to pull the robe closed.

"So?" he asked. "What do you want to do this morning?"

"I don't know. Read? Catch up on my studying?"

He placed his hand on her bare knee. "Really? You want to study? We can do that later."

She smiled but pushed his hand away. "Not now. I'm reading." He put the hand back on her knee and slid it up her thigh.

She shifted on the couch and let the hand continue for a moment. "Patrick, no." She pushed the hand away again.

"Why not?"

"We can't."

"Why not? Come on, Mary! Let's go!"

"So many reasons."

"What?"

"It's Lent, for one. And we can't do it. We can fool around a little at night like we do, but we're not married. So we can't do more. And anyway, I've got to study."

"We've got plenty of time this morning. You can study later. So, why not?" He began stroking her leg again. For a moment she allowed it, then stopped him again. She pushed her hair back with both hands. *Why can't he just stop? Why must he persist? I have to be strong. I can't give in.*

Mary looked Patrick in the eyes. "Like I said, if we got going we'd have to stop. We're not married. So, let's not start. It'll be easier this way." He paused. Then he stopped and pulled his hand back, frustrated.

He stood and went to the window, looking out at the blowing snow as it piled up on the street. He shifted from one foot to the other. He put his hands on his hips. Then he folded his arms restlessly across his chest. Next his hands went up, pushing his hair back, a gesture common to Mary but unusual for Patrick. Mary sat silently on the sofa, watching him. Her finger marked her place in her book.

What is with her? Come on Mary! I can't live like this. "This is impossible," he said, turning to confront her. "I've never done this with a girl I loved before. There was that one time, but the girl meant nothing to me. That was just experimenting. I've been waiting for the right one, and now I've found you. You're the one. I love you. So, why can't we?"

Mary pulled her robe closer. "I've never done this before either. Not at all. Not with anyone just to experiment. I love you too, but you know how I feel about this. I just can't. Particularly during Lent."

"It's not like you're giving it up for Lent if we've never gone all the way. Hell, if we're being honest, we really have done it. All the things we've done are sex, maybe not the sexual act, but close enough."

The priest at confession told me, "You have not sinned if what you say about your relationship is true." I've memorized his words. I recite them to myself every day since that confession. We haven't had intercourse. All we've done is a little fooling around and that's okay. The priest said so. "No we haven't!" she protested. "We always make sure we end it before we actually do it. It would be a sin if we did more. It would be wrong."

"God, Mary, you know I love you. Jesus, this is unnatural. Always so close and then stopping."

"I know, but you need to listen to me. We can't do it. And please don't swear like that."

"What do you expect me to do? Just go on like this, month after month? We love each other, right? You know I love you. Do you really love me?"

"Yes, but not when you're yelling at me. Please keep your voice down. Of course I love you."

"And don't you want to make love, too?"

Mary let out an exasperated sigh. She pulled her robe tight again and sat straighter on the sofa, planting her bare feet together on the floor. She looked away, past him out the window at the snow. "Yes, I want to make love with you. It's an awful temptation some nights. But we can't. We're not married."

"Do you want to get married?" Patrick let the words out before he had a moment to consider what he was saying.

Mary stopped. She turned and looked at Patrick. "You're proposing so we can have sex?"

There was silence, as they weighed the consequence of what they had said. *I feel trapped. I never expected the conversation to go in this direction. One moment we're talking about making love, about having sex. The next I've proposed. I need to reassure her that this is about love, not sex.*

He stood across the room by the window, looking back at her, meeting her eyes. She remained on the sofa, folded into her robe, watching him.

Patrick composed himself and spoke, his voice steady, his manner serious. "No, of course not. Look, I can't imagine going on without you. I want to be with you forever. Yes, I want to make love with you, but this is about a lot more than that."

Mary put her book aside and looked at him, wondering if this was the moment. *He means it! I've been wanting to talk marriage with him and now he's proposed. I've been thinking about it and wanting to bring up marriage. And now it's happening!*

"This is for real. Not about sex," he concluded. "I've been giving this a lot of thought."

"I want that, too. I've been giving it a lot of thought, too. Yes, I think we need to think this through some more, but yes."

"Yes to getting married?"

"Yes. What did you think I meant?"

"I wasn't sure if you meant yes to married or to sex. Or both."

"Married. Sex comes later."

He sat beside her and took her hand. "Mary, will you marry me?"

She leaned over and kissed him on the cheek. "Yes, but let's give it more thought. This is serious."

I'm still unfulfilled. But she said yes. Didn't she? I'm getting accustomed to waiting for her to allow me more but this is something. "Yes, this is a serious moment. I know that." He sighed when she didn't respond. "So. What do we do today?"

"Let's take the morning to study and see what the weather's like this afternoon. Maybe we could go out for a walk later."

"Fine. I'll go upstairs and get my paints and paint for a while."

She picked up her book. "Why don't you come back and paint here, with me?"

Patrick climbed the stairs to his apartment and closed the door, resting his head against the wall. *I can't believe I just proposed. I love her, sure. But why am I so confused and frustrated? Man, what's happening? I need to talk to Uncle Win.* The call went to voice mail. "Hi, Uncle Win. Patrick here. It's snowing in Providence. Call when you can. I'd like to talk."

He gathered his paints and went back to Mary's.

As soon as Patrick left, Mary dressed and called Sister Catherine. "Hi, it's Mary."

"Well, hello, young lady. It's good to hear from you. Has it started snowing there yet?"

"Yes, they've canceled classes today so I'm home."

"That's nice. What are your plans?"

"We're staying in and studying. I'm reading poetry and Molière. Patrick's gone to get his paints, but he'll be coming back in a few minutes to paint here."

"That's nice. I like that the two of you will be spending the day that way, together."

Mary paused. "He proposed. Just a few minutes ago."

"Excuse me? What'd you say?"

"He proposed. He wants to get married. I can't tell my parents or anyone. But I wanted to share this with you."

"That's wonderful news, Mary! I'm so happy for you."

"Yes, me too. I want to say yes. I did, actually. But I'm still confused." *I don't know what I'm getting myself into with him. I never intended for it to get to this point. Sister Catherine knows that. I'm thrilled every day that I've found Patrick and we're together, but I'm confused.*

"Is this because he's not Catholic? I told you that shouldn't be a problem. Maybe he'll become Catholic, but as long as you raise your children Catholic it's not an issue."

"Yes. Of course I would. But there's so much to think about. I don't know."

"He loves you, Mary. I could see that when I met him. And you love him, too. So relax. Enjoy it. This is a special time for the two of you."

"I know."

Patrick's door closed at the top of the stairs. "I've got to go. He's coming back."

"Take care of yourself, dear Mary. And thank you for calling and sharing this wonderful news. Goodbye." Mary hung up as Patrick opened the door.

Patrick set up at the table by the front window. He got a glass of water and paper towels to use with his watercolors. What should I paint? He looked around for inspiration; something to paint. Outside, a squirrel huddled on the bare branch of a tree. Patrick squeezed out black, brown, blue, and green paint; tiny daubs of color on his white palette. He dipped his brush in the water and mixed colors. He blocked in the body of the squirrel with its fluff of a tail curled up along its back.

Minutes later, he stepped back to assess the picture. *That's no good. It lacks energy and depth. The colors are wrong. How about a still life?* He grabbed the wine bottle left over from their dinner several nights before. A bit of wine remained in the bottle, refracting the light. An old leather-bound French book sat next to the bottle. That might work as a nice still life. He set to work but once again was disappointed in the finished product. He set the second picture aside with the first one.

His phone rang. "It's my Uncle Win. I'll take this outside so I won't disturb you." He went out onto the front steps. Snow blew around him. "Hi!"

"Hello, my young friend. How's the weather down there in sunny Providence?"

"We're snowed in. They canceled classes today."

"Yes, it's supposed to start here in a few hours."

"Snowed in with Mary."

"Oh my! That should be fun. And can I ask? What are you two up to?"

"Unfortunately, nothing."

"Patrick, relationships settle into patterns. The way you start can become the way a relationship continues. You need to do something new if you want something new to happen with her. You love each other. Take charge. Do something."

"Um, I kind of did this morning." Patrick hesitated. "I proposed to her."

"You did what?" Win exclaimed.

"I proposed. I said I thought we ought to consider getting married."

There was silence on the line. Uncle Win took a deep breath. "Okay, I'm not surprised. What did Mary say?"

"She said yes, but we're still going to think about this a bit. Please don't tell Mother or my father."

"Of course not. What led you to ask her this morning?"

"I don't know." *What am I supposed to say? We were fooling around, but stopped as usual and then…* "I'm in love. It doesn't make much sense, does it?"

"Love has nothing to do with what makes sense. It's about emotions, not logic. You need to take time," he advised. "Talk with her more when you've both had time to let the feelings and emotions settle in. Your parents aren't the best role models for talking things through. But you need to do this with Mary."

"Yeah, okay, sure."

"I imagine that what you said this morning was more emotional than logical. But you're talking about a lifelong commitment. It might be the right thing for the two of you. But it might not be. Take time to think this through."

"Yeah. Thanks for calling me back, Uncle Win. I just needed to talk with you."

"Of course. You know I'll be here any time, but you need to be talking with Mary about this, not me. Take your time, dear Patrick."

"Okay. I've got to go. I'm on the porch, and it's snowing and cold. I've got to get back inside."

"Yes. Get back in where it's warm. And say hi to that wonderful young lady for me."

"I sure will."

"I love you, Patrick. Take good care of yourself."

"Love you too, Uncle Win." Patrick hurried inside to the warmth of Mary's apartment.

Patrick began a third painting. This was of Mary curled on the couch. He got the line of her body, the folds of her sweater, her bare feet tucked beneath her on the couch. It looked exactly like her but the picture lacked the passion he usually found when he painted her from memory. *That's odd. How could painting her from memory produce art that's so much more vibrant than this, painted with her right here to inspire me?* He set it aside with the first two failed paintings.

As they finished lunch Mary suggested, "Let's go for a walk. It's stopped snowing. We need to get some fresh air."

Chapter Twenty

IT WAS LATE MARCH AND each day more snow melted in the warm sunshine. Puddles dominated the street gutters, and lawns on college hill were green, if muddy. Breezes swept away the moisture during the daytime. At night there was fog. The mood of the warming world was optimistic.

Patrick drove to Aaron's at dawn with four of his best paintings framed and covered with taped bubble wrap. He set them behind Aaron's truck seat and helped load one of his steel sculptures, covering it with a blue tarpaulin. They packed into the front seat with coffee and pulled out for the trip north to Boston, riding behind the tail end of rush hour traffic.

As they neared Back Bay, Aaron called a gallery on Newbury Street so a loading zone parking place was open for them upon arrival. Two men from the gallery waited on the sidewalk with a low, wheeled dolly. Aaron pulled in and parked, leaving his hazard flashers on.

Patrick helped Aaron and the two gallery workers load the heavy sculpture onto the dolly. Then, while Aaron and the men rolled into the gallery, Patrick brought his four paintings and backpack and followed them in.

Aaron introduced Patrick to the gallery owner. "Sylvie, this is my friend, Patrick Chamberlain. I told you about him. He's brought several paintings with him. Patrick, this is Sylvie. She decides what work will be displayed here."

Sylvie was tall and slender, her dark brown hair cut with bangs. She appeared middle aged, though careful attention to her hair and makeup made it hard to tell; she could have been much older. She wore wide-cuffed black slacks and a red silk blouse unbuttoned half way down her torso. Long gold chains were braided around her neck. Gold earrings looped below her ears. She extended a thin hand and took Patrick's hand just by the fingers. She spoke in a voice faintly accented, maybe French. "It's a pleasure to meet you, young man. Your reputation precedes you, and I am familiar with your uncle's work."

"Thank you. I hope you like what I've brought. Can I show it to you?"

"I'll have one of my assistants take a look. I have business to conduct upstairs with Aaron."

A younger woman, short, pretty, and blonde, approached with a smile. Sylvie spoke. "This is Lisa. She'll be helping you. She knows the terms if she thinks your work can sell here."

"Hi, Lisa." Patrick extended his hand. She took it and pulled him close, brushing his cheek with a light kiss. "Let's see what you've got."

They sat on upholstered arm chairs near the back of the gallery. Aaron and Sylvie disappeared up the stairs. Patrick set down his paintings and began peeling the tape off the bubble wrap.

"So, you're a grad student at RISD. That's a great school. I love going to Providence to visit. I have a few friends who live there. They play in a band."

"Yes, it's a great little city. I don't get out much to the club scene but I enjoy living there. Where did you go to school?"

"Bennington. Vermont. It's a tiny little town, a small school. I majored in art history and found my way here after graduation."

"I'm from Maine. Bowdoin undergrad. Do you paint?"

"No. I did a little when I was in college. Not now. But I love art. And artists. I love the whole art scene."

Patrick set out the first painting, propping it on a chair. Lisa assessed it. "I love it! I love the textures in the trees. And the contrast, the colors, the chiaroscuro. Magnificent!"

Patrick set up another, leaning it against the wall.

"This one's even better," Lisa said. "Aaron was right. You're good." Pleased, Patrick unwrapped the third painting and set it out along the wall next to his second one.

"These are really good," Lisa raved, a hand raised to her throat. Patrick pulled the fourth one from the bubble wrap and stood back, setting the painting on his chair. Lisa stood and took his arm, wrapping her hand around his bicep. Together they reviewed the four paintings.

"Oh my," she said. "You have some very good work here. We'll definitely want to show these. If we were to take two on consignment, what would you want? We usually start with new artists by taking their work on consignment."

Patrick slipped his arm from her grip. "I'm not familiar with the Boston market. I don't know what to expect. I've sold in Maine and Providence. But I don't know what to ask." He had talked with Uncle Win and Aaron and had a good understanding that this was an expensive market. Both had advised him to allow the gallery to set the terms.

Lisa answered, analyzing the business as she spoke. "Watercolors don't command the prices we get for oil. But these are original, not limited editions. And you're a new artist. People don't know you yet. We could list these at 1,000 each, maybe as much as 1,500."

"Okay. And what would be my share if they sell?"

"Like I said, we sell on consignment with a new artist. With someone like Aaron, we buy directly and set a price where we can make our money back. But with you, we would give you sixty percent of the price if we sell your paintings. So we want to price them where we can move them. Maybe start a little higher and then negotiate a price with a buyer. Does that seem okay?"

Patrick calculated in his head. If they sell a painting for 1,500 dollars, sixty percent would be almost 1,000 dollars. I wonder how many paintings they'll take? "Do you think you could sell them for 1,500?"

"Yes, I think so. Most people will pay the asking price, a few will try to negotiate down, but these are good. Yes, we could sell for that price."

"How many would you take?"

Lisa reassessed the four paintings, then scanned the available wall space.

"All four. I would set up an alcove or a corner for these four paintings. Do you have a small bio we could include?"

"Yes, I have something we used at an exhibit down at RISD." He reached into his backpack and pulled out a one-page biography that included a color photo.

"This is perfect. And I like that you have the photograph, too. You're a handsome young man. People will appreciate that."

"They buy the paintings because they like the paintings, right? Not because of my appearance."

"Of course. But it doesn't hurt that they will read about you and like your portrait. If you email me a copy for this bio sheet, I could print a stack of them to give to people."

"Sure. I'll do that as soon as I get back to Providence. So, what's next?"

"I'll take the four paintings and the bio. I'll set up a space to display everything and get your bio framed. I'll need to do paperwork to take the paintings into our inventory. And I'll prepare a contract for you. It'll take a few minutes. Feel free to look around the gallery while I work on that." She walked to a desk in a back corner of the gallery. Patrick followed.

"Okay. And do you have a restroom I could use?"

"Of course. Upstairs. Through that doorway in the back. Straight ahead at the top of the stairs."

As he was leaving the bathroom, a door opened across the hall and Aaron came out. Behind him stood Sylvie, buttoning her red silk blouse, tucking it into her pants. Her hair was tousled.

Aaron saw Patrick and quickly pulled the door closed behind him. "How's it going? Did Lisa like your work?"

Patrick paused. *What did I just see? What is Aaron doing?* "Yes." Patrick glanced at the closed door a moment. "She's taking all four paintings. She's doing the paperwork now."

They started down the stairs together.

"Excellent! You've had a good morning then. With a bit of luck, the money will start to come in before you finish the school year."

What the hell? How could he do that to Melanie? Aaron in the room with Sylvie, and Sylvie buttoning her blouse? Aaron, my best friend, my role model and mentor? Aaron, Melanie's special love?

"Yes, it'll be nice to start making money. I can't wait." Patrick kept his words measured.

"Let's see how they're doing with setting up my sculpture."

They were in the truck, heading through Back Bay side streets when Aaron said, "So, all four paintings you brought were taken by Sylvie's gallery. That's great. I planned to take you to another gallery out in Chestnut Hill. But since you didn't bring more of your work, let's leave that for another day."

"Sure." Patrick stared out the window at the bleak vista of dirty ice along the edges of the sidewalks. *I can't look at him.*

"Are you okay? You seem upset. You just got four paintings displayed in a major Boston art gallery. What's going on?"

"Nothing. I'm fine."

Aaron navigated the maze of downtown streets to the expressway. Once they hit the highway, Aaron cleared his throat. "Does this have to do with Sylvie?"

Patrick sat in silence for a moment, looking out the window at the traffic. When he answered, it was carefully, picking his words. "Yes. I thought you and Melanie were a solid couple. I'm still trying to get my head around what I saw."

"Melanie and I are solid. And don't bring this up to her. Or with Mary for that matter. Mary and Melanie talk. Sylvie's just a friend."

"It looked like she's more than a friend."

"She's just a lonely old lady, really. She sells my sculpture, and I give her a little something on the side. It's a business transaction. It's not a big deal. And now she'll be selling your paintings, as well."

"You have sex and then she sells your art? Is that the way this business works?"

"No. I didn't have sex with her today. We fooled around a little. Nothing more."

"It looked like there was more going on."

"Not today. If sex was the plan, Sylvie and I would've gone back to her place and told the gallery staff we were going out to lunch. That's how it is with her."

"Is she going to expect me to have sex with her, too?"

"She won't expect it, but you could probably make it happen if you wanted to."

"I don't."

"What about with Lisa? She's pretty cute."

"No. I'm not looking for that. I just want to sell my paintings. That's all."

Aaron turned back, focused on the traffic, accelerating. They got back to Providence in time for a late lunch.

"I just got a big check from Sylvie's gallery. Can I take you out to lunch?" Aaron offered.

Patrick shook his head. "No, I'm good. I've got things to do. Work to catch up on."

"Come on, Patrick. Let it go. So, I fuck Sylvie sometimes while I'm up there. Let it go."

"Yeah, we're fine, you and me. I just have things I've got to do."

"All right. But remember. Not a word of this to Melanie or Mary. Okay?"

"Sure."

—

Patrick had trouble finding a focus with his artwork for the rest of the day. He skipped lunch and was hungry when he got back to the house. More than for food, he was desperate for Mary.

Mary was waiting for him on her couch. She leaped up and gave him a kiss. "Well? Tell me all about it. Did the gallery like your paintings? Did you sell anything?"

"Yes, they took all four paintings on consignment."

"Wonderful! That's fantastic news. Congratulations!" She hugged him.

"Yes."

"So, let's celebrate! Let's go out for dinner. Consignment means you don't have the money yet. But it's still a reason to celebrate. Let's go to our pub by the river; nothing fancy."

"Sure. Sounds good."

Mary stepped back, checking on Patrick. He wasn't smiling. "Are you okay?"

"Yes." His voice cracked.

She pulled him to the couch and sat beside him. "What's wrong?"

"Nothing." His voice was little more than a tight whisper.

She took his hands and held them. She waited. Suddenly his eyes filled with tears.

"What's wrong? What happened today?"

"Nothing," he insisted, but he continued to cry.

She held him and he sobbed onto her shoulder, his shoulders shaking.

He scrubbed his hand across his eyes. "This is what's wrong," he said. "It's all wrong. I'm an artist. And I guess artists are too emotional. We feel too much, get emotional over nothing. That's all. It was great. We went in this gallery downtown. And in less than an hour they took my paintings. I'll make several thousand dollars when they sell them. It's all good."

"That's wonderful, Patrick. But that's not what's bothering you. I know you too well for that."

"I don't want to talk about it. I can't talk about it." He took a deep breath and exhaled slowly, looking up to the ceiling. "You're so good to me. All afternoon I've been dying to get back here. I just needed to be with you."

Mary waited. She took his hand again and sat with him.

I need to get it out of my head, out of my mind, out of my soul. He looked up into Mary's lapis-blue eyes and started.

"Aaron's cheating on Melanie. He's having an affair." Patrick began to tear up again. "I've always looked up to him. Respected him. He's my role model. I've always thought I wanted to be like him. Making great art and selling it in galleries everywhere. And I dreamed that we would have that together. You and me, living like Aaron and Melanie. Having a cool loft apartment and being together happily ever after." Patrick paused.

Mary nodded and sat quietly, still holding his hand.

"But we're up there. And then Aaron comes out of the gallery owner's office. Sylvie. And she's half undressed, buttoning up her blouse. I can't get that picture out of my mind."

Mary digested that thought. *How many times has he talked about how he remembers everything he sees, storing it away, images indelibly etched into his brain, ready to be painted someday. Now he has this terrible image of Aaron and the gallery owner haunting him. I can't imagine how awful that must be for him, being unable to forget.*

Patrick went on. "I don't want to be like him anymore. He doesn't think it's a big deal. He says he loves Melanie and this thing with Sylvie is nothing. But it's not. At least not for me. That's not who I am or who I want to be. I don't know what to think. Don't know what to do. I promised him I wouldn't tell you because he thinks you'll tell Melanie. And I can't tell Melanie, either. But I needed to tell you. I need you right now."

She held him, soothing him, but now she was upset. *Poor Melanie. Aaron's an ass. But what about Melanie?* "Melanie doesn't know?"

"No. And I shouldn't have told you. And you can't tell Melanie."

"I ought to. She needs to know."

"Wait. She'll figure it out sooner or later."

"Okay. But I'll need to be there with her once she finds out. She'll need a friend when that happens."

They reheated leftovers for dinner. "It will hurt Melanie so much when she finds out what he's done." Mary settled on the sofa next to Patrick. "Why does love have to be so complicated?"

"Maybe that's just the way it works." Patrick sighed. "I certainly don't know any more about love than you do. But being in love is worth it. We just have to work at it to do the right thing. I would never do that to you."

Mary put her head on his chest. "I know. I won't ever hurt you, either."

"I wish I could know for sure that he'll do the right thing when she finds out. That he'll end it with Sylvie, the gallery owner."

"I believe the woman will always find out. I think we know our men well enough to know when they do this." *I know so little about love and how these things work. Melanie will find out, I know it.*

"But Melanie didn't see this. She didn't know him well enough for that."

"None of us did."

They went to bed and held each other as they drifted off, emotionally exhausted and worried.

Chapter Twenty-One

THE NEXT MORNING, MARY'S CELL phone buzzed in her purse during her morning class. She checked it quickly. A text message from Melanie. "I need to talk with you. Meet me at 11 on the street outside RISD."

Mary replied, "Okay."

The class ended. Mary hurried down the hill and waited at the door of the RISD classroom building. An old woman in a stained raincoat sat on the steps smoking a cigarette. She seemed out of place with the young art students rushing in and out, but she looked familiar to Mary.

One of the students paused for a moment. "Hey, Sadie, are you posing today?"

"Yeah. I'll be right in." The woman snubbed her cigarette out on the stone step and stood. *Sadie. The woman from Patrick's nude sketches. She's posing for his class again today.* Mary pushed the thought aside and waited for Melanie. *The craziness of the art world is overwhelming me. There's Aaron's affair, this woman posing nude for Patrick, and now Melanie wanting to talk with me.*

Melanie burst through the door. Her appearance had changed again. Now her hair was honey brown, pulled back into a bouncing ponytail. She wore a pastel pink cardigan sweater over a white blouse buttoned to her throat. A short, gray pleated skirt above argyle pink and gray knee socks completed the ensemble. On her back was a Wonder Woman cartoon backpack. She finished the outfit with black canvas sneakers. She was as cute as ever.

But when she came closer to Mary, it was obvious that things weren't right. She wore no makeup and her usual grin was gone, replaced with a thin-lipped, set mouth. Her eyes were shadowed and red-rimmed. "Let's get out of here," Melanie said.

"Where do you want to go?"

"I don't care. Nowhere. Anywhere. Someplace quiet, where we can talk."

"Let's go to my apartment."

"Don't you have classes?"

"Yes, but this is more important. What's going on?"

"I'm running away from home."

Once at Mary's apartment, Melanie dropped the backpack and darted to the sofa. She sprawled across the couch like a broken doll. Her head was back, staring at the ceiling. Her arms flopped at her sides. Her legs splayed out, apart.

For a moment there was a flash of pastel pink panties beneath the gray pleats. Then she hunched forward, pulling her feet back under her, her knees together. Her elbows turned in to her waist and her forearms rested along her thighs. She tucked in like a downhill skier and leaned her head into her palms. She made no sound, but her shoulders shook with her sobs. Mary sat next to her and pulled her close, an arm around her shoulders. After a minute Melanie sat back and dabbed with a pink handkerchief at her red, wet face.

"Aaron's been cheating on me." Melanie's voice was a thin squeak.

"I know. Patrick found out yesterday and told me. We feel awful about it. I wanted to call you but Patrick had promised not to say anything."

"Aaron told me. He said Patrick knew and Aaron was afraid one of you guys would tell me. That's why he told me."

What am I supposed to say? This is new for me. I want to help her, but I don't know what to do. Mary waited.

"I still love him. It would be easier if I didn't. Then I could just walk away.

I've broken up with plenty of men in the past, so I know how that works. But I love him." She started to cry again. Her voice cracked. "It really hurts. I don't know what to do."

"Are you leaving him?"

"I don't know. Right now, today, yes. I need time to think. We were up most of the night talking about it. We didn't fight. Just talked. He apologized and told me he loves me. That the other women don't really matter to him. Did you know there were other women?"

Mary shook her head.

"This morning I got up and threw some clothes in my Wonder Woman backpack and walked out to go to class. He doesn't know I'm leaving him."

"Perfect! Let him worry a bit when he finds out you're gone. He deserves it. How he reacts will tell you a lot about where his head is with this."

"My head tells me he's a no-good piece of shit, and I should never go back. But I love him. I don't know what to do." Melanie spoke now with hard anger, her fists clenched in her lap.

"You say there are other women?"

"Yes. I don't know how many. The woman who owns a gallery in Boston. That's who he was with when he was there with Patrick yesterday. But he let it slip that there might have been others."

"He needs to stop. I mean, he's a good-looking man. There's a lot of charisma there. Maybe girls are always available to him. But he's got to stop. He can't keep doing that."

"No. And he promised it would never happen again. But I don't know if I can believe him. I don't know if I trust him anymore."

"Tell me about you and him. How did you meet?"

"I was a student in his class a few years ago. It happens. I know I wasn't the first student to sleep with him. But one night led to another and the next thing we knew we were always together. He didn't have time for anyone else. Or energy for them maybe, after me. And I didn't want anyone else."

"Yes, it surprised me last night when Patrick told me. I always saw the two of you as a perfect couple."

"We are. Were. It's so odd now. So different."

"What will you do?"

"I don't know. I don't know where I'll stay. I'm lost."

"You can stay here as long as you want."

"Really? You'd let me do that? What about Patrick?"

"He'll be fine with it. Patrick and I are both fine with you staying here. Shouldn't you let Aaron know you'll be staying here?"

"Fuck Aaron. Where I decide to sleep is not his concern."

"That's right. Stay here with Patrick and me."

Melanie reached for Mary's hand. "You're the best friend I have in the whole world."

Mary fixed sandwiches for the two of them and then led Melanie into the bedroom for a nap.

Mary met Patrick at the apartment door late that afternoon. "Sshh, quiet," she whispered. "Melanie's here. She's asleep."

He came in on tiptoe and sat next to Mary on the couch. "Aaron said he told her everything and they fought all night. He didn't say that she'd left him. Should we tell him she's here?"

"Why?"

"So he won't worry. So he'll know she's safe?"

"Let him worry. It might do him some good."

Melanie appeared in the bedroom doorway. She now wore baggy khaki pants and a white tank top with thin straps. She appeared rumpled from her nap but her hair was still in the perfect ponytail.

"I heard what you said, Mary," she interjected. "Yeah, that's right. Let him worry. Don't tell him I'm here."

They sat together, Mary and Melanie on the sofa, Patrick shifting to one of the straight-backed chairs from the dining area. They were out of food but Patrick ordered pizza. They ate and headed to bed much earlier than any of them were used to. Patrick went back to his apartment alone. Mary made up the sofa for herself and gave Melanie her bed.

Late at night, with the apartment dark, Mary awoke to someone crawling onto the futon with her. "Patrick?"

"No, it's me. Melanie."

Mary slid over to make room. *What is happening? These artists and their uninhibited social and sexual ways, what is Melanie doing?* Then Melanie settled in, lying on her side with her back to Mary. She pulled herself into a small ball and fell asleep. Mary reached over for a moment and rested her hand on Melanie's shoulder. When she was sure Melanie was asleep, she withdrew her hand.

—

They woke at daylight. "Take the bathroom first," Mary offered. "You're my guest."

"No, no. You have to get ready for school. And I'm sure Patrick's coming soon."

"Thank you."

Melanie dressed and made a pot of coffee. Patrick knocked a few minutes later. "You've got a new color for your hair," Patrick said. "I noticed it last night but it didn't seem the time to comment about it. I like it."

Melanie flipped the ponytail and primped with her hands. "Yes, it's my natural color. I got tired of always dreaming up new ways to look, new costumes for every season, every month. I've decided to go back to my natural self."

"It looks good."

Mary took a sip of her coffee. "So, what are your plans for the day?"

"I don't know. Can I stay here? I don't want to go to RISD and risk running into Aaron."

"Of course. Here's a spare key. I'll be back after lunch. It's Good Friday. Patrick and I are going to Mass this afternoon. Would you like to join us?"

Melanie paused. "Sure. I'd like that. I may need to borrow something to wear. I just brought a couple of changes of clothes."

"We can do that."

Mary and Patrick left for classes. When they returned after lunch the apartment was sparkling. Dishes were washed and put away. The whole apartment was scrubbed; the first time in weeks, though Mary was a fastidious housekeeper. Fresh daffodils were in a pitcher on the coffee table next to the tree with the crystal birds.

"You cleaned!" Mary exclaimed. "I've been so busy with my class work I'd let things go. And where did you get the flowers?"

"At a little market up the street. I bought us some food, too. I thought it would be a nice way to thank both of you."

"You bought food? Thank you," Patrick said.

They talked eagerly about everything; their classes, their art, everything except Aaron. Bright sunshine filled the room, making the flowers glow as Melanie laid out lunch.

Mary sat back, satisfied after lunch. "Mass begins at three. Do you still want to come?"

"Yes. I think it'll be nice."

All three of them sat in the pew; Mary on the aisle, Melanie in the middle where Margie had sat when they went to Mass during her visit. Patrick noticed Melanie genuflected before she entered the pew. He leaned closer and whispered, "Are you Catholic?"

"Sort of. It's how I was raised."

When it came time for communion, Mary went forward to receive the sacraments but Melanie remained seated with Patrick. Neither Mary nor Patrick asked Melanie why she wasn't taking communion.

Mary looped her arm through Melanie's as they walked home. "What'd you think of the Mass?"

"It was nice."

"When was the last time you went?"

"I don't know. Maybe high school? Maybe my first year of art school?"

"Do you want to join us again on Easter?"

"If I'm still here on Easter. Sure, that would be nice."

"Okay, I've figured out dinner," Melanie announced over a glass of wine. "I figured Good Friday means seafood for dinner. So, we're having a pasta Alfredo dish with salmon, scallops, and shrimp. Patrick, we'll take care of the pasta and the seafood if you could cook up the mushrooms and add sun-dried tomatoes and scallions to the sauce."

They set to work, bumping into each other in the tiny kitchen. Mary pondered the situation. *The mood is subdued. Maybe that's because of the solemnity of Good Friday. Or maybe it's because Melanie's situation with Aaron is hanging over all of us.*

By Saturday, Melanie's presence was becoming part of their routine. They had just finished lunch when Patrick's phone rang. "Hello?"

"Is this Patrick Chamberlain? The artist?" It was an eager woman's voice.

"Yes. Who's this?"

"It's Lisa! From the gallery in Boston. Remember the paintings you brought up on Wednesday? I sold one of them."

"Which one?"

"The seascape. I've got your commission check."

"Fantastic! How do we work this? Do you mail it to me?"

"I could do that. But I'm coming to Providence tonight to see friends. That band I told you about is playing. Why don't you meet me at the club? We could have a drink, listen to music, and dance a little?"

Patrick paused. *She wants me to meet her? This is not what I want. Certainly not after what happened with Aaron and Sylvie.* He looked up. Both Mary and Melanie were watching him, curiosity clear on their features, listening to the bits of Lisa's voice they could hear. *I know the right thing to do.*

"No, I don't think so. I've got a lot going on this weekend. Easter weekend plans with my girlfriend."

"Bring her. I don't mind. That might be fun. Come on!"

"No. Thanks for the offer, but like I said, there's a lot going on. Could you mail me the check?"

"Sure. Of course. But I'd also like a replacement painting to fill the space of the painting that sold. When are you coming back up to Boston?"

"I don't know. Let me check my schedule and get back to you."

"Okay." Lisa paused. "If you want to sell your artwork here find time to bring me something soon." The line disconnected.

Is she mad I'm not meeting her? He turned to Mary. "That was Lisa from the gallery in Boston. They sold one of my paintings and want me to bring another one. And they've got a check for me."

"You should go. Take another painting and pick up the check."

Melanie spoke cautiously. "Lisa? From the gallery on Newbury Street?"

"Yes." Patrick nodded.

"I know her. She's like a younger version of that woman Sylvie. I've heard things about her. Be careful. But you do need to keep the business relationship growing. Mary, do you have an afternoon free during the week?"

"Thursdays I'm out of my last class by one."

Melanie took charge. "Okay. Here's what we're going to do. Patrick, call her back and offer to come up Thursday afternoon. Mary, you'll go with him. That way Lisa will keep her hands off him."

He'd just hung up with Lisa when Melanie's phone rang. "Aaron." She let it go to voice mail.

Melanie waited for the message light to flash, then played it for them all to hear. Aaron's deep voice filled the room. "Hey, Melanie. Where are you? I'm worried to death about you. Are you okay? Call and let me know you're okay. And I'm sorry about all that's happened. Please call me."

Melanie shook her head. "I'm probably going to go back to him. But I'm not ready yet. God, why does it have to be so hard to be in love?"

Patrick and Mary both sat in silence. Neither had an answer to Melanie's question.

Patrick's phone rang. "Hello, this is Patrick."

"Patrick. It's Aaron. Have you seen Melanie?"

Patrick looked up. Melanie waved her hands, shook her head, and mouthed the word, "No."

"Yes. Mary and I've seen her. She's okay but she's somewhere where she can think things out. And she doesn't want to see you yet. Maybe later, but she wants her space right now."

"Is she with you guys?"

"She's somewhere safe. Give her time."

"Okay. Well, if you see her, please tell her that I love her, and I'm sorry. And I miss her, and I need her back. God, this is killing me." Patrick held the phone out so they could all hear the call. Aaron's voice was shaking. "You'll tell her?"

"I'll tell her if I see her. Hang in there, man."

"Sure. I've got nothing else I can do." Aaron hung up.

⌐

A final call came from Uncle Win. "How's my boy Patrick?"

"Just fine, Uncle Win. How are things in Maine? Are you and Robert planning to cook Easter dinner?"

"Everything's good here. No, I'm going over to your parents' house for Easter dinner. Robert's gone to Vermont to be with his children and grandchildren. He doesn't really feel welcome with Tom and Susan at your house. It seemed like a good thing for me to do for Easter, not to eat alone, you know."

"Mary's cooking lamb. Her special recipe."

"You'll be going to Mass with her?"

"Yes."

"Enjoy. I didn't want to call when I was with your parents. They'd ask too many questions. Your painting's coming along?"

"Yes, and I sold one at a gallery in Boston. They just called to tell me."

"That's wonderful. We'll get you in several galleries here this summer and you might have a steady income in a few months. And Mary? She's well? You're talking with her about things?"

"Yes. She's fine. We're doing well."

"And your friends. Aaron and Melanie. How are they?"

Patrick looked at Melanie. She looked back at him, impassive. "They're okay."

"All good news. Say hello to Mary for me. Give her a kiss from me."

"Will do. I love you, Uncle Win."

When he hung up Mary started right in. "Are Uncle Win and Robert having Easter together?"

"No, Robert's going to have Easter dinner with his children and grandchildren."

"He has children?"

"Yes. From his first marriage. He's divorced."

"Ah." Mary nodded. *Always there are new questions. Uncle Win is such a good person. But he's gay and his partner is divorced. The Church disapproves of both of those things. How can Uncle Win be so good if his life is so wrong?*

Melanie clasped her hands in a prayerful gesture. "You're cooking lamb tomorrow? I love lamb. Can I stay one more day, please?"

Mary smiled. "I was counting on it. I don't know if you'll like it. This is my first time cooking it, but most of my dishes have turned out pretty well. There was that one…"

Patrick laughed. "She misread the amount of garlic to put in a stew. She ended up putting in a whole head of garlic instead of a clove."

"It was awful," Mary admitted.

"And I lied and ate a whole helping," Patrick added, still laughing. "I had to pretend I liked it. The apartment smelled for days."

"Learning to cook is a lot like learning to make love," Melanie declared. "Most recipes turn out okay in the end. There will be a few mistakes along the way and even some of those will be good. But you can't be afraid to try new things."

—

Easter morning Mary put the lamb in the oven and they headed up the hill to St. Joseph's. After the Mass they walked out into warm sunshine, still feeling the joy of the service.

"That was beautiful." Melanie glowed. "I'd forgotten what a good time Easter is."

"Resurrection. Salvation," Mary declared. "Christ is risen."

Patrick only nodded. To him it was little more than any other Sunday.

Melanie smiled. "It's like springtime itself; the end of a dark time in the winter and the beginning of new life. And if Jesus is raised from the dead maybe there's hope for all of us."

"Amen." Mary gave her a quick hug. "That's the message right there."

"And for me with Aaron. Maybe we can work things out and start over. Get our life back together."

"Do you trust him now?"

"No. That'll take time. But I think I should try with him again."

Patrick stopped. "He's a bastard to have done this to you, Melanie. I still get angry when I think about what I saw in Boston. I don't know if I can forgive him as easily."

"I understand," Melanie said. "But this is me. And believe me, I'll walk away if he screws around again."

When they got back to the apartment, Mary and Patrick set up for dinner. Melanie went out to the front steps and called Aaron. A few minutes later she was back. "He wanted to come right over to get me. I don't want to mess up our dinner, so I told him I'd call when I'm ready to go home."

They sat down to dinner. The lamb was magnificent. Melanie helped them clean up then called Aaron.

Ten minutes later he arrived, parked on the street across from the apartment house, and walked in, right past Mary and Patrick to hug Melanie, sinking his face into her hair. He held her for a long moment.

When he eased back, he was crying. "I'm sorry. I love you so much. I've missed you. I'm so sorry for what I've done. Come back to me."

Melanie took his hands. She looked him in the eyes, not smiling. "I love you too, but if you ever do that again, we're done! Don't even think about it. Do you understand?" He nodded.

She picked up her Wonder Woman backpack and led the way out.

Aaron gave a cursory wave to Mary and Patrick and followed her.

Mary turned to Patrick. "Do you think he's changed?"

"I don't know. This might have made him wake up and realize what he's got with Melanie. What do you think?"

"I still think he's a son of a bitch." Mary's face flushed.

"Hey! I don't know if I've ever heard you swear!"

"Well, about Aaron I've got reason to be angry."

"Do you think Melanie and he can work things out?"

"I hope so. Time will tell."

"I hope so too. Aaron's an idiot. I'm glad you're coming with me to the gallery in Boston. I didn't want to go back and have to confront Sylvie and Lisa. It will be easier with you there."

"Happy to do it. But Lisa better not come on to you. So help me, I'll kill her."

Chapter Twenty-Two

THEY PARKED IN THE ECHOING concrete garage beneath the Boston Common and walked through the Public Garden. Patrick cradled a bubble-wrapped painting in his right hand and held Mary's hand with his left. Mary was into her city-walking mode, making no eye contact with the people around her, hurrying along. Patrick remembered her walking like this on the first morning he saw her back in September.

The Public Garden was crowded; business people, college students, and tourists walking the winding paths, stopping on the duck pond bridge, and filling the Swan Boats. Patrick and Mary crossed Arlington Street and turned onto Newbury Street. The gallery was several blocks down. Inside the gallery they paused, looking for one of the staff.

Lisa was the first to see them. "Patrick! It's so good to see you." She rushed to him, gave him a brief hug and a longer kiss on the cheek. "I'm thrilled your first painting sold so quickly. And I had another young couple in yesterday who were very interested in another one. They're coming back this weekend to decide if they'll buy it. This is working out well. We'll be seeing a lot of each other." She gave his arm a squeeze.

Patrick pulled back. "Lisa, this is my girlfriend, Mary."

Lisa suddenly became more formal. She turned to Mary and shook her hand as she smiled. "Mary. It's so nice to meet you. You must be very proud to have a talented young artist like Patrick for your boyfriend."

"Yes, I am." Mary wasn't smiling.

"And Patrick! Look at her. She's beautiful. She should pose for you. You could do a series of pictures of her. It would be fabulous."

"I have. I've painted her several times."

"Good. Okay, well—I've got your check; 900 dollars. And I'll log this new one into our inventory."

"Great."

It only took a few moments. Patrick looked around the gallery. He kept Mary at his side. Mary stood, her arms folded, watching Lisa working at her desk. When Lisa was finished, Patrick asked, "Is there a good restaurant nearby where I could take Mary for dinner?"

"There's a pub a couple of blocks down where a few of us go after work. I could wrap things up here early and show you where it is."

"No, thanks. Mary and I want a quiet dinner together. Just the two of us. How about a seafood place?"

Lisa gave them directions. They found the restaurant and settled in over a glass of wine while they waited for their dinners.

Mary started. "That Lisa. I don't like her. She was hitting on you."

"I don't know. Was she?"

"Don't be foolish. If I hadn't been there, she would have been all over you."

"You think so?"

"Yes. Be careful with her. Melanie warned you."

"There's nothing going on. It's just business."

"Sure. That's what Aaron said about her boss. Sell your paintings, yes, that's okay. But watch out for her. She's bad news."

"Trust me. I don't want anything to do with her."

They finished their dinner and left Boston, following the tail end of rush-hour out of the city.

"Mary?" Patrick hesitated glancing at her as he drove. "Do you think we should talk about marriage? I proposed several weeks ago but we haven't talked about it again."

"I know, but right now, I'm tired and want to get back home to

Providence." Mary reclined her seat and closed her eyes.

Patrick took a deep breath. *We need to talk about this. But how? I can't force her.*

⸺

Several days later, as they began dinner in Patrick's apartment, Mary paused and put her fork down. "I have news," she said.

Patrick waited.

"Companies are starting to come around for job interviews. I have two lined up for late tomorrow afternoon. Both jobs are in Canada."

"Where?"

"One is in Montreal with CBC, the Canadian Broadcast Company. The other is with a small company in Quebec City."

"They'll be a breeze. You're the top of your class, you're perfect. Why wouldn't they want you?"

She shrugged. "I know I have good grades, but this is the real world. All I can do is go in there and tell them what I can do for them."

Patrick lifted his wine glass. "To our future!"

Mary smiled and clicked his glass. "Yes, to our future."

The next afternoon, Patrick cut class and went back to Mary's apartment. He wanted to be there to offer support before her interview. He let himself in and heard the shower running. Moments later Mary came out to the bedroom wrapped in a towel.

"Oh hi. What are you doing here?" she said, stepping into the bright light of the living room.

"I wanted to see you off."

"I'm glad you came. Thank you."

He studied her delicate features in the bright afternoon sun. "You are so beautiful."

She paused. Then she lifted a foot onto a chair next to the bedroom door, unwrapped the towel and dried her leg and foot. Her whole body was exposed to Patrick. She switched feet, putting her other foot on the chair and drying the other leg. Patrick stared, storing this new image.

Mary looked up and caught his eye. "What?" she challenged. "It's not like you've never seen me before. We sleep together every night. Most nights we end up nude in bed. You see me heading into the shower every morning."

"This is different. Middle of the day and broad daylight here in the living room. Not that I'm complaining."

"You see your nude models in your class. This is nothing new."

"You're not some model posing for a class. You're you. You're my girlfriend and I love you."

"We haven't got time for me to pose for you. I have to get back to school for my interviews."

"Of course. Get ready." He was grinning.

"Thanks." Mary turned and went into the bedroom. Minutes later she returned in a conservative navy-blue dress and low heels. Her hair was brushed. She kissed Patrick and picked up a notebook.

"You look great." He kissed her. "Good luck. I'll see you for dinner?"

"I'll be back in a couple of hours." She was out the door.

Patrick went to his apartment and set out a large piece of watercolor paper. His mind was empty except for the fresh vision of Mary. He had no need to block out the painting with a sketch; he started right in. He let the dark wall of the room provide a backdrop to the light silhouette of the woman's body. Sun, through gauze-like curtains in the window, lit the top of her arms and torso, making her glow. Her nearest leg was raised, the foot on the straight chair. The lifted leg hid her sexuality, giving a demure feel to the pose. Her closest arm hid one breast as she leaned forward to towel her foot. In the gap between her other arm and her body was the small cone of the other breast, pink tipped and silhouetted in profile. Her dark hair, also lit by the diffused sunlight, fell in a long cascade behind her shoulder, enhancing the shape of her face. The towel draped over her shin to the floor. Folds of the towel repeated the waves of her hair.

He finished in less than an hour and stood back to evaluate the still damp painting. He had done landscapes, still-lifes, and occasional portraits, but none came close to the emotional power of this. He came back into the painting for a moment, adding a touch of light to a lock of Mary's hair. *Done. It's perfect. She's perfection. My own Aphrodite, Bathsheba, Helen, or Cleopatra. He smiled at the thought. I'll never sell this one.* Patrick sorted through a stack of empty frames and found a big one that fit. He waited with impatience for the painting to dry so he could matte it and seal it forever in the frame.

—

Mary burst through the door. "I got it!"

He tucked the painting and frame aside. "Which company?"

"CBC. Canadian Broadcasting. I'm doing verification of bilingual broadcast scripts to make sure they say the same thing in both languages, even with the idioms. I have to be in Montreal starting in July. Six weeks for orientation. Then in August or September, I'll be based in New York, sending stories in French to Montreal." She laughed.

Patrick hugged her. "And the money?"

"More than I imagined. More than you can imagine. More than my father makes." She continued laughing. "I can't wait for July!"

"I've still got the money from the painting I sold in Boston. Let's go to the pub. Dinner's on me."

They sat in the pub, nursing their second beers and halfway through a plate of nachos when Patrick spoke. "You'll be in New York by the fall. I don't know how I'd handle living in a city that big, but I want to stay close to you. Could we live outside New York and commute?"

"I suppose. New York has tons of galleries where you could sell your paintings."

"I know. Aaron promised to introduce me to a few of them."

"Not like what he did with the Boston one, I hope."

"Yes, let's hope. And Uncle Win has connected me with a couple of places in Maine and New Hampshire; Portland, and Portsmouth, and maybe Camden. But where do I want to live?"

"I start in Montreal and then go to New York."

"Maybe I could find a place half way between them. I might teach for a year while you get set in New York. Maybe Vermont? I could see you during the summer in Canada and then in New York when you start there."

"That'll work. Maybe you can find a gallery in Montreal, too. I'll stay with Margie at first when they send me to the city. Then I'll need my own apartment in New York."

"I've got a passport. Uncle Win took me to Quebec City a couple of years ago. You'll need one to get in and out of Canada."

"They're taking care of that for me. It's all coming together."

Patrick took a sip of his beer. "Now I need to find a teaching job. Something till I can depend on until my art starts to sell. And somewhere close enough that I can be with you in Montreal and New York. Maybe we could get a loft together in New York."

"That would be amazing. Once we're married, that would be the way for us to live."

"Let's plan on it."

"Can RISD help you find a teaching job? You won't be graduating till next year."

"I'll see what's available. Anywhere close enough to get to you and to the galleries."

⟶

The next day it was Patrick's turn to celebrate. He danced into Mary's apartment at the end of the day. "I've got it! I've got it!"

She smiled at his antics. "Got what?"

"I walked into the placement office just as a guy from Phillips Exeter Academy was checking in to set up interviews. He said they need an art instructor. We started talking, and I showed him my work and he hired me for next fall. It's like it was meant to happen."

Mary hugged him. "Where is it?"

"Exeter, New Hampshire. About an hour north of Boston on the coast. Two hours to my parent's house, a little less to Portland and Uncle Win. Maybe four to either Montreal or New York. I could leave mid-afternoon on a Friday and be with you for a late dinner."

"Or I could come visit you."

"Yes. We've got it all figured out. I knew we would."

"The money's good?"

"No. It's terrible. But I need to be certified to teach in a public school. I'd have to take education classes and finish my Master's degree. The Academy is private. So the degree and certification aren't so important. They said I'd be an asset to their faculty because of what the recruiter called 'life experience'. They like that I'm a real working artist. The pay isn't great, but I'll have money coming in from several galleries. I'll be fine."

"Yes, we both will." She paused. "But you won't have your Master's degree. You won't be completing your MFA?"

"No. I've gotten what I need from RISD, even without the degree. I've grown in my art. I'm getting established in galleries, and I've got the teaching job. And with you not here, why would I stay?"

"If you think it's the right thing to do, that's okay. I want you to be happy."

Two days later, Mary worked on dinner in his kitchen while Patrick matted the painting he'd done of her two days earlier. He took the frame and began to insert the matted painting.

"Dinner's in the oven." She came though the bedroom door and stopped in her tracks.

"Patrick! It's beautiful. You know how I feel about you and your nudes. But this is different, alluring…" She took a closer look at the face. "Is this me?"

"Yes." Patrick watched her reaction to the painting. "It's what I saw when you came out of the shower getting ready for your interview a couple of days ago. I did it while you were at your interview."

"But I'm not that beautiful. And my body isn't that great."

"Yes, this is you. You're wonderful, amazing."

"What are you going to do with this? It's great, even if I don't think I look this good. It's a wonderful painting. You've got to put it up somewhere. But somewhere private. You can't show it in a gallery or anything."

"No, I won't ever sell this. I could never let this go. I'm thinking I'll put it in this frame and then hang it here in the bedroom. This is just for me. And you."

"Okay. Can I ask one thing?"

"Sure." Patrick relaxed. *She's accepting the nude as art now, not as something objectionable. She's come a long way with her understanding of art. Maybe she's evolved with her views on sexuality as well.*

"Remember the quote I wrote on the matte for the painting we gave Melanie and Aaron? Could I find a quote for this and add it on the matte?"

"Of course. But small letters like you did with Aaron and Melanie's picture. I want the focus to be on the painting."

"I'll do that." She ran down to her apartment and returned with her calligraphy pen and ink and a sheet of paper covered with quotes by French writers and philosophers. "Here's two I think might fit." She pointed out the quotations.

"The unique and supreme voluptuousness of love lies in the certainty of committing evil. And men and women know from birth that in evil is found all sensual delight." - Charles Baudelaire

"Art ought never to be considered except in its relationship with its ideal beauty." - Alfred de Vigny

Patrick read the quotations and thought for a few seconds. "The second one is perfect. I don't know who Alfred de Vigny is, but this fits my vision for the painting. Before I set this in the frame could you write that in small calligraphy on the matte beneath the painting?"

"Of course. I kind of like the Baudelaire quote. Love really is about committing evil. Sensual delight is what leads to sin. But I can live with the 'ideal beauty' phrase."

The lasagna still needed to bake for a while. Mary took her calligraphy pen and ink and carefully added the de Vigny quotation in tiny letters beneath the nude painting. When she finished, Patrick sealed it into the frame and hung it across from the foot of their bed.

Chapter Twenty-Three

TWO GRADUATIONS WERE UP THE hill from their apartment. First was the Rhode Island School of Design. Patrick was a year short of the classes needed for graduation, but he was planning to leave school and teach in New Hampshire. He and Mary watched as the small crowd of graduating art students marched along the street. As artists, they saw their world as an opportunity awaiting their expression. Many of the mortar boards and a few of the gowns were decked out with additions; decorations designed to make political statements, reflect the graduate's artistic specialty, make a satirical comment about the post-graduate world. It was a light-hearted, noisy parade.

Two days later, the graduation at Brown University took place. This was a larger, more sedate event transitioning the graduates from academia to their impending lives of success. Patrick sat with her family as Mary's name was called and she walked across the platform. Graduation speakers were noted celebrities from the worlds of international diplomacy and the corporate world.

Uncle Win gave Mary a congratulatory hug and then departed for Maine.

Shortly after, Mary's party gathered around a table for eight in a quiet corner of a small store-front Italian restaurant. Mary sat at the head of the table between her father and mother. Patrick and Margie were next, facing each other. Then Aaron and Melanie; Patrick had made certain that Aaron was on his side of the table and Melanie was next to Margie. Finally, at the other end of the table sat Sister Catherine.

Sister Catherine led the table in a prayer, blessing Mary's graduation and the start of her career.

They ordered dinner, picking from a long list of northern Italian specialties. Mary's dad announced, "This meal is on me." He waved off the appreciation from around the table. "It's not a big deal." He picked his glass up off the table. "But what is a big deal is our daughter, Mary. We're so proud of you. You're smart, you're kind, and you deserve the best of everything in life. Cheers." He settled in next to Patrick again and carefully placed his beer on the table. "You're not graduating from art school? Mary says you're dropping out." He kept his voice low.

"I don't know if I would say I was dropping out. A degree isn't necessary for me with my art. People will buy my work and I have a teaching job in New Hampshire in the fall to supplement my income."

"Dad," Mary whispered. "Patrick will be fine. Let him be."

"I think he should be the kind of man to stick it out, that's all I'm saying. I've never liked quitters." He waved the waitress over for another round of drinks. Then he turned again to Patrick. "Mary's done what she set out to do. She's graduated and has a great job. Can you say that?"

Patrick flushed. "As a matter of fact, I can. I've learned a lot this year. That's what I came to RISD for. But this is Mary's day. Leave me out of this."

"All right." Her dad nodded. "As long as you've got a job earning a living with your paintings. You've got to earn a living. A man's got to pay his own way in the world. That's the way it is."

Dad finished by toasting Mary, lifting his glass of beer. "To my daughter; a young lady with perfect grades and a Master's degree. I am so proud of you. I barely finished high school before I went to work and here you are, my baby, with a Master's degree from Brown University. You can't imagine how this makes me feel."

Mom beamed and reached over to squeeze her daughter's hand.

On the sidewalk outside the restaurant, Sister Catherine pulled Patrick aside. "I'm so proud of Mary. I can see that you are, too. Don't let her dad get on your nerves. He's concerned and wants the best for his daughter."

"I know, he told me."

"I'm aware that you're planning a future together with Mary, but he doesn't know that. He worries about Margie and her boyfriend, how they're living together without being married. I think he doubts whether or not you'll do right by Mary. But I know that with your teaching job and your art in the galleries, you'll be able to provide for her when you get married."

"Mary told you we're thinking about that?"

"Yes, of course. And I'm very pleased for Mary. And for you, too. She'll need your support when she starts her job."

"Yes. But she'll be making more money than me. I don't need to support her."

"What she needs from you is emotional support. Right now you need to be there for her. When you have children, she'll need your financial support."

"Of course I'll do that for her."

After goodbye hugs, everyone headed back to New York, leaving Mary and Patrick with Aaron and Melanie.

Patrick fussed as soon as the car was gone. "Man, your father and Sister Catherine had plenty of advice for me."

"They mean well." Mary slipped her arm through his as they walked along Hope Street.

"You're fine," Aaron said. "I'll get you in a few more galleries, word will get around. Your work is excellent. It's already selling. Don't worry."

"I'm not worried. But I hate people telling me how I should live my life, giving me advice and telling me what I should do. Why won't they leave me and Mary alone to do what we want?"

Aaron looped his arm around Melanie's shoulders. "Hey, we've taken a cottage near the ocean on Block Island next weekend. It's got two bedrooms, so why don't you both come with us? Continue the graduation party for another few days."

"Late May? In Maine the ocean's still brutally cold." Patrick gave an involuntary shiver. "I don't know. Is it warm enough?"

"Sure. Maybe not real beach weather yet. But it's a pretty place, and it's got good restaurants and pubs."

"Come on," coaxed Melanie. "It'll be fun. We can play on the beach." Patrick turned to Mary. "What do you think?"

"Sure. I don't have to go to Canada till July. I don't have any place else to be. Let's go."

Later, back at their house, Mary spoke with more concern. "Do you think Aaron and Melanie have gotten past his affair?"

"I don't know. I don't see any hints of trouble between them."

"I want things to be good with them."

"Me too. I want it all to be perfect."

⚬

The ferry left at dawn on Saturday. The ride to Block Island was chilly, with a stiff wind. Gulls followed the boat all the way to the harbor at New Shoreham. Aaron drove his BMW off the boat and turned left. The road rolled over hills, winding around turns. They drove slowly, circling the southern half of the island, past a brick lighthouse, ponds, and meadows. Tumbled rock walls lined the road and the fields. Shallow woods, mostly oak, fit around the fields.

A few minutes later they parked in front of a small, white cottage set in the woods down a sandy lane on the northern spit of the island. After unpacking, they took sandwiches and beer to a small table on a sun-washed wooden deck behind the house.

When her meal was finished, Melanie stood. "Time to check out the beach. Did you see the little path going off from the back yard? I bet that goes right down to the water."

She trotted off the deck and onto a narrow sand track worn through low bushes and oak forest. Aaron followed, with Mary and Patrick right behind. The path wove downhill for no more than a minute. They broke out of the bushes and the overhanging trees into sunlight on a long, hard-packed, sandy beach. Large red and brown boulders marked the wide shoreline.

Melanie kicked off her sandals and stood in front of the group, hands on hips surveying the scene. There was no one on the beach but the four of them. "Perfect!" exulted Melanie. "It's like our own private beach. Let's go skinny dipping!" She crossed her arms over her body and pulled her t-shirt up over her head. She dropped it on the sand and walked alone toward the water. Aaron, Mary, and Patrick stood where they were, speechless, watching her go. Still walking, Melanie unhooked her bra, tossing it off. With her bare back still facing her friends, she pushed her shorts and panties to her ankles and kicked them free. Suddenly she ran toward the low surf. She splashed in, high stepping and screaming for a moment. She waded a few more steps, arms swinging wide, till she was hip deep. Then she dove forward beneath the dark waves. She surfaced, stood and turned to them, hands at her face.

"It's freezing!" she screamed. "Oh, god, it's cold!" She ran out of the water, leaning forward against the slope of the beach, head down, pumping her little fists. Her small breasts bounced. She ran to Aaron, slammed into his denim clad bulk, and wrapped her wet arms around him. Instinctively he hugged her to him. "It's freezing!" she repeated. "God, the water's cold. Warm me up, Aaron!"

Patrick looked away, concentrating on the water. Mary looked at Melanie's miniature body, enveloped by the mass of Aaron's welder's arms. Melanie turned her head, pressing her damp cheek against Aaron's hard chest. Peeking over his arm, she caught Mary's eyes. For an instant she flashed her imp grin at Mary and winked. The moment was their secret; nobody saw the wink but Mary.

"Come on," Aaron said, embarrassed. "Get dressed. Get warm."

She wriggled out of his embrace and trotted over to the path of her clothes, dropped along the beach. She pulled on the t-shirt, no bra. Then she struggled into her shorts, dragging them up, sticking, over her wet legs. No panties. She went back to Aaron and handed him her underwear. "Could you hold these for me?" she begged.

He crumpled them and tucked them it into the pocket of his shorts. "Come on," he said. "Let's take a walk."

They strolled along the shoreline, holding hands, heads down, talking quietly. Mary and Patrick went to one of the flat boulders at the edge of the surf and sat, feet in the cold water.

"What are we to make of that?" Patrick asked.

Mary swished her feet in the shallow water. "Melanie's back; full force, as wild and unpredictable as ever. At least she didn't insist we follow her in." She looked at her feet in the shallow in front of them. "And she's right; the water is cold."

"It's still early in the summer. But that's not the point."

"With Melanie, you never know for sure what the point is. That's part of her charm."

"Come on, Mary. We're both kind of uptight about these things. But I always thought you were more conservative than me. You weren't bothered by what she did?"

"We're among friends. No, I would never do that, and I'm glad the water was too cold for her to get us all naked and swimming with her. I don't know why Melanie did it. But it really isn't something that shocked me. It's the sort of thing I'd have expected of her."

Patrick nodded. But then he added, "I brought shorts to swim in. If we come back to the beach, I'm wearing my shorts."

"I have my suit, too. I just hope Aaron doesn't get naked in front of us."

Patrick agreed. "Peer pressure. We were supposed to outgrow that when we left junior high school."

⁓

Back at the cottage after a seafood dinner in New Shoreham, Aaron turned to the Red Sox game. Patrick joined him. Mary pulled Melanie aside. "Let's take a walk."

Mary took Melanie out on the deck and led her through the dark, down the path to the beach. The surf rolled quietly up the sand and flowed back out. It was low tide, and the shallows smelled of seaweed and salt. They sat on the boulder where Mary had sat with Patrick in the afternoon.

"The skinny dipping. Why did you do it?"

"It's fun. Don't tell me you've never been skinny dipping."

"No, I really haven't. I learned to swim at a pool back in the city. And when I'm at my parents' place, there's a lake where I've gone swimming in the summer. But it's a public beach. So, no, I've never gone skinny dipping."

"You should."

"I don't know about that. Maybe you and Aaron can do it. It's not what I would do. But why did you do it in front of me and Patrick?"

"Is that it? You're upset that I was nude in front of Patrick?"

"No. Yes. A bit, yes. But why? You didn't have to do that."

"Okay. The four of us are friends. We're adults. I'm not coming on to Patrick if that's what you're worried about."

"No, I'm not worried about that. I just don't understand why you did it."

Melanie kicked her feet in the trickling flow of sea water. She looked out into the darkness of the ocean.

Mary waited.

"Okay. Here's the thing. I don't ever want to lose Aaron. Not again. So I'll be as seductive as possible. I plan on being as alluring, as sensual and sexy, as he can possibly imagine, so he won't even dream of going to anyone else. It's all I've got."

"Melanie, you've got so much else. You're a beautiful person, a wonderful being. You can just be you and he'll love you. You know that."

"I always thought so. But then he ran around with that woman Sylvie and god knows who else. I won't let that happen again."

Mary nodded. *I'm still baffled. Melanie's wild. But she doesn't need to do this. Aaron must still love her just because of who she is.* "Aaron will love you no matter what. And you know that if there ever are any problems with him, Patrick and I will be there for you again."

"I know. You two were wonderful back when it all fell apart."

They walked back up from the beach in silence, stumbling once or twice on the shadowed path.

Much later, Mary and Patrick lay in the narrow bed in the cottage bedroom. Through the thin wall to the other bedroom they heard bumping. It continued, again. And again. Then a thin voice, barely audible through the wall, "Aaron! Oh! God!"

On Sunday morning, Mary was up at dawn. She pulled Patrick out of bed. "Come on. We're going to be late for Mass."

They borrowed Aaron's car and arrived in time for the seven o'clock mass; practically nobody was there. The service concluded quickly. They were back at the cottage, showered, and dressed again before they heard from Aaron or Melanie.

In the afternoon the four of them went for another drive on the country roads of the island. Patrick stopped them at one spot and pulled out his pad to sketch. He sat on a rock wall above a meadow that dropped off toward the ocean. He worked quickly, silently, intent on the view. His two fellow artists sat with Mary and waited, watching as he worked. When he finished, he had a good drawing, the meadow dipping into a small pond, with rock walls fending off low woodlands. The gleam of the sea was on the horizon.

"I thought you stored nice views, landscapes like this in your mind for future paintings," Mary said.

"I do. But sometimes doing a sketch 'en plein air' is a good way to go. Right then and there, in the moment. Remember that first sketch of the alley in Providence I gave you?"

"Oh my!" marveled Mary. "A year with me and suddenly you're speaking French."

Patrick laughed and needlessly clarified his French. "Yeah, 'en plein air.' It's a term we use for sketching or painting outside. It means something like 'out in the open air'."

"Tres bien, mon amour."

"Oh, Aaron," Melanie chirped. "They're speaking French to each other. How romantic!"

"Should we give them the house alone for an hour or two?" Aaron chuckled.

"That won't be necessary," Melanie giggled. "Maybe we should be the ones to go back to the house and leave them out here to do it en plein air."

Patrick stopped it. "Enough. We're fine right here, the four of us together. There are no secrets between us. Let's discuss where to go for dinner."

Mary and Patrick lay awake for another hour after they all went to bed, distracted by the noisy lovemaking in the next room. Mary rolled to Patrick and whispered, "We don't make noise like that, do we?"

"No, but we don't quite do the whole thing."

"We do enough. But we're not that noisy, are we?"

"No. Maybe they're showing off for us."

"Maybe. Making sure we know they're together and happy again."

"I hope everything is back the way it should be with them." They kissed quietly and went to sleep.

—

Late Monday afternoon, Aaron and Patrick leaned on the rail, watching the water rush past as the ferry carried them back to the mainland. Mary and Melanie dozed on seats behind them. All four were sunburned, windblown. Their minds were fuzzy from the drinks they'd had in a bar overlooking the harbor while they waited for the ferry.

"Did you and Mary have a good time?" Aaron asked, his words hidden from the women by the wind.

"Yes. It's a pretty island. Maybe we'll come again sometime, just the two of us."

"Melanie and I didn't get in the way of you two, did we?"

"No."

"I realize it was a small cottage. Like you said, there are no secrets between any of us anymore."

"No."

"You and Mary, I know you're going to make it. You've got a better relationship than I've been able to give Melanie. You know that?"

"Mary and I are in a good place. You and Melanie are working things out?"

"Oh, yeah. All that's far in the past. We're fine."

Chapter Twenty-four

THE LEASES ON THEIR TWO apartments in the wonderful house on Wickenden Street expired at the end of June. They spent early June clearing out the apartments, loading their cars with their few belongings. They were ready to move before the end of the month.

Patrick's car was jammed full of finished artwork; framed and matted paintings, stacks of more paintings and drawings, his portfolio. His box of artist supplies, unused watercolor paper, and sketch pads took only a bit of room. His bags of clothes and other personal items took even less.

Mary's car was loaded with her clothes. In the back seat she stacked her collection of Patrick's artwork. The iron tree with the glass birds that Aaron and Melanie had given them at Christmas was in a box. Patrick had explained, "You keep the tree and the paintings. You'll need to decorate your apartment in Montreal and it will make you feel at home when you settle in New York. I've got plenty of artwork."

Patrick kept the luminous nude of Mary that had hung in their bedroom. *I'll keep it forever in my bedroom wherever I settle.*

With help from Aaron and Uncle Win, Patrick was getting established in new art galleries. In addition to Sylvie's gallery in Boston, Aaron convinced a second gallery, outside Boston, to accept Patrick's work.

RISD agreed to continue to show two of Patrick's paintings. Uncle Win set him up with three galleries in New Hampshire and Maine. Aaron was connecting him with New York galleries as well. The framed paintings in his car were ready to fill any new gallery space that became available.

Mary outlined her plans. "Canadian Broadcasting will provide me with a temporary apartment for the weeks when I'm in training. Could you help me settle there?"

"Of course. Let's go to Maine for a few days and then head to Montreal. When you're settled in Montreal, I'll return to New England to find an apartment in New Hampshire, near the school in Exeter."

They drove north in their two cars. Patrick led her along the rural roads out to his home. His father met them at the front door. "Come on in," he said, shaking their hands. "Drop your bags in the front hall. I'll take care of getting them to your rooms. We don't want to go there right now. Mother is resting."

The welcoming finished, Tom went back to his study and closed the door. Mary and Patrick were left alone in the hall. "Let's take a walk," suggested Patrick. He led her out the back and down a mowed path through the tall grass of the meadow.

They came to a rocky shoal of a beach on a channel, the tide racing out to Casco Bay. Gulls wheeled overhead and sat in rows on the beach facing the wind. Thick stands of pine watched over the granite shoreline. Patrick led her to a sheltered spot with driftwood logs to sit on. It was his favorite place; the spot where he and Uncle Win had come at Thanksgiving to talk about Mary. Patrick sat on a driftwood log. Mary squeezed on a flat spot next to him. They held hands and watched the water flow by, dragging kelp with it.

"Your house is quiet today," Mary said. "And you've gotten quiet, too. Is everything okay?"

"Mother's not happy with me right now."

"Why not?"

"Because I've quit school at RISD. She doesn't care that my art is starting to sell or that I've got the teaching job lined up at Phillips Exeter Academy. She thinks I should get my Master's degree and my PhD and become a professor somewhere. But that's not how it works with art. That's not what

I want to do."

"Uncle Win is a professor. She wants you to be like him. Where is he?"

"He'll be along this afternoon. Yes, he's a professor, but he makes his living selling paintings. He teaches a couple of classes a semester."

"He has a PhD? Most colleges want their professors to have that."

"He's got an MFA. But with art, the degrees are less important than they are in academic areas. My father has his PhD, of course. So does Mother."

"She has a PhD? Is she a professor?"

"Sort of. She was, here at Bowdoin before I was born. European History. She quit so she could take care of me when I was little. She teaches a bit now, but just as adjunct faculty, one or two courses a year at most. But she has the PhD. It matters greatly to her. It defines her."

"And that's why she's not pleased that you've left RISD."

"Yes. And that I've chosen to degrade myself by teaching at a level below college. She doesn't care about my art being in galleries. That's retail work, as far as she's concerned. No different than if I was selling clothes at a store in a mall. Hardly respectable."

"Are you going to be okay while we're here? We're staying a couple of days before going to Montreal."

"Yeah, I'll be fine. She'll leave me alone, I expect. That's what she does. She'll spend most of the time in her room. And we'll take a couple of days to see the sights along the coast. So we'll be out of the house most of the time. It'll be fine."

Down the beach, a chubby man pushed through the blueberry bushes from the path and turned toward them. Uncle Win. Wearing sandals, he stepped carefully on the sliding stones. He sat on a granite rock across from them.

"Thought you two would be here." He smiled. "I know you, Patrick. When I saw your cars out front of the house but you weren't inside, I knew where you'd come. Welcome home!"

Patrick stood and went to give him a hug. Mary followed, leaning over to give Win a hug and a kiss as well. "It's good to be home," Patrick said.

"Tom called when you arrived. I came right out. I'm here to cook, of course. We'll grill salmon steaks tonight. And I brought wine."

"Perfect," Patrick said as he and Mary sat back on the driftwood. "I'll need the wine. Mother's locked away in her tower."

Win laughed, roaring and leaning back on his rock. "Of course she is. You've disgraced the Chamberlain legacy. You've dropped out of school. Next thing you know you'll be smoking cigarettes, drinking beer, stealing hub caps from cars, or teaching at a snooty prep school in New Hampshire, for God's sake. It's a tragedy! What's to become of you? Or of Mother? Or her?" He pointed at Mary.

"I can't change Mother. I've come to accept that," Patrick said.

"No, you can't change her. Don't even try. Enjoy life as it comes at you. Take Mary out on the mail boat from Portland while she's here. Ride around Casco Bay for a day. Have a picnic on one of the islands. Come home drunk. Why not? You're a disgrace as it is. It can't get worse, so go live a little."

"The picnic sounds like fun," Mary said, hoping to brighten Patrick's mood. "Let's do it!"

"Sure. Riding out in the bay would be a good way to spend a day. We'll do it." He smiled and relaxed when she took his hand.

Uncle Win turned serious. "You leave for Montreal Sunday morning?"

"Yes. We want to get Mary settled in her apartment before dinner that night. We'll leave right after Mass."

"Good. That means you'll be here for the croquet then." Uncle Win began to grin.

Mary was startled to see Patrick grinning as well. "It's on," he answered. "Mary, have you ever played croquet?"

"No, not really. It's a kids' lawn game, right?"

"A kids' game? Hardly. Not here at the Chamberlain house," Patrick explained. "Here it's war. We usually have the big Fourth of July battles. But that's a week away."

Uncle Win picked up the conversation. "Yes. But seeing as you're both here we moved it to Saturday afternoon. Here's what happens, Mary. We play teams. Patrick and I might be a team and Tom and Susan might be a team. And we play for very important family bragging rights. Then, once things are established and one team has won, we reorganize the teams. It might be boys against girls, for example. Tom and Patrick on a team, and Susan would get paired with me. I have no idea why. Then brothers against others; Tom and me against the world of Susan and Patrick. We really get carried away with it. You should see how worked up Tom and Susan get over it!"

Mary asked, "Can you explain the rules to me? I've never played before."

"Each player has a ball," Patrick explained. "And you start at one end of the lawn next to a wooden post. You hit the ball through wickets, little metal arches, playing down the field to the other end. Then you work your way back to the start. As long as you go through a wicket you get another shot on your turn. The first player back wins."

"And if your ball hits another player's ball, you get to put your ball up next to theirs, put your foot on top of your ball to hold it in place and then whack your ball," Win said. "That will send theirs flying off somewhere. It's a lot of fun."

"Sounds like it," Mary said.

"And another thing," Patrick added, smiling. "In a few spots rocks poke up through the lawn in the middle of the croquet court. They're like sand traps on a golf course. The game wasn't designed with rocks in the way. But at the Chamberlain's there are obstacles on the course."

"Even more fun!" declared Uncle Win. "You'll love it, Mary."

Dinner that first night was chilly, served at a table set up on the lawn overlooking the channel to the bay. Win marinated the salmon and cooked on charcoal with hickory chips added to smoke more flavor into the flesh. The wine was a light Pinot Grigio. Win bought chocolate cake from a Portland bakery for dessert. Mother sat silently throughout the meal. She hadn't acknowledged Mary's presence. As soon as the cake was served, she stood and picked up her plate and fork.

"I'm very tired," she announced. "I believe I'll finish my meal inside. If you will kindly excuse me."

She walked alone back across the lawn and into the old house. Tom remained with Uncle Win, Patrick, and Mary, but he didn't speak.

Uncle Win set things up for them. "You're planning to take Mary around the bay on the ferry tomorrow?"

"Yes. It's a pretty ride. And we'll pack a picnic."

"Come by my place when the ferry gets back to Portland," Uncle Win said. "Let me take you both to dinner."

Tom nodded. "Always a good day when you tour Casco Bay," he stated. "Enjoy yourselves." He stood and followed Mother into the house.

Mary and Patrick were out early the following morning. They knew that Tom would explain to Mother where they'd gone. They took a bag filled with chicken salad sandwiches, a shallow plastic tub of pasta salad bought at the local supermarket deli, and another bottle of the Pinot Grigio. They were on the mail boat ferry by mid-morning, standing on the deck in the bow watching the perfect Maine seacoast flow by. The ferry stopped at several islands before they got off on Chebeague Island. Patrick led Mary down a narrow lane to a quiet cove. Granite boulders defined a ragged edge between the hard shore and the cold Atlantic. They went to a wide stone slab above the high tide line and sat, holding hands. They watched the waves for a while and then set out their lunch between them on the rock and relaxed, easing in the warmth of the sunshine. Patrick worked the cork out of the wine and poured two small cups. Mary opened the container of pasta salad and placed the sandwiches on paper napkins.

Gulls gathered, settling onto the rocks close by. "Guard your lunch," Patrick cautioned. "Mind the gulls. They'll steal everything but the wine."

They ate in silence, watching sailboats. It was quiet except for the sound of the ocean tumbling onto the rocks close in front of them. After lunch they sat, leaning in to each other, with a second glass of wine. Soothed, they closed their eyes.

"This is perfect," Mary said. "It's heaven. So quiet. So beautiful. You should paint this."

"I have. Many times. I can always catch the look of the bay, the light, the air. But the feel of the place, the mood, everything about it with the sounds, the smells, is hard to get in a painting. It's always changing. The same place is different from day to day, moment to moment."

"Could you do a new picture of this place? Just for me, the way it is today?

I want to keep this moment with me forever. I'll put it in my apartment when I settle in New York."

"Of course. When you're ready to move there, I'll have it for you. No place on the planet is less like New York City than here."

"It will be perfect to have this place, this moment, this day always with me when I get there."

"Should we talk about marriage?"

"And ruin the mood of this perfect moment? Let's do that another time."

Patrick shook his head and started to speak but stopped. He gave up without a word.

We need to talk about the future. But she's right. She's always right. This isn't the time for that talk. This is a perfect day. It can't get any better. Our future can wait.

They met Uncle Win when the ferry brought them back to Portland. He led them to a small street, little more than a cobblestone and brick alleyway a block up from Commercial Street. They found a narrow restaurant in an old brick-front warehouse building and settled in for a leisurely seafood dinner, lobster for Mary. There was more wine and more chocolate for dessert. The meal itself was spectacular. It also gave them a refuge from Mother's tension back at the house.

When they got home after dark, Mother had gone to bed. "She's resting to be ready for the big croquet showdown tomorrow," Tom said with a wry laugh. "She said that winning matters. As though we didn't know that!"

The sun was barely up and the grass was still soaked with dew when Tom began setting up the croquet court. He measured exact distances on the trimmed grass, hammered the stakes and aligned the wickets, making sure the level lawn was perfectly symmetrical for the game. The area was bordered on one side by gardens near the house, newly blooming flowers clustering above the grass. The far side was bound by a low, fieldstone wall. Beyond the wall, a meadow fell away to the bay. Tall grass, green- tasseled at the top, filled the meadow.

After lunch, Tom and Mother joined Patrick and Mary. They sat in white-painted Adirondack chairs next to one end of the croquet court. Little was said; this was not a time for small talk. They watched the sunshine on the meadow grass and enjoyed the breeze blowing off the water. Uncle Win arrived, and they were ready to begin the games.

"There are five of us this year. Not the usual four. How do we set up teams for the first game?" Patrick asked.

Mother smirked. "Yes, it would be so much easier if she hadn't come. It would be like every other year. But now she's here. What to do?"

The comment was met by silence. Mary shifted in her chair.

Tom sought peace. "I'll sit the first game out," he said. "Patrick, why don't you and Mary take on Mother and Winthrop?"

There was nodded agreement. Uncle Win grinned at Mother. "Looks like you're stuck with me, Susan. But they're just kids. What do they know about croquet? We'll take them!"

"Sure, Uncle Win," Patrick taunted. "Good luck. Should we give a couple of strokes to make things fair?"

"Not necessary," Mother replied. She looked grim, almost angry, as she selected the mallet and ball with black stripes. Patrick picked green and gave Mary blue. Uncle Win went with yellow. Tom reclined at the end of the court in one of the Adirondack chairs, his legs crossed, watching.

"And so it begins!" Uncle Win announced. "The world famous, somewhat annual Chamberlain Croquet Classic is on!" He took the first shot.

Things went well at the start. Mary got her ball through the beginning wickets and was moving nicely into the middle of the lawn. Patrick led her, giving instructions, directing her where to point her ball. Uncle Win played odd, bouncing ricochet shots off the white granite that poked through the lawn. Mother took an early lead, hit the end post and began working her way back.

Then the game changed. Mother lined up her next shot, ready to move back to the middle wicket, ready to head into the home stretch for the win. Mary's blue ball was across the lawn, several wickets behind.

In a moment Mother turned, and drove her ball bounding across the lawn, hitting Mary's. Without a word she walked to the two balls, her black one, Mary's blue one. Mary and the rest of the family watched, confused. Mother set her ball next to Mary's, pushing her own ball down onto the lawn with her foot. Then she smacked her ball, driving Mary's in recoil up into a low trajectory above the grass. The ball clacked onto the top of the border wall of granite and sailed off into the meadow of high grass beyond.

"Mother!" Patrick shouted. "What are you doing?"

Tom was on his feet. "Now, Mother, that was uncalled for."

Mary was speechless. She turned to Patrick in distress. "What do I do now? How do I play my ball when it's somewhere in that field?"

"You don't," he replied grimly. He dropped his mallet, jogged to the wall, hopped over, and began looking for Mary's ball in the meadow.

Uncle Win went to Mary and put his arm around her shoulder. "Don't you worry, young lady. This is all going to be fine."

Mary stood in shock, red-faced, on the edge of tears.

Mother surveyed the scene. Tom was scolding her, Patrick had gone to rescue Mary's ball, and Winthrop was comforting the girl.

"Fine," she screamed. "All of you can take her side if you want to. But it serves her right for coming here and making our boy lose his way. Making him drop out of college when he doesn't even have a worthwhile job. When he could have become a professor at a fine college, a prestigious school where we could have been so proud of him. He's not even respectable now, and it's all because of this girl."

Mother slammed her mallet down, bouncing it across the lawn. She stormed into the house, crashing past the wood-framed screen door. The game was over.

—

The rest of the day was tense. Tom stayed inside with Mother. Uncle Win stayed outside with Patrick and Mary. Dinner wasn't a possibility at the house so Win took Patrick and Mary back into Brunswick for a light meal at a tourist-oriented restaurant on Route one. Mary sat in the booth, her arms on the table, still stunned.

"I don't know what I did," she began. "I tried so hard to make her like me. I don't know what I should do now."

Patrick took Mary's hand and held it. He didn't know where to start, what to say to comfort her.

"Leave Mother out of it," Uncle Win said. "What matters isn't what she thinks. It's what you both think. You want to be together, to have a life together. You've got that. Tom will be fine. He'll come around, but he's got to manage Mother. He's got to keep the peace so he can live with her. And if Mother can't get her head around it, that's her loss."

"I needed for her to like me," said Mary. "After Christmas, I thought she did."

Win patted her hand. "She tried to like you. You didn't do anything wrong. It's less about what you did than what Patrick's done. She blames you for Patrick leaving RISD. It was Patrick's decision, and I think you did the right thing, Patrick. But Mother won't blame you for it. You're her boy. She'll blame Mary."

"I'm not turning back," Patrick said. "I'm going to teach at Exeter, sell my paintings, and stay with Mary. I know all of this is the right thing to do."

Uncle Win nodded. He reached over and held Patrick's and Mary's hands in his. "It is. You're both doing the right things. The next few months will be hard, being away from each other. Be strong. Hold on to each other. Don't worry about Mother. Let Tom do that."

After dinner, outside the restaurant, Win put an arm around them, a three-person hug. "You'll be fine," he said. "Have a safe trip to Montreal tomorrow. Patrick, I'll see you after you get Mary settled. I'll help you find an apartment in New Hampshire."

CHAPTER TWENTY-FIVE

THEY GOT UP AT DAWN on Sunday and left without seeing Mother or Tom. Their first stop was at a large, modern-looking Catholic church near the Bowdoin campus.

"Where is the Methodist church you go to?" Mary asked.

"A couple of miles further south. There's more Baptist churches in Brunswick than Methodist, but we go to the Methodist church."

"What's the difference between Baptist and Methodist?"

"I'm not sure. Something to do with baptism, I think. They immerse people to baptize them. John Wesley founded the Methodist church." Patrick was suddenly aware of how little he had paid attention when he was growing up in his church. He was learning the Catholic Church, but he knew very little about his own.

"Nothing about communion? You do take communion, don't you?" Mary asked.

"Yes. Usually on the first Sunday of a month."

"Just once a month?"

"Yes. It's not a problem, is it?"

"No, I guess not for you."

They settled in for Mass. It was traditional, the prayers and sacraments the same as back in Providence or New York. For a moment, the familiarity made Mary feel at ease.

They left after Mass, Patrick following Mary's car in his, across New Hampshire and Vermont, past customs and were in Canada. As though decreed by Provincial law, the land became flat and the forest was replaced by wide open farm land. A representative from Canadian Broadcasting had agreed to meet them at her new apartment.

They crossed a river and climbed hills into the city. Several blocks along Rue Sherbrooke, Mary turned onto a side street, checking the numbers on the doors of the buildings. She stopped. Patrick stopped behind her. The man from CBC came out from the door of an apartment building and directed them to a parking area across the street.

After they parked, he escorted them into the stone apartment building to a second-floor apartment. It was furnished sparingly, but it was far nicer than the student housing they had left behind in Providence. He shook Patrick's hand, saying "Bonjour," and continuing on in rapid French. Patrick smiled and let Mary carry the conversation. Finally, the man excused himself and left Mary with Patrick in her new home.

It took several trips to transfer all of her belongings into the apartment. The paintings were the last things they carried up the stairs. Generic prints decorated the walls, but Patrick took them down. They evaluated the wall space and decided where to hang Patrick's paintings and drawings. The tree with the crystal birds went on the coffee table just as it had in Mary's apartment in Providence. Finally, with the rooms decorated, they sat on the sofa. It was a real sofa with throw pillows, not a futon.

They went to an ATM and used their credit cards to get Canadian money. Then they shopped for food. Back at her new apartment, Mary cooked hamburgers for dinner. They went to bed, exhausted, fumbling as they tried to transform their old bedtime routine to the new place. They slept restlessly.

They were up early, Mary eager for her first day at CBC, Patrick excited for her but dreading the drive home. They had agreed that she might be working late at her new job and it made no sense for him to hang around the French city all day waiting for her.

After a quick breakfast, they left in Patrick's car, driving side streets toward the river and the CBC building. Mary checked the map on her phone and called out, "This is good. You'll turn left at the next corner to head out of the city. And I only have a couple of blocks to go. I can walk. Pull over here so I can say goodbye."

Patrick did as he was told. Mary turned to him. Her eyes showed nervousness, maybe fright, certainly excitement. She smiled. "Here I go!" she said. "I love you, Patrick. Be safe driving home, and be good with your mother. I'll be thinking of you all day. And I'll call tonight."

"Good luck today. I love you, too."

She leaned across to him and they hugged and kissed. After a moment more, she was out of the car and walking, her eyes on the ground.

Patrick watched her go. Then he pulled back into the traffic and turned toward the border. The car felt empty. He was alone. He snapped on the radio and searched till he found a rock-and-roll station. It was Canadian, playing outdated rock music. The DJ spoke French. Patrick left the radio playing; it was better than driving alone.

Shortly before he crossed the border, he lost the Canadian station. He searched on the dial again and found a station from the University of Vermont, playing strange new rock music by obscure bands. He retraced his route from the day before back to Montpelier, then into the mountains toward Maine. In the mountains he lost all the radio stations, hearing only static. He snapped off the radio and drove the last hours in silence, absolutely alone.

He was in Brunswick by mid-afternoon.

He approached his house with dread. Tom met him at the door. "Come on in, son. I'm glad you got back safe and sound. Come along and let's talk with Mother."

She was in her spot on the sofa in the living room. Tom sat next to her. Patrick sat across from them on the other sofa. He waited. It was up to her how this conversation would go.

"I understand that I was rude to your girlfriend. And I would—"

"Her name is Mary."

Mother took a breath. "I understand that I was rude to your girlfriend Mary. And I would like to apologize. It was wrong of me, and I am very sorry. Could you please tell her on my behalf?"

Patrick took a moment. "Yes. Sure. I'll talk to her tonight."

"Will you please accept my apology?" Mother's face was taut, hard, pale with her effort to apologize.

Again, Patrick paused. "Yes. Apology accepted. Let's move on," he said, looking at the floor.

"Patrick," she continued. "Why did you drop out of grad school? You would have had your MFA in another year."

"I don't know," he confessed. "I went to RISD to improve my painting, to get to that next level with my art. And to meet people who could help me get a start in the business. I've done all of that. There wasn't much else I could have gained by staying there. And yes, when Mary got her job, there wasn't any other reason for me to stay. If she had planned to be there another year, I probably would have stayed with her. But when she got the job and began to prepare to leave Providence—"

"So, it was her!" Mother crowed.

"No. It was my decision all the way. Whether or not I have an MFA won't make that much difference. Getting the year at RISD did. But with her leaving, I wanted to get a job too, something where I could be near her. And then, just like that, there was the job at Phillips Exeter Academy. It felt like it was meant to be. It's where I'm supposed to go next year."

"You said she'll be in New York by the fall? New Hampshire will be farther away than Providence. Why don't you go back to grad school? You'd be closer if you were still in Providence."

Patrick thought about that for a moment. It made sense. He looked over at his father. Tom was detached, looking away, out the window.

Patrick let out a slow breath. "I understand what you're saying, Mother. But I've made my decision. I've taken the position in Exeter. I can't leave them on such short notice. I have my paintings in galleries in Maine and Boston. And my friend Aaron is getting me connected with two galleries in New York. This is my moment. I'm on the edge of something good and I have to see it through."

"Your Uncle Win has his pictures in galleries, but at least he completed his MFA. And he's a professor. Why couldn't you do that? You admire your uncle."

"Yes, Mother, I admire Uncle Win. He's an inspiration. But I have to follow my own path. Uncle Win understands what I'm doing. This is right for me."

"So where will you live? Not in Montreal or New York. Have you thought this through?"

"I'm going to Exeter tomorrow to look for an apartment near the academy. If Mary's career works out so she's permanently in New York, I'll probably move close to New York City to be with her when I'm done at Exeter. I don't know. Right now I have to find a place to live in New Hampshire and see how it goes next year."

Finally Tom spoke. "That's good. Patrick, we're proud of how your art has developed this year. And we're pleased that you've found such a wonderful young lady with Mary. However things go for you and her over this next year, we support you both in your careers. Your uncle will be joining us for dinner. You probably want to rest up after your long drive back from Canada so you'll be fresh at suppertime."

Tom stood. "Come along now, Mother. Why don't we leave our boy so he can get some rest? Let's go out and walk a while."

—

Uncle Win baked fish for dinner. They ate at a table set up on the lawn where the croquet match had been held. When they were finished, Tom and Mother took the dishes to the house to wash. Patrick folded the tablecloth and left it sitting on the table. Uncle Win poured the last of the wine into two glasses and called to Patrick, "Come along boy. Let's go watch the tide come in." They walked down the path to the rocky beach, found their places, and sat on the driftwood log sipping their wine.

"Can I give you some direction, some pointers?" Uncle Win began.

"Of course."

"You're like my own child. You're the boy I would have wanted to have if I could have had children. And while Tom and Susan have raised you, I believe I can take credit for much of where you are with your painting and with your life."

"I agree. I've tuned my parents out since high school. What they want for me isn't what I want for myself."

"Yes. I've always told you to find your own direction, to pursue your own dreams. If you copy other peoples' art, everything you do is derivative. It's no better than a poor imitation of someone else's vision. And if you chase other peoples' dreams with your life you may satisfy them, but you will never suit yourself. Does that make sense?"

"Yes."

"You're doing that now. Following Mary and trying to work out how to build a life together. Leaving RISD and taking the position at Phillips Exeter Academy. Getting your work in galleries. It may turn out fine for you; I hope it does. If it works out, you can be proud. And if any of it doesn't, you can blame yourself, nobody else. Win or lose, it's your life and you can make it work. I'm confident you'll do fine."

"I hope so. It seems to be working out well so far."

"Yes. So far. But the thing is that you're blazing a trail here. You're following your dream, not your mother's or your father's. And not mine, either. Not even Mary's, though she's very much a part of this. You get to make the rules, write the script."

"Yes. What's your point?"

"Ask for help when you need it, don't be afraid to ask for direction. Ask me, ask Mary, ask your parents. But go your own way whenever you can. Don't make derivative art. And live your life your way, by your rules, but with consideration for others. Most of all you have to be considerate of Mary since your life and hers are deeply connected now. You also should respect the wishes of your parents. Do what you need to do, but keep their concerns in mind."

"I'm trying to."

"I know, and I'm proud of you. So are your parents."

"I wish they could tell me that." Patrick took a sip of wine and watched the evening light shine on the rushing water in the channel next to the beach. Win waited.

"Okay," Patrick said, ready to move on. "Tomorrow I find an apartment in New Hampshire."

"Here we go," Win replied. "If I can give some more advice?"

"Of course."

"Exeter is an interesting town. I've been there. Parts are very preppy and upscale, near the school. Those will be expensive. Parts are small-town New England, full of farmers and families that used to work in the mills. Those will be less expensive. You'll find better places at a better price if you go north."

"Good tip. Thanks."

The two artists sat, drinking their wine and watching the tide and the sunset.

His phone rang just before bedtime. It was Mary. He walked out into the cool of the summer evening to talk. "How was your first day at CBC?"

"Great! I was terrified when I first got there. I don't know anyone of course, and I don't really know for sure what it is I'll be doing yet. But they took good care of me."

"Good! Tell me more."

"My boss is a manager named Justine. She had everything ready for me. I had a lot of paperwork to fill out, and they had a cube waiting for me with a computer and a phone and everything. She assigned me a couple of projects I'll be working on with her. And I went through the orientation with a few other new employees. It was nice. They took me to lunch."

"Very nice. How did you get home?"

"I walked. It's about twenty minutes. They keep the apartment I'm in for people like me who are just here for assignment for a few weeks. So it's convenient. How was your drive home?"

"Lonely. I was missing you the whole way."

"And when you got home?"

"Mom apologized. And she told me to apologize to you as well."

"Uh huh. Okay. That's good, I guess."

"Yes. For her it was a big thing. I'll take it."

"Good. What are your plans for tomorrow?"

"Apartment hunting in New Hampshire. You?"

"Work, of course. I have a career now. They're paying me really well."

"Good. I'll let you go. Sleep well. I love you."

"I love you too."

It was their first night alone in months. They didn't sleep well.

Before noon the next day, Patrick was in Portsmouth with a real estate agent. They reviewed a series of apartment listings and visited several in Portsmouth. Then they drove to the other side of Great Bay, to the small town of Newmarket. The main street was dominated by a massive granite mill building, now converted into offices, restaurants, and expensive condos with views of a river. Instead of the pricey condos in the mill, Patrick settled on a one-bedroom apartment at a good price on the second floor of an old house. *I like that it's right across from St. Mary's. It's a Catholic Church. That'll make Mary happy when she comes to visit. I could paint it too, maybe catching the way it looks at sunrise looking out my window. It's such a modest, white clapboard church. Mary would love that picture.* Patrick made a deposit and planned to move in the following day.

That evening he called Mary. "How was your second day?"

"Fine. I'm settling in. I had to buy my own lunch today, but that's okay. I like it here. What did you do today?"

"I found an apartment in an old house down in New Hampshire. It's in a little town about fifteen minutes away from Exeter. I'm moving in before the end of the week."

"Wonderful. Could you come back to Montreal this weekend? I want to show you around. This is a beautiful old city."

"Sure, I can do that. What time should I get there? When do you get out of work?"

"I'm usually done a bit after five. Can you meet me at my apartment around six?"

"Perfect. See you in a couple of days."

He moved into the Newmarket apartment the next day. Uncle Win rented a truck and contributed some old furniture he had kept stored: a kitchen set with a stained table and three chairs, a hard sofa, a coffee table and two end tables. For the bedroom he provided an old queen-size bed. With the furniture in, they went to a nearby mall and found dishes, pans, stainless silverware, and the other essentials. Uncle Win paid for it all.

I'm set. I'll hang my paintings, and I'll place the nude of Mary in the bedroom.

CHAPTER TWENTY-SIX

PATRICK LEFT AFTER LUNCH ON Friday. He passed into Quebec and was in Montreal shortly after six. He had called ahead while he waited in the line at the border customs stop and Mary was watching for him, sitting on her front steps. She ran to his car and they held each other.

"Come on," she said. "I've got chili in the crock pot and a bottle of wine in the refrigerator."

"Remember when we didn't know much about wine?" he said as he pulled the cork.

"Yes. Aaron and Melanie taught us a lot," she answered. She served the chili.

"They taught us many things," Patrick said, pouring the wine.

They talked excitedly during dinner, about Montreal, her co-workers, and her job. They made plans to see the old city the next day. But they were rushing to finish the meal, feeling a need to pretend it was like any other night, eating dinner together and relaxing for a while before bed.

It was barely nine o'clock when Patrick suggested, "We've both had a long week. Why don't we get to bed early?"

At first, she protested. "Tell me more about your week and the apartment first." She fiddled with the trim on the arm of the sofa, delaying even though she too was anxious to get to bed.

"Didn't I tell you about it on the phone?"

"Yes, but I want to know more."

"There's not much to say."

"Okay. Have you done any painting this week?"

"No. A couple of sketches, but there hasn't been much time. I drove around a little. There are great places for me to paint in Newmarket. That's my new hometown. There are rivers, waterfalls, woodlands, and Great Bay. I'll get back into painting soon. Oh, Aaron called. He's setting up appointments for me with New York galleries in a couple of weeks. Melanie says hi."

"Great. It will be nice if you're in New York galleries. You can work with them when you visit me in the city. Say hi to Melanie when you talk with her."

Then Mary gave in. *I know how eager Patrick is. And I've missed him so much. We're both ready to be together again, sharing love, leading each other along. But I need to be careful tonight even more than every other night. We need to stay on this side of the edge of what I know is wrong. I'm trying to delay because I'm scared after being away from him for so long, but I can't postpone it forever.*

"You're right," she whispered. "It has been a hard week. Let's go to bed." She led him to the bedroom.

They had barely gotten to bed when they began. They craved each other, frantic and desperate after their time apart. But as they always did, they stopped short of the final act, bringing each other some satisfaction but not completion. Before she fell asleep, Mary recited the priest's words to herself. "You have not sinned if what you say about your relationship is true." *I know it's a rationalization, but it's the best I can do.*

⌐

Saturday they walked the old city, enjoying the easy weekend pace. In the old section, Patrick stopped, opened his sketch book, and began sketching a wide cobblestone street bordered by canopied sidewalk restaurants. A small crowd of tourists gathered behind him, watching him work. Mary stood back, enjoying his workmanship as she always did and feeling proud that the crowd was also admiring his artistry.

When he was finished, he looked up. One of the tourists, a middle-aged man with his wife, asked, "So you're an artist?"

Patrick smiled, suppressing laughter at the obvious question. "Yes."

"Are you in galleries here in Montreal? Are you local?"

"No. I'm American. I'm in a few galleries in Boston, Providence, and Portland. And I'm about to start with a couple of places in New York."

"Really! New York. I'm from down there, in the city a lot for business. I'll look for your work the next time I'm in New York. What's your name?"

"Patrick Chamberlain."

"How much do you want for the drawing?"

"How much would you pay?"

The man took a moment, assessing the work. "I love Montreal. My wife loves this city. I'd like to take home a souvenir piece of art. But this isn't framed."

"No, but you can always tell people you saw me do it. That's worth something. You can get it framed."

"Yes. I can do that when I get home. Would you take two-hundred fifty dollars Canadian for it?"

Patrick leaned over the drawing without talking. He accented an edge of a restaurant awning and touched up a spot on the flagstone sidewalk. Then he signed the drawing. He looked up at the man.

"Sure." He tore it carefully out of the sketchbook.

Patrick took the money. They shook hands, and the man walked away with his arm around his wife and the drawing tucked in her shopping bag.

Patrick kissed Mary. He laughed. "Dinner's on me tonight!"

They made a reservation at a French restaurant in old Montreal. Then they toured the old Cathedral. The ancient building, the stained glass, the stone work was compelling to Patrick. The angles of the arches and windows begged to be drawn and painted.

"Is this where you go to Mass?" he asked.

"This weekend will be my first Mass in Montreal," Mary replied. "I've found a smaller church closer to my apartment. We'll go there tomorrow morning."

Dinner was incredible.

⸺

Patrick sat next to Mary at Mass. He was starting to understand the Mass in the United States but in Montreal he was lost again. The rituals were the same, familiar movements, the smoke over the altar, raising the communion wafer, wiping the cup clean. But here, the Mass switched back and forth between French and Latin. Patrick didn't understand a word of it.

After Mass, they spent another quiet day together. Finally, they had one more night sharing the bed, almost making love.

At dawn on Monday they were up. Mary rushed through her preparation for work, eager to go but reluctant to say goodbye to Patrick. Outside her apartment they walked to his car. "Can I give you a ride?" he asked.

"I'd like that, but you have to turn in a couple of blocks to head out of the city. And I go straight to CBC."

"Come on. We can be together for a couple of minutes more."

As he was dropping her off, he asked, "Can you come this weekend to New Hampshire? I'll send directions."

"Okay, but I'm working till five. It'll be late when I get there."

"I'll snack while I wait for you, and we'll have dinner as soon as you arrive."

"Okay. I'll see you Friday. Drive carefully and call to let me know you got home safely. I love you."

"Love you too."

They separated, him heading south, her walking to her job.

⸺

He arrived in Newmarket mid-afternoon. He dropped his bag and walked straight to the kitchen table. He laid out a large piece of watercolor paper and set out his paints, palette, and brushes. Still feeling inspiration from his time with Mary, he began to paint, barely pausing to block out the scene. The painting worked up effortlessly, drawn out of his memory of the mail boat ride with Mary in Casco Bay. Kelp-coated rocks and a tidal pool dominated the foreground. Above that he left a low line of paper unpainted, white for the surf on the rocks. He added the ocean and the rippled bay shining with the afternoon sunlight. One sailboat tipped in the breeze in the middle of the channel. Gulls wheeled above. The far shore of the bay was an edge of dark pine, broken here and there with suggestions of gabled houses. The sky was a deep blue fading to pale nothingness above the treetops; no clouds.

Finished, Patrick set the painting up and evaluated it. He had caught the perfect peace of that afternoon with Mary. He took his pencil and signed the painting. Then he added a title, lettering carefully in small print at the bottom.

"Chebeague Island, Casco Bay – This is Heaven"

On Friday, Mary came to Newmarket, arriving after ten, exhausted. They ate a quick meal then went to bed. Their time together was becoming more important. It became increasingly powerful, tempting them more each time.

They spent Saturday morning and the early afternoon driving together, stopping whenever Patrick was captivated by the scenery. They drove to Portsmouth and crossed causeways to Newcastle, a historic village with narrow streets and clapboard houses. Heading south along the coast they passed mansions to Rye and North Hampton. The afternoon concluded with Mass at St. Mary's, across the street from Patrick's apartment.

After lunch on Sunday, Mary left to drive back to Montreal. He had kept the Chebeague Island painting hidden, a surprise he would deliver once she got to New York.

They found a rhythm for their lives. Every weekend they were together. One weekend Patrick drove north to Canada, the next she drove south to New Hampshire. They spoke on the phone every night. They began to feel comfortable in each other's new homes. Their lovemaking was increasingly passionate, but cautious. They always backed away at the final crucial moment.

In mid-August, Mary prepared to move to New York and start her work with CBC in Manhattan. She called Patrick. "I'll be leaving Montreal mid-afternoon on Friday and staying at Margie's apartment while I get settled. Could you meet me there Saturday?"

"What about Margie and Javier?"

"I'll be sharing her place with them for a few weeks. But you can stay with me. It's okay because Javier is working out of state for several weeks."

Patrick drove to the city Saturday morning. The trip left him shaking. *I've never been good in big cities. The traffic makes me anxious. And now I'm lost.* He drove around blocks, dodging taxis, checking his directions. He arrived late in the morning, just as Margie was leaving the apartment. She was already packed, ready to drive to their parents' weekend home in Connecticut. She hugged Patrick as she headed out the door. "Behave yourselves, you two," she ordered with a smile. "I don't want to come home on Monday and hear from the neighbors about all sorts of noise or wild parties."

Mary replied, "We'll be good."

Patrick laughed. "No promises!"

With Margie gone, Patrick gave Mary a large package, wrapped in paper. "This is for your new apartment," he said.

She pulled the paper away and propped the framed painting on the sofa. "Chebeague Island," she read. "This is Heaven. This is where we picnicked. It's perfect!" She kissed him.

She took him to Central Park that afternoon. "I know you like the country," Mary said. "The woods, the seacoast, all the little towns. This is the best we've got in Manhattan. It's not New Hampshire, but don't you think it's nice?"

He nodded, looking around, unconvinced.

They sat on a wood and iron bench beside a park road way. Crowds surged past them, joggers, walkers, bicyclists, and rollerbladers. There were street musicians. He saw sad-looking horses pulling outdated open carriages with tourist families or young couples in them. Elderly couples walked slowly, hand-in-hand. Noisy groups of teenagers rushed past, jostling, singing, and shouting.

"Yes, this is nice," he said.

He began to relax, but then he heard sirens squealing in the distance and became aware of the closeness of the buildings looming above the park and of the noise from the constant traffic just past the trees. *My art requires that I spend time in cities, visiting galleries. I need to become comfortable in Mary's world to be successful working with the art galleries. I need to find peace here. But it's so crowded, so noisy, so confusing.*

"Monday, when you go to work, I have an appointment with a gallery here," he said. He showed her an address. "I have four paintings to take to them. Aaron got me the appointment."

"That's only a few blocks from where I'll be working. Maybe I can stop by when they set your work up."

"I meet them at nine Monday morning. I'll head back to New Hampshire right after that. Classes start next week. I have to set up the studio at the school."

"So, let's enjoy every moment while you're here."

That night they lay in bed. They had finished as much of their lovemaking as Mary would permit. She fell asleep. Patrick tossed restlessly on the bed. Outside the apartment building there was incessant noise; sirens, the sounds of passing cars, honking horns, even occasional footsteps and voices downstairs on the sidewalk, one floor below. He remembered the trite phrase, "the city that never sleeps." He couldn't. He finally dozed and woke on Sunday with a headache.

Walking to Mass, Mary asked, "How did you sleep?"

"Terrible. All the traffic outside. All the noise."

"I don't even hear it. For me it might be like the sound of the ocean is for you when you're home in Maine. It's just noise."

The weekend passed too quickly. Monday morning, Patrick dropped Mary near her new office and headed toward the gallery with his paintings. As he was kissing Mary goodbye, he asked, "Will you come to see me next weekend? I'll be starting my teaching job and I'd love to see you."

"Of course I will. Every weekend we'll be together."

Then Mary was out of the car and off to work. He found a parking lot a block further up the street, parked, and walked to the gallery, carrying his stack of wrapped paintings. The gallery owner evaluated the paintings and accepted all four. He set prices with Patrick and discussed where the paintings would be displayed. *This is it! I'm in galleries from Maine to New*

York City. With a bit of luck, I'll be able to earn a living this way.

With the deal in place, Patrick began the long drive back to New Hampshire. He needed to leave the city, the traffic, and the chaos behind. *I can relax when I get to New Hampshire. That's where I belong.* He hurried back to peace.

Chapter Twenty-Seven

MARY ARRIVED LATE FRIDAY NIGHT. They had both grabbed quick meals earlier in the evening, Mary's at a rest area off the highway. Patrick welcomed her with a long hug and a kiss and led her upstairs to his apartment. He brought two glasses of chardonnay into the living room and set out two plates on the table in front of the sofa. Then he produced a box of chocolates and strawberries in a bowl. He put on Camille Saint-Saens, music he knew she liked, playing it quietly, setting the mood.

"A little dessert while you settle in," he explained.

They eased back on the couch, sipping the wine and eating the chocolate and berries. When the food was gone Patrick stood and reached to her. "Time for bed," he said. "I want to show you some new places I found along the coast tomorrow. We'll head out first thing in the morning." He led her to the bedroom.

The stress of her new job and the move to the city left her vulnerable. The wine weakened her even more. Though they went to bed wearing the scant clothing they always wore at night, it was discarded moments after he turned the light out. They began their love-making, intending as always to find ways for release without committing the sinful act of actual intercourse.

There came a moment when everything aligned. There was a spasm as they shifted positions, a slipping and he was in. Mary gasped. Neither of them was certain whether it was a sound of panic or pleasure or dismay. Then both of them lost control. They felt like they were tumbling, falling together. They grabbed at each other like drowning people. Their bodies moved in the same rhythm, pulling them further down. The intensity continued to build, leaving them both wanting it to stop and hoping that it never would.

As suddenly as it had begun, it was over. Patrick slumped and rolled onto his back beside her, still holding her hand. Her body continued moving, aftershocks rocking her, making her legs twitch. He reached over to kiss her and found that her face was wet.

"Are you crying?" he asked.

"I don't know."

"Did I hurt you?"

"No."

She turned to him and kissed him, the way she always did at night, holding his face between her two hands. "God, I love you!" she said.

Then she turned again onto her back. They fell asleep embracing. Outside, the autumn moon shone. It was done. It was perfect. It was heaven.

—

He awoke to his dark, silent apartment. He reached for Mary but she was gone. He felt the bed. It still retained a pink trace of her body heat and a hint of her perfume. He stood up. "Mary?" he called quietly. There was no answer.

The apartment was small. He looked in the bathroom, the dark living room, and finally the kitchen. She was nowhere. He checked out the window. Her car was still parked outside, lit by a streetlight. She had to be nearby.

He dressed quickly, grabbing shorts, a t-shirt, and flip-flops. He left the apartment and went to look outside. On a hunch he crossed the silent, middle-of-the-night street to the church. The door was always unlocked; it was a small town where everybody knew everybody. There was no need for locked doors on a Catholic church in the little town.

He pulled the heavy door open and stepped inside. The sanctuary was dimly lit by a thousand votive candles. In the flickering light he could see Mary's tiny figure kneeling, bowed in a pew, one row back from the front. Quietly he walked up to her. She had her eyes closed, praying, the beads moving through her fingers, clicking. She slid over without stopping her prayers to allow him room to sit. He did and waited in silence while she prayed.

Several minutes later she stopped, sat back in the pew, opened her eyes, and looked at him. Then she stood. Her prayers were said. There was nothing more she could do. For the moment at least, she was at peace. "All right," she said. "Let's go home."

He stepped out of the pew and allowed her to lead him down the aisle, out the door and across the street through the night to his apartment. She hurried up the stairs to his unlocked door. Once they were inside, she turned, locked the door and cut across the living room toward the bedroom.

For a brief moment Mary paused, frowning, distracted and disturbed. *A line has been crossed. It can never be undone. I know I can never change my new, imperfect life. This will always be with me.*

"Let's go back to bed," she commanded. She pulled her t-shirt over her head as she walked. Looking at her bare back as she stripped, Patrick was reminded for a moment of Melanie heading toward the surf at the beach on Block Island. Then Mary was at the bed, her shorts were gone, and she was pulling Patrick to her. Hastily, in the dark bedroom, they made love again. Then they slept.

—

When they woke it was mid-morning and the sun filled the room. "Good morning," Patrick said.

"And a good morning to you!" She rolled on top of him and it began again, this time in the bright light of day.

When they had showered and dressed, Patrick took her to breakfast in a crowded place by the river on the ground floor of the old brick mill in the center of Newmarket. The restaurant was packed, it being a Saturday morning. Families with small children, older couples, a bunch of hard-working men in baseball caps and baggy jeans; it was a congenial place. Greetings were called across the room as a new family came in. No one knew Patrick and Mary but they felt welcomed.

After they had ordered their eggs, Mary leaned over to Patrick and whispered, "We might be the only people here who had sex last night. Do you think everybody knows we made love? Do you think it shows?"

Patrick chuckled and whispered back. "Friday night? The end of the week? Some others might have done the same thing we did. And no, it doesn't show. They don't know."

After that, they were quiet among the noise of the breakfast place. It occurred to Patrick that what Mary had said was the first time she had spoken so openly with him about their lovemaking.

They spent the day driving the brief, twisting New Hampshire seacoast, following a route similar to one they had driven several weeks earlier. It felt different this time. Because of the night before, everything felt different.

They bought sandwiches and Cokes and sat on a bluff, watching the ocean beneath them.

"This place is a lot like that island you took me to in Maine," Mary said.

"Too crowded," Patrick replied. "Too much traffic. Chebeague Island is better, quieter. But this is nice."

"I plan to find my new apartment next week. That painting you did of that island? I'll hang it in the living room wherever I end up living."

"Are you happy to be in New York?"

"Yes. You can't imagine how good it is to be back. It's my home. I know my way around. I know where to go, what to do. I never got settled in Providence. Certainly not in Montreal. It's great being with my sister right now. I know she likes me being there. And I've got plans to see Sister Catherine this coming week. It'll be good to have them both right there for me. I miss Sister Catherine."

"That's great. I'll come down and see you next weekend?"

"Maybe."

Maybe? We see each other every weekend, either at her place or here in New Hampshire. Maybe? What does she mean by maybe?

They got back to the apartment too late for Saturday Mass. "I feel awful missing it," Mary said. Then she brightened. "We can go tomorrow morning. I might be ready by then."

They had bought sole in a seafood market on the coast before they came home. They cooked it in a skillet with wine, capers, and lemon juice. "We've finally learned how to cook like Melanie," Patrick laughed.

Mary smiled. *Remember Melanie's declaration that learning to cook is like learning to make love? "There will be a few mistakes along the way," Melanie said. "And even some of those will be good. But you can't be afraid to try new things." I know I've made a mistake. I can't change what I've done. And it was so good. God forgive me, but I love him. It was wonderful. But I've sinned, I'm lost. How can I ever make it right again?*

After dinner, they finished the strawberries left over from the night before. Then they rushed back to bed for more lovemaking.

———

Sunday morning Patrick cooked breakfast for Mary, a cheese and mushroom omelet and fried potatoes. With breakfast done and the dishes stacked, they crossed the street to the church. Patrick noticed that Mary skipped dipping of her fingers in the font as she went in, but she genuflected before she entered the pew. When it came time for communion, Mary stayed in the pew.

"Aren't you going up for communion?" Patrick whispered.

"I need to go to confession first," Mary said, her head down.

Mid-afternoon, Mary led Patrick to her car. "I've got to go," she said. "Sunday evening traffic can be slow getting into the city."

"I wish you would never go. I love you." Mary smiled but said nothing.

Patrick continued. "It will only be a few days. I start my first week of classes at the Academy tomorrow morning. I'll leave early Friday afternoon and be with you in time for dinner."

Again Mary smiled. She hugged him and held on. She kissed him and said, "God, I love you. You can't imagine how much I love you. You need to always remember how much I love you. Don't ever forget that." She was in her car, her seatbelt was fastened, and the door was locked. Without another word she started the car and drove away. She turned the corner, passed by the church, and was gone.

⟋⟍

Patrick waited on the dusty parking lot and watched until her car was out of sight. Then he walked back up the stairs to his apartment. He felt light, loose-jointed, relaxed. He sprawled on his sofa, grinning.

So this is what it's like to make love all weekend with the woman you love! After all this time we finally finished it. It was perfect. Maybe I should paint what I'm feeling. No, there's nothing here, no images, no visions that could convey my emotions. Elation and satisfaction are feelings, not pictures I can paint. I'm hungry, but for what? Certainly not dinner. I'm satisfied. For the moment food isn't the answer.

I know it's irrational but I want her to come back right now. Maybe she'll miss me, wanting more. Maybe she'll get home, quit her job in New York, and drive back to me. Maybe she'll stop wherever she is on her drive and come back this afternoon. Then we can spend the rest of our lives making love every night in New Hampshire. I want to call her right now and ask her to come back. No. I can't. She has to get back to New York and her job. That makes sense. I have to let her go. At least for today. There's always next weekend. It's only five days till I see her again on Friday.

⟋⟍

Mary was numb. She drove blindly till she was on the interstate heading south. Finally, it was too much for her and she pulled into a rest area and slumped over the steering wheel, sobbing.

I've fallen. I've failed. I'm broken now and I'm lost.

Part of it is the sin. To have intercourse, to make love when we aren't married, that's a sin. The priest made that clear to me back in Providence. I memorized his words and I've been reciting them to myself for months. As long as I didn't succumb to temptation, as long as we didn't have real intercourse, I had nothing to confess. We tight-roped a fine line for so long. It was a rationalization. But it worked. I loved him without committing a sin. Until the last two nights. Now it's over.

My prayers that first night in the church helped me feel a little better. I'll need to go to confession as soon as I get to New York. But that won't take away the terrible truth of what I've done with Patrick.

There's so much more than my Catholic discipline involved. What Patrick and I did was wrong. It's that simple, that clear. Once we started, there was no turning back. I gave in again and again to everything I've resisted for so long. It's been an unforgettable weekend. It was wonderful. It was awful.

It's hopeless now. I've sinned. I've failed. Would it be so wrong, since I'm already lost, if I turned around and drove back to him? That feels like the perfectly natural and right thing to do right now. Why not give up everything and return to him? I want him so badly, even now as I remember moments from the weekend. But no, there's no way I could ever go back. Not now. Everything about my time with him, I have to cut that from my life. I can never go back.

I've betrayed myself. That's the worst part of it; even more than the sin. I was always the big sister, the good girl, the one who got perfect grades in school and college, daddy's favorite. I've found the perfect job. Now it's all over. I've succumbed to temptation. I've failed. Nothing is right anymore. Everything is wrong.

Margie is living with Javier and that's wrong; they aren't married. I'm no better. And Melanie. Look at Melanie and Aaron, living together and happily in love with each other. Maybe that was all an illusion, a relationship built on lies. I was determined to be better than either Margie or Melanie. I was supposed to be perfect. Now I know that I'm not.

She sat up in the car and took a deep breath. *I have to do something, go somewhere to deal with what I've done. What should I do? Where can I go? To go back to Patrick is to give up and go back to a life I shouldn't be living. He's at the center of my failure. He's the reason for everything I've done. I love him and that's why I've failed. It was sinful, it was wrong; it was less than who I want to be. I can never be with Patrick again.*

She took out her phone, took another deep breath, and dialed Sister Catherine. As soon as Sister Catherine answered, Mary lost it again. "I've done something awful," she cried into the telephone. "I've committed a sin and disgraced myself. I can't go back to Patrick. Not now."

Sister Catherine listened in shock. "What have you done, dear Mary?"

"We had intercourse. I have sinned. I was weak and now everything is wrong. Can I come home now?"

"Of course. I'll take care of you while we figure this out. Have you told your parents or your sister?"

"No. I can't. They've always thought so much of me. I'm supposed to be better than this. I'm supposed to be the perfect one but I've failed. I've let them down. I've let myself down. They can't know what I've done."

"You don't have to give up on Patrick. You love him. You were planning to marry him."

"I know. Yes, I love him. But I can't go back to him. I can't live like this. Everything I've done is a lie. I don't even know about my job anymore. Everything I believe in is lost."

"Come home, dear child. We'll sort this out. You can do this. You're going to be all right."

Mary hung up. She took a final deep breath and drove out of the rest area, back onto the interstate, heading south to New York, driving at exactly the speed limit.

CHAPTER TWENTY-EIGHT

PATRICK SAT AT THE KITCHEN table watching out the apartment window as the sky lightened into dawn. Late autumn fog washed in off Great Bay; the sunrise colors filtering from violet to gray and then turning a pale, cheerless yellow. He picked up his coffee and took a sip. The mug was handmade by a pottery-major classmate back at the art school in Rhode Island. The coffee was strong, the way he liked it, but cold, bitter, brewed hours ago. The facade of the church across the street was beginning to catch the first rays of sunlight. *I'm so tired of how much Mary's faith meant to her. Not that one church, but the church as a whole. It still means so little to me.*

His work table was across the kitchen. Brushes and paint tubes littered the tabletop. Otherwise the table was empty; squares of brush- stroked paint on the flat surface silhouetted the places where paper had once laid. Tacked to the wall behind the table was the last picture he'd finished, a watercolor portrait of Mary. Her dark hair cascaded to her bare shoulders. Her head was turned; only the lashes of her magnificent eyes could be seen at the edge of her profile, defined by a single thin brushstroke. Mary had been gone for almost two weeks now.

I haven't been able to paint at all for over a week. Not since she left me. Was I foolish to think it could last? Maybe we were both naïve, but I never saw the end coming.

Patrick roused himself from the table and walked zombie-like to the bathroom. He turned on the shower to heat the water then set out his clothes for the day. He would bathe and dress as he had every day since Mary vanished. Then he would drive down from Newmarket, through the village of Newfields, past the rolling woodland hills and farm meadows to Exeter. He would go to the art studio at the Academy and be bright and inspiring for his young student artists. They had seen his paintings on the wall in the hall outside the classroom. They had heard that his works sold in galleries in Boston and New York. Already several of the young students idolized him.

The students couldn't see past the cheerful facade he gave them in the studio classroom to know the pain he was feeling. They couldn't understand his emptiness. What they saw was that his portfolio of finished watercolors was full. They didn't know that he could not paint again until his muse returned.

Showered and dressed, Patrick walked down the apartment stairs and out the door to his aged Volvo. The car turned over slowly but started. Patrick put it into gear and backed away from the old house. He guessed he would need a newer car before the New Hampshire winter set in. He would get to it in time. Today he must focus on getting on with his life without Mary.

He dragged himself home after his classes to the hollow apartment in Newmarket. He ate a dull dinner alone; a hamburger fried in his skillet, a slice of cheese melted on top, the cheeseburger set between two pieces of toast. A bottle of iced tea washed it down. He didn't want anything more to eat.

He had to talk to somebody. He called Uncle Win first. "Hi, this is Patrick."

"Patrick, my boy! I haven't heard from you for a couple of weeks. How goes the career at the academy?"

"It's fine. But I'm not. Mary's gone."

"What? Oh Patrick, I'm sorry. What happened?"

"I don't know. I thought we were doing fine. It was hard this summer, with her in Montreal and me in New Hampshire. She just moved down to New York which I thought would make it easier. She would be closer. She came up a couple of weeks ago, and we had a good time, a great weekend together. Then she left and I thought everything was okay. But I haven't heard from her since, I can't track her down, I don't know what happened."

For a moment speaking about it with Uncle Win, he thought he might cry. But there were no tears. He was beyond that. He was empty and felt little emotion.

Uncle Win asked, "Have you called her parents? What about her sister? And who was her college advisor? The nun? What about Sister Catherine?"

"I talked to her parents and they said she's fine but that she doesn't want to be with me anymore. No reason why. I don't know how to get hold of her sister unless I drive down there and show up at her door. That could be awkward. And I have no way of contacting Sister Catherine."

"Could you call Canadian Broadcasting? That's where she works."

"I did. She quit. And she was about to get an apartment but I don't have her new address. She's vanished. I don't know why, and I don't have any way to find out."

Now he felt the tears. The loss was bad enough, but the lack of understanding why she left was what really burned. That and the lack of any way to find out.

Win listened to the silence as Patrick held himself together, struggling with the pain.

"Listen, Patrick. Today's Wednesday. I have classes tomorrow. But I'm wide open after that. Can I come down Friday?"

"I have classes every day till two o'clock. But yes, I'd like to see you." His voice broke.

"I'll come by the school after two on Friday and find you. I know my way around the campus. I know where the art building is."

"Okay."

"Have you called your parents?"

"No. I've hardly talked to them since Mother tore into Mary. I don't want to talk to them about this. Mother will just gloat and say, 'I told you that girl was no good'."

"You need to call them. Call them now, before nine o'clock. After that, it would be too late, they'd be in bed. Ask to speak with your father. He can tell your mother. And let me say that I think she'll be sympathetic. She won't want you to be hurting the way I know you are."

"Okay. I'll call them in a couple of minutes and I'll see you Friday."

After he hung up with Win, he took a moment, gathering his courage. Then he called his house. The line was busy. He waited a moment and dialed again. His father picked up.

"Hello?"

"Hi father, it's Patrick."

"Yes. I just got off the phone with Win. He gave me a quick call to alert me to what you're dealing with. Patrick, I'm sorry to hear about Mary. She seemed like a nice enough girl. I genuinely enjoyed her visits."

"She's gone. I don't know why."

"Any chance she'll come back? Maybe she's out of town on a business trip or something."

"No, if it had to do with business I would know. She would have told me. She's just gone."

"I'm sorry to hear that. Is there anything I can do to help?"

"Could you tell Mother? I don't want to have to face her with this. She'll probably celebrate. She didn't like Mary."

"Now Patrick, she cares about you. She had that little run-in with the girl, but I think she's past that. She'll be sorry to hear about this. She won't celebrate. But I'll let her know."

"Okay, thanks."

"Listen, son, why don't you come here over the Columbus Day weekend? That's only a few weeks away. It'll do you good to take some time, get away, and come home for a couple of days. The long weekend will make things better for you. We'd love to see you."

"Okay. I'll do that."

"All right then. Get a good night's sleep, son. The rest will help. You'll feel better about things in the morning. And we'll plan on your visit in a few weeks. I'll call again in a while to see how you're doing."

"Okay. And I'll call again to make plans before Columbus Day. Thanks, father."

"You're welcome. Goodnight Patrick."

—

Finally, he called Aaron.

"Hey Patrick! How're you doing?"

"Mary left."

"Yeah, you said she was moving down to New York."

It felt foolish to repeat the story again. He had already told Uncle Win and then his father. But he had to do it. "No. She left me. I don't know why. A couple of weeks ago she came up and we had a really great weekend together, but then she drove off and went back to New York I guess. I haven't heard from her since. Her parents told me she doesn't want to be with me anymore but that she's okay. She quit her job, and I don't know where her new apartment is. Just like that I've lost touch and she's gone."

"Oh man. That's rough. What are you going to do about it?"

"I don't know. What would you do? You've always been kind of like my guide through these sorts of things."

"I don't know. I've never been in love with a woman the way you and she were in love. I don't know what I should say, what advice to give you."

"But you must have had girls leave you. What did you do? How did you deal with what you were feeling after they left?"

"I moved on. There are always other girls out there. You'll find one. Hey, I was up in Boston a couple of weeks ago, working a deal at that Newbury Street gallery, and Lisa, the girl you worked with there? She was asking about you. Give her a call."

"I don't want to call Lisa. I'll work with her when she sells one of my pictures and needs a new one. But I don't want to see her. Particularly right now."

"Take your time. When you're ready, there will be girls there for you."

"Yeah, okay. But I'm not ready. Could you say hi to Melanie for me?

And tell her what's happened with Mary. I know they were close, so she should know."

"I'll let her know. Hang in there, buddy. Hey, I'm going down to New York next week. I'll be checking some business at the gallery where we got your paintings displayed and I'll keep an eye out for Mary while I'm there. But it's a big city."

"Okay. You do that. It was good talking with you."

"You too, Patrick. Good night."

Patrick sat back. Everyone knew who needed to know. He was on his own. The rest was up to him.

—

Patrick was setting up for his one o'clock class the next day, waiting for his students to arrive. A group of boys burst through the door several minutes early.

"Hey Mr. Chamberlain," one of them called. "There's a girl out in the hall looking for you."

"What? Really?"

Mary! He ran to the hall. There was Melanie.

"Hi," she said. "Aaron told me. I knew how you'd be feeling so I came right up. How are you?"

"Awful."

Students were passing them in the hall, turning into the studio classroom. All of them checked out the new art teacher and the stunning woman who had come to visit him.

"When are you done with your classes?"

"Two."

"Can we talk? I'll meet you someplace."

"Sure, come back at two. We'll go get a cup of coffee. Or a drink."

"Okay. I'll be back." She kissed him quickly on the cheek and walked away. He went back in the classroom.

"Ow! Mr. Chamberlain, that girl is hot! Is she your girlfriend?"

"No, she's just a friend. She's an artist too."

"Come on man, give it up! She's your girlfriend."

After class, Patrick met Melanie and they left the campus, walking past the bandstand to the center of town. He bought a cup of coffee. Melanie got herbal tea. They walked down the hill to a park running along the river's edge and found a bench.

The two artists sat, watching the shallow river flow by over the mud and rocks. Neither spoke. Finally, Melanie started. "What happened?" she asked.

He leaned over, elbows on knees, looking at the ground, saying nothing. Beneath his feet, early autumn leaves had blown under the bench, golden flecks patterning the grass. He imagined it as a painting, his mind leaping ahead to how he might lay it out, what colors he could use, how he would define the edges. It was a good sign, he realized. It was the first time since Mary left that he had conceived an image that could become a new painting. It was a small step, but it was progress.

He looked up and leaned back, his elbows resting on the back of the bench, his legs stretched in front, crossed at the ankles. He couldn't make eye contact with Melanie, but he could talk.

"You probably know more about my relationship with Mary than anyone. Maybe even more than my Uncle Win. I expect you know that Mary and I went a long time without ever actually making love."

Melanie nodded but didn't say anything. She turned toward Patrick on the bench.

"She was always worried that if we did more it would be a sin. We did things, though. We found ways."

Melanie nodded again. "Yes, Mary told me that."

"Well, the last weekend before she vanished, we did it. It was a pretty intense weekend. I knew she was upset by having gone through with it, but I thought everything was okay. She prayed about it, that I know. Then she vanished. That was it. She's just gone."

Melanie reached over and put her hand on his shoulder, patting gently. She waited to see if there was more he might say. He took a deep breath and turned to look at her but said nothing. There was nothing more he could say. His eyes went glassy with tears for a moment. Then he forced himself to try a smile.

She folded her hands in her lap. "Okay. I always wondered how she would deal with it once you two finally broke down and made love. Now we know."

"Do you think she's coming back?"

"No, I don't think so. This was always very hard for her. She's very much in love with you, but to actually make love? I think it made her do something, I don't know what, I don't know why, but she's not coming back. Take comfort that she's okay. Aaron told me her parents said she's okay."

"Yes. At least there is that."

They sat again in silence, digesting what had been said. Then Patrick started again. "Aaron said I should move on. He said I should just go find a new girl and get on with it. I'm not ready for that."

"No, you're not. You'll know when you are. And yes, there will be a girl waiting for you when you're ready."

"How do you and Aaron have such a great relationship? I wish Mary and I could have had that."

Melanie gave a short, sardonic laugh. "Huh! You want a relationship like Aaron and I have? Don't you remember everything that happened back at Easter?"

"Yes, but you guys worked through it. Everything worked out for you."

"We got past that time. But it's not good. Yes, I love Aaron. And I think he loves me. But it's a matter of time. I don't trust him at all. I worry all the time that he's still fooling around behind my back, but now he's hiding it better. It's great when he's with me. But I know the time will come when I catch him doing something he shouldn't. Maybe I'll come home and find him with someone. The day that happens is the day I'm gone. I've opened a small bank account to save money from the artwork I sell, so I'll be ready."

"But I thought you were doing fine. I saw how you were with him that weekend on Block Island."

Melanie smiled. "Yeah, that was a pretty good time."

"Why did you come up here to New Hampshire?"

"To see you. I heard Aaron talking with you on the phone. I knew that what he said to you wasn't helpful. And I knew you'd need a friend right about now. So I came."

"Thanks."

"I want you to know this, Patrick. You and Mary saved me last spring.

I was in a very bad place after I found out what Aaron was doing. I was thinking terrible things, frightening things. You saved me. I'd do this for anyone who needed a friend. But I'll always be there for you. I'd be there for Mary too, if she called me. But I doubt she ever will now. I've lost a friend too."

Patrick nodded, looking at the leaves under the bench again. Melanie continued. "You call me any time things are worrying you. And I'll check in from time to time. You matter to me. Let me know how things are for you."

"I will."

Melanie stood. "I've got to go now," she said. "It's a long drive back to Providence. I'll call Aaron so he'll know where I am and not worry. I've got to let him know when to expect me to get back home."

Patrick stood too. They walked back to the Exeter campus where Melanie had parked. At her car, she turned and hugged Patrick and gave him a kiss. "You're a good man, Patrick. You're going to be fine. Take your time. We'll stay in touch."

She got in her car and headed home to Aaron.

Uncle Win arrived the next afternoon before Patrick's last class let out. He didn't cause nearly the stir with Patrick's students that Melanie had. The students filed out as the week ended and Uncle Win came in. He pulled a chair over and sat across from Patrick.

"You doing okay today?" Uncle Win asked.

"Yeah. Every day it gets a little better. I get a little more distance between her and me. And Melanie came yesterday to talk with me about it."

"Melanie's something special, a beautiful soul. What did she have to say?"

"Yeah, she's special. Most people can't see past her appearance but she's a good friend. She listened and told me it was going to be all right."

"She's right. You might not be able to see it yet. But this will work out okay for you."

Patrick nodded.

"So here's what we're going to do," Win stated. "I'll drive you back to your apartment. Then I'll cook dinner. I brought groceries. We'll talk about it tonight if you want to. And I'm planning to stay the night, sleeping on your sofa. Tomorrow morning we'll come back here to get your car. We'll sort all of this out, you and me."

Patrick didn't know what Uncle Win had in mind, but he knew that whenever Uncle Win became this focused, it always turned out well. Win's plans were too clear-cut, too well thought out for Patrick to protest. He followed Uncle Win to his car.

After dinner, they sat in Patrick's living room. "It seems like I've explained what happened so many times. To you, my parents, Aaron and Melanie. I'm sick of talking about it. But it still doesn't make sense. I don't understand why she left."

"Why do you always hope that love will make sense? It's love. There's nothing at all sensible about it."

"What do you know about love, Uncle Win? Not for nothing, but you're gay. What do you know about love between a man and a woman?"

"Love is love, Patrick. Gay or straight, being in love is the same. So is heartbreak. I understand that because I've been through it all." Patrick nodded and waited for more from Uncle Win.

"Robert and I have been together twenty-one years now. We're as settled as any couple I know. But it wasn't easy getting there. He used to be married, of course, and he has children. When I met him after his divorce, he was broken down like you are. And missing his little kids. He loves his wife and kids very much, but he couldn't stay with them. It was hard for him, and difficult for me, too, when we first met. It's never easy. You have to work at it every day."

"I thought Mary and I were doing that."

"I expect you were. But whatever got in the way was too much for her to handle. Sometimes, no matter how much love you have, it's still not enough to overcome whatever issues come up."

"I told you about our last weekend. We finally made love. Was that too much? Is that what did it?"

"Probably. For her. And maybe it's best that it happened the way it did."

"How is that?"

"If it had happened earlier, you never would have had the experiences you did with her. You're different now because of everything that happened with her. You're a better man with a new outlook on life. And if it had happened later, you might have already been married to her, and that could have become really messy. Sooner or later it would have happened."

"I can never paint a picture of her again. It's too hard."

"Did you ever stop to think about the pictures you painted of her? The one you did with her right there that snowy day? You showed that to me and it wasn't very good, no life in it. It hardly even looked like her. Your best ones of her were done from your memory. They were fantasies. The reality of Mary wasn't nearly as beautiful or emotionally powerful as your vision of her."

Patrick nodded. "Maybe everything I loved about her wasn't real. I loved that fantasy of her, though. What do I do now?"

"You get up every day. You paint. You live. Each day you'll go out and see what it brings. A new set of experiences, a new series of visions to paint."

They drove to Exeter on Saturday and went into Patrick's studio classroom. Uncle Win laid out the plan for the day.

"Before I go back to Maine, here's what we're going to do. You express yourself best with your paints, not with your words. So I'm going to go out for a walk for a couple of hours. You're going to stay here in your studio. You told me you can't paint anymore. That's nonsense. You can. You will. You're going to start right now. I want you to think about everything you're feeling about Mary. I want you to think about everything that's happened. Remember the best times with her and think about the bad things, too. I want you to feel it all, painful as it may be. And I want you to paint it. I'll be gone till lunch time, and when I come back, I want you to show me a full-size watercolor that has everything you've been feeling. Pull it all out of your soul and paint it."

He left no room for argument, no discussion, no options. Uncle Win turned and walked out of the studio, down the hall, and onto the Phillips Exeter Academy campus. It was up to Patrick now. Painting might begin to bring him back.

Patrick sat alone in the quiet studio and began to think. After a moment he pulled over a big piece of rough watercolor paper.

Uncle Win walked across the campus absorbing the atmosphere of his alma mater. Boys and girls flirted in the autumn sunshine. Across the river people were gathering at the stadium for a Saturday football game. Win found a spot on the riverbank beneath an overhanging tree, sat and stretched out, reclining on the grassy bank looking up through the tree limbs. He daydreamed, imagining the students' stories caught among the branches. Students walked by, chatting and laughing. In the distance a band was playing.

When the time was right, when Patrick was ready, Win knew that Patrick would encounter the new woman and that would be that.

After enough time had passed, Uncle Win walked back to Patrick's studio classroom. Patrick stood at a sink washing out his brushes.

"Ah, you're cleaning up. You must have painted something. Let's see."

Patrick dried the last brush in silence, then walked Uncle Win to an easel. Propped on the easel was the new painting. Recalling the painting he had done of Chebeague Island for Mary, Patrick had recreated the exact same seascape. But where Mary's picture was filled with sunshine and breezes, this one was different. The water was flecked with small white caps. Dark storm clouds covered most of the sky. Beyond the clouds on the horizon was a brilliant slice of light, the clouds swept away. Sunset was there, illuminating the tips of some clouds, and reflecting like gold on the water, lighting the tops of the trees.

The image was spectacular, as good as any that Patrick had on display in the galleries in New York and Boston. It was hopeful, inspiring.

Uncle Win looked at the bottom of the picture where Patrick had penciled in a small title. "Chebeague Island, Casco Bay – The end of the day. The storm is over."

Uncle Win looked up at Patrick, grinned, and hugged him. "You're back," he said.

Chapter Twenty-Nine

IN LATE FEBRUARY, UNCLE WIN drove Patrick to Providence. They met Aaron and Melanie and caught the train for New York City. His paintings had been selling regularly in the gallery there and they had rewarded him with a one-man show. Three rooms on the second floor of the gallery were turned over to a collection of Patrick's artwork. Patrick was going to the opening reception triumphantly, bringing his friends.

They checked into their hotel in Manhattan and prepared for the exhibit's opening. Patrick dressed in a new dark, pin-striped suit. He wore a gray shirt with French cuffs, gold cufflinks, and a trendy necktie. He looked handsome, very successful, very New York.

Uncle Win, Aaron, and Melanie began to coach him for the reception. "Keep your right hand free to shake peoples' hands," Aaron advised.

"Hold your wine in the left hand if you can."

"That'll be easy," Patrick said. "I'm left handed, anyway."

"But don't drink much," Melanie suggested. "I know the city and the crowds stress you out, but stay sober through the evening. Take it easy."

Patrick nodded.

"Sample the hors d'oeuvres," Win said. "We took you to dinner so you don't need to eat, but I expect the food at the reception will be exceptional."

"Take it easy with the food," Aaron added. "You're here so people can meet you. If they like you, they'll buy your art. You don't want greasy fingers or crumbs on your suit."

Melanie came to him. She centered his tie behind the jacket, buttoned it, smoothed his lapel, and smiled. "You'll do fine. Now let's go to the gallery and have some fun."

They got out of the cab and went in from the cold to the warmth and bright lights inside the gallery. Wide stairs turned up from the first floor and opened into the three white-walled rooms where his show was displayed. Patrick stationed himself in the middle of the front room. Behind him, tall windows looked down on the street. The windows were sound-proofed so he couldn't hear the traffic, but there was a never- ending parade of cars and cabs pushing past the building, their headlights lit.

Music played. Waiters circulated trays of food. The rooms were filled with well-dressed New Yorkers, all accustomed to going to openings; galleries, theaters, and concerts. All of them wanted to meet the new young artist from Maine. Patrick held his wine glass as he had been instructed. It was half full. He smiled and shook hands and posed for photographs. He made small talk and answered the same questions again and again.

"Yes, I grew up on the coast of Maine."

"Winthrop Chamberlain? He's my uncle. He's had a lot of influence on my work. He's right over there."

"I studied at Bowdoin, but then spent a year at the Rhode Island School of Design. A lot of what you see here reflects my times living in Maine and Providence."

"I live on the New Hampshire seacoast now. I'm teaching at Phillips Exeter Academy."

He believed he was over Mary. It had been five months since their breakup. The last time he had been in New York he stayed with her at her sister's apartment. He had sent his paintings to the gallery, reluctant to return to the city. Even so, he kept catching himself whenever he saw a new person come up the stairs. Maybe she had heard about the show.

Maybe she had read about it in the New York Times. Maybe she would come. She didn't.

The evening ended. Patrick, Win, Aaron, and Melanie crowded into a cab for the ride back to their hotel. They settled into the hotel lounge for a nightcap. Uncle Win glowed. "That was incredible! You sold several pieces tonight alone."

"Five," Melanie specified. "And three more were sold before the show even opened."

"How does this work?" Patrick asked. "Do I have to replace everything as fast as they sell it? I don't know if I can keep three rooms filled if they keep selling them like this the whole month the show runs."

Aaron explained. "No, they'll keep them up till the end of the show. They mark the ones that are sold, but they leave them all up. It actually helps to sell more. People come in and see that a lot are already sold and it makes them eager to get in on the action. They'll want to get a piece of your work before they've all been sold and before their value goes up."

Uncle Win concluded the evening. "It's already been a successful show and it's only been up a few days. I also think you've driven off some of your demons by selling a few of these pieces. I know where they came from in your soul. And now you'll need to keep painting. Your work will be very much in demand once word of this show gets around. Your parents will be proud of you and your success here."

Several days later, Mary slipped into the gallery and went up the stairs to view the show. She had read in the paper about the special exhibit of watercolors by Patrick Chamberlain. She had made a point not to be near the gallery on the evening of the reception. As she looked around the gallery now, it was all so familiar to her. Several of the paintings in the show she remembered hanging on the wall of his apartment in Providence. She left the top of the stairs and moved to the front room. While she surveyed the paintings, Mary was approached by a salesman from the gallery. He stood beside her as she looked at a landscape; a meadow and pond surrounded by woodland, the light of the ocean reflecting beyond the trees. She realized that the painting was derived from the image Patrick had sketched en plein air during their weekend on Block Island.

"It's magnificent, isn't it?" offered the salesman.

"Yes, it is."

"It makes me imagine spending a romantic weekend near the ocean," said the salesman, trying an approach he hoped might sell this painting to the woman.

"Yes."

"He's an incredible young artist. Did you come to the reception last week?"

"No, I missed it."

"You should have been here to meet him. I believe he's gone back to Maine now."

"Maine? I thought he lived in New Hampshire."

The salesman turned to her, surprised that she knew this detail about the new artist. "You're right. He's from Maine originally, but now he's living in New Hampshire. Did you read his bio in the paper?"

"No. I just knew."

"Let me go get you a copy of his bio." The salesman hurried away.

Mary moved further along the wall. She stopped. In front of her was a stormy seascape. She knew this scene; it matched the one she had on the wall in her living room. She knew hers by heart. Hers was a sunny day on Casco Bay, a memory of their best day together. This one was filled with storm clouds but it was the same island, the same coastline, the same channel. Hers was titled, "Chebeague Island, Casco Bay – This is Heaven".

She leaned forward and looked at the label next to the picture in the gallery. "Chebeague Island, Casco Bay – The end of the day. The storm is over." She read Patrick's handwritten inscription beneath the painting with the same title. Then she read the date and realized it was painted just a few days after she had left him. She looked at the stormy painting again and became aware of the bright light breaking through the clouds on the horizon. It suggested better days ahead.

The salesman hurried up and handed her Patrick's bio. "Isn't this one wonderful?" he asked, looking at the seascape. "He's so good at capturing a scene, getting the mood of a place. But this painting. He was dealing with something very emotional when he painted this. It's a very moving, powerful painting, isn't it?"

Mary folded the bio and put it in her purse. "What does the red dot on the label next to the painting mean?" she asked.

"That means it's been sold. But if you like his work let me show you some other things he's done."

Mary remembered Patrick telling her how hard it was to part with his paintings, to sell them when they meant a lot to him. He had said that it was like giving away his children.

"Come," said the salesman. "This room is all landscapes and seascapes. The first room back at the top of the stairs has city scenes. We tried to set up the show by grouping similar themes in each room. We have three rooms and three sets of paintings."

Mary followed the salesman to the second room. The cityscapes were also familiar to her. Many were from their time in Providence. Every one brought back memories of places they had gone during their year together.

"You said there are three rooms?" she asked.

"Yes. Right over here is the third room. We have a series of portraits he did of a woman he used to know."

He led her into the third room. Everywhere she looked she saw herself. The salesman watched her. "She's a beautiful woman, don't you think?"

Mary nodded.

"She looks a lot like you."

"Yes. Yes, she does."

"We have ten pictures here. He might have painted more but these ten are all we have. She had to be a lucky woman to have been close enough to inspire him to paint her like this. You can see from the pictures in the other rooms that he loves the places he's lived in New England. He must have loved this woman, too, but I don't know if they're still together. He was alone at the opening reception. There was no woman with him."

"Yes, she would have been a very lucky woman to have been with him."

Mary turned around. There was the spectacular nude, toweling off after her shower. This was the painting he was never going to share with anyone but her. This was the one painting he said he could never give up. She looked at the bottom of the painting and read in her own careful calligraphy, "Art ought never to be considered except in its relationship with its ideal beauty." - Alfred de Vigny

She saw the label for the painting. It was titled, "The Goddess of Love".

There was a red dot on the label. Her painting had been sold.

The salesman spoke rapturously, leaning back, his arms folded across his thin chest, one hand raised, fingers at his mouth, all the while contemplating the painting. "Of everything of his we have in this show, I feel this one is the most magnificent. It's absolutely breathtaking, don't you think?"

The salesman turned to speak with her, but Mary was already on the stairs rushing for the door to the street.

Epilogue

IT HAS BECOME PATRICK'S HABIT over the long winter to get out early each Saturday, driving to Portsmouth for breakfast. After he eats, he spends the day driving along the coastline with his sketchbook seeking inspiration.

It is now late March, almost Easter, and a chill drizzle is soaking the Portsmouth streets, melting the dirty ice that lingers in the gutters. Patrick walks into the coffee shop he goes to every Saturday and finds the table he likes, set back in a corner. He prefers to sit here, out of the way, observing people as they come to the shop, sketching some of them. He plans to get his usual breakfast, but he is startled when a young woman comes out from behind the counter and approaches him with a mug of coffee and a pastry on a plate.

"Here you go," she says, her voice husky. "Kenyan Dark Roast, black. And the croissant with almonds and honey. That's what you always get, right?"

He looks up, surprised, speechless. The girl is smiling as she sets the cup and plate in front of him. He notes, as he has noted on the past Saturday mornings, that her dark blonde hair is pulled back, clasped behind her head, hanging to her shoulders, her eyes are very light blue, and her eyebrows arch when she talks to people, making her whole face light up. She is talking to him now, her eyebrows arching.

"I did get it right, didn't I? This is what you always order but you seem unsure about it."

He is distracted by looking at her but he answers. "Oh no. It's right. I'm surprised that you remembered."

"Of course I remember. You're here every Saturday morning, so I was ready for you when you came in. My name is Diana."

"Patrick."

"Okay then Patrick. Enjoy your coffee. I'll stop back in a bit."

The girl leaves, returning to the counter to wait on other customers. Patrick sips the coffee and opens his sketchbook. He surveys the room and settles on an old couple sitting several tables away next to the window. The old man is lost behind his newspaper. His wife, Patrick assumes she must be his wife, sits silently, engrossed in her coffee, looking out at the rain, and back to her husband. Is she hoping for conversation? Have they had a fight? Is she lonely, even though she's sitting with him?

Have they been married so long, Patrick wonders, that they have nothing left to say to each other? Can that happen? He remembers Uncle Win's advice on love from the terrible time after he lost Mary. "Sometimes no matter how much love you have, it's still not enough to overcome whatever issues come up." Have these two people gotten to a point where they can't overcome their differences? Patrick decides instead that they must be at a point in their marriage where they can communicate without speaking. Maybe that intuitive bond is what love is. That is how he decides to draw them.

Patrick begins to sketch the woman, catching the shadowless light from the foggy street on her wrinkled face. As he works, he notes that he is making the woman appear happy, serene as she looks to her husband. He goes to work on the husband, sketching him as being connected with his wife even though he is almost hidden from her behind the newspaper. Their hands almost touch on the tabletop.

A voice is speaking behind his shoulder, quietly, barely more than a whisper. "Nice. I don't want to speak loudly and alert them to what you're doing. It's like bird-watching where a noise could startle the birds. But this is a very nice drawing. Well done."

He turns. It's Diana. She smiles. It has been six months. He has had no one smile like that with him for too long. In spite of himself Patrick smiles back.

"I'm on break. Can I sit down?" she asks.

"Certainly. Please do."

She sits. "I've seen you sketching every week when you come in, but I've never seen what you do till now. You're very good."

"Thanks. I enjoy it."

"Are you an artist? I mean, is this a hobby or is it what you do?"

"I'm an artist. It's what I do."

"Very good. Are you in galleries? Do you sell your artwork?"

"Yes. I do mostly watercolor. And I'm in a few galleries. I sell a bit. I work during the week, teaching art at Phillips Exeter Academy. What about you?"

"I'm a grad student at UNH. Occupational Therapy. I work here to make a little extra money, a grad student budget being what it is."

"I understand. I was a grad student last year."

"Where?"

"In Providence. Rhode Island School of Design."

"Can I look at your sketchbook? I'd like to see more of your work." Patrick says nothing but hands her the book. Diana turns through it. Behind the drawing of the two old people she sees landscapes, drawings of the coastline, and street scenes from Newcastle and Newmarket and Portsmouth. She sees other sketches of people from the coffee shop and recognizes a few of them as her regular customers. She comes to a portrait of herself.

"Oh my," she says, smiling. "You drew me. I feel honored. And you made me pretty. Thank you."

"I draw what I see."

She hands the sketchbook back.

"Here," Patrick says. "I'll give you a couple of drawings and your portrait. Is there another one you like?"

"Thank you. That's very nice of you. Let me think about which one I like best."

"I'm happy to give them to you."

"I'm happy to get them. I'd like to talk more with you about your art. But I've got to get back to work. What are your plans for today?" She is standing up, getting ready to leave the table.

"I'm wide open. No plans. What time are you done here?"

"Two."

"I'll wait to eat lunch till then. I'll come back to see you at two. We'll find someplace to go for lunch."

Patrick drives out to Newcastle. He does a cursory walk through the narrow lanes, his umbrella tipped against the wind. He sees places that could become paintings but he doesn't take the time to sketch them. Not yet. He drives back across the causeways to Portsmouth, parks his new Volvo and returns to the coffee shop at two. He waits outside. The rain has abated and the sun is breaking through. Clouds race away toward the sea scattered by a warm breeze. Blue sky returns above.

Diana comes through the door carrying a paper bag and two tall cups on a cardboard rack. "You said you would want lunch so I took the liberty of buying for you. I've got two of my favorite sandwiches. A curried chicken with raisins and a black forest ham and cheese. You can have either. I'll take whichever one you don't."

"The curried chicken sounds good."

"It's yours. And I've got two iced teas."

"Perfect. It's warming up. I know the place to go for an impromptu picnic. Walking distance."

Patrick leads her down the hill to a spot along a brick walkway overlooking the Piscataqua River. They find a bench and sit with the tray of lunch between them. They look out at the river. The tide is coming in, pushing up from the sea out by the Isles of Shoals, rushing into the river, tipping the buoys, flooding Great Bay.

"Tell me about your art," she says. "Tell me how you do it."

"There's so much to say," he says. "Where do I start?"

Acknowledgements

Writing is a solitary endeavor. Yet I have discovered that getting a book published requires the collaboration of many people. I enjoyed the support of many friends to bring this, my first full novel, to life. Narielle Living, my publisher and editor, has been wonderfully supportive and a good friend throughout the process of preparing my story for publication. She has been patient with me and restrained while bringing life to my story.

Sections of this book have been reviewed by members of my two writers' groups in Williamsburg. These writers are Tim Holland, Elizabeth Brown, Pat Ryther, Cynthia Fridgen, Dave Pistorese, Barbara McLennan, Cindy Freeman, Sharon Dillon, and Jack Lott. Their reading and critique of my work and our discussions of the themes in this story have been engaging. Other writer friends have also offered valuable suggestions, notably Brian Schulz, Ellen Smith and Liz Haskins.

My children, David and Carey, both of whom have careers in the arts and spend a lot of their time working on college campuses, have also weighed in with their views.

Finally, my wife Debbie has read and re-read this entire book. She has kept me from becoming discouraged with the long process of creating this novel.

Thank you all.

About the Author

Peter Stipe has an extensive background in the arts. He has artwork on display at On the Hill Gallery in Yorktown, Virginia and is a past-president and board member of the Yorktown Arts Foundation. He also served on the board of directors of the Chesapeake Bay Writers and the Williamsburg Book Festival. His first book, *Finding Our Way*, a collection of short stories, was initially published in 2015. *The Art of Love* is his first full novel. He is also the author of *Remember Me*, a book that explores the truth behind his family's traditional stories. A New Englander most of his life, Peter now lives and writes in Williamsburg, Virginia.

* 9 7 8 1 9 4 8 9 7 9 3 4 4 *